GOODBYE
SISTER DISCO

GOODBYE
SISTER DISCO

JAMES PATRICK HUNT

 ST. MARTIN'S MINOTAUR ❦ NEW YORK

GOODBYE SISTER DISCO. Copyright © 2008 by James Patrick Hunt. All rights reserved. Printed in the United States of America. No part of this book may be used or reproduced in any manner whatsoever without written permission except in the case of brief quotations embodied in critical articles or reviews. For information, address St. Martin's Press, 175 Fifth Avenue, New York, N.Y. 10010.

www.minotaurbooks.com

Library of Congress Cataloging-in-Publication Data
Hunt, James Patrick, 1964–
    Goodbye Sister Disco / James Patrick Hunt.—1st ed.
        p. cm.
    ISBN-13: 978-0-312-36156-3
    ISBN-10: 0-312-36156-4
    1. Police—Missouri—Saint Louis—Fiction. 2. Saint Louis (Mo.)—Fiction.
3. Kidnapping—Fiction. I.Title.

PS3608.U577G66 2008
813'.6—dc22

                                                      2007042580

First Edition: March 2008

10 9 8 7 6 5 4 3 2 1

This book is dedicated to Joseph Hunt.

ACKNOWLEDGMENTS

The author wishes to extend his gratitude to his editor, Kelley Ragland. Also to Lieutenant Darrell Hatfield, Oklahoma City Police Department (Ret.), and Special Agent John Jones, Oklahoma State Bureau of Investigation (OSBI).

There ought to be no prisons.

—CLARENCE DARROW

Thank God for penitentiaries.

—RICHARD PRYOR

GOODBYE
SISTER DISCO

ONE

Tom Myers was a cautious, intelligent person. He was aware of the dangers of trying to be too familiar with Sam as well as with any senior partners. They liked to be flattered, but one could not be obvious about such things. Sam had seen him lurking by the study and called him in to join them in conversation. Tom was aware that what Sam wanted was an audience for his stories, but he still felt lucky at being called in. Tom Myers was twenty-five years old and hoped to be a partner by the time he was thirty. His starting salary at the firm was $130,000; more than most judges received. Twice the annual salary his father—a line worker with Chrysler—had ever earned. Tom was aware that his life was going through a significant transition and that it was perhaps happening very quickly. But Tom Myers did not think in terms of luck or even of fortune. He felt that he had been planning such things since the age of twelve. Hard work, good grades, scholarship, avoiding the things that get in the way of a good career and life. Plan your work, then work your plan.

At one point in the conversation, he felt it was safe to say, "And where did he get the authority for that?"

It made the men in the room laugh. Even Sam, as it flattered him. And Sam went on with his story, eventually getting to the part he liked. Something about his closing argument that had made one of the jurors actually *cry*. And, as Sam pointed out, he was the one defending the big bad corporation. Much laughter.

Beneath the study, in the basement of the house, there was a bar. You could go there if you wanted hard liquor rather than wine or beer. But the room was more or less dominated by Sam's kids and their friends who were home from college and they seemed a little raucous and territorial.

There was a young woman at the bar, waiting for a vodka tonic. She was twenty-two, her fair skin contrasting with her black cocktail dress. The dress was not something she would have picked for herself; it was something that Tom wanted her to wear. It didn't much matter to her one way or the other. She was an attractive woman, though not strikingly pretty. But she looked good in the dress and she knew that Tom Myers took pride in having her escort him to the party. The girl's name was Cordelia.

In its way, St. Louis is a large small town. Consequently, Cordelia Penmark was familiar with the children of Sam Fisher. She didn't like them. She thought they were vulgar. Yet some part of her knew that she didn't quite belong with someone like Tom Myers either. She knew that she would have to make a decision about Tom fairly soon. Because if ever a boy had marriage on his mind, it was Tom Myers. Cordelia did not begrudge him his ambition. And he was not a bad sort. But a marriage with him would be disastrous. Though she wouldn't be able to convince him of that. Not that she intended to try to convince him. Maybe later in her life, a Tom Myers would work. But not now.

Tim Fisher was saying something to her.

"What?" Cordelia said.

Tim said, "You going to Bodie's tomorrow night? He's having a party."

Tim Fisher standing next to her in his baggy jeans and his ridiculous facial hair, trying to be street. God, speaking to her as if they were old friends or something.

Cordelia looked at him briefly. Giving him that much, she said, "No." And walked away with her drink.

She drifted out to the back patio to have a cigarette. She smoked and looked out at the dead leaves on the pool cover. Cold out here. Her coat was somewhere inside. It would be warm in the spring and she would graduate from Washington University. And then what? Europe? The Hamptons? She was welcome in both of those places, had family homes in those places. But the social strata required that she play a certain part when she was there. Dinner parties, clubs, fund-raisers, etc. It required her to pretend. It was like work. It was hard to talk about it with people. Certainly she never talked about it with Tom Myers. He would hardly be sympathetic to the plight of the poor little rich girl. Tom *wanted* to be in the Hamptons. Would work his tail off his whole life to be a part of something that was vague, something that probably didn't quite exist. It's not quite Pamela and Averell Harriman, dahling. It's Tim Fisher in baggy pants trying to be Eminem.

Cordelia looked down into her drink. It was two-thirds drained. God, now she was becoming an alcoholic. Sucking down vodka like it was Hi-C. She would have to watch the drinking. She lifted her cigarette. Yeah, maybe cut down on the smoking too. It was what happened when you got bored at parties. Smoke and drink just to have something to do.

"Nice night, isn't it?"

Cordelia turned to see a man standing next to her. He lit a cigarette. An older fellow, perhaps around her dad's age.

"Yes," she said. "A little warm for this time of year."

The man nodded and gave her a polite smile. He wasn't bad-
looking for an older guy. Maybe he wasn't wanting anything from
her. Maybe an old guy who wouldn't try to hit on her because she
was half his age. More often than not, they just wanted to talk to a
pretty girl. Or a young one.

She said, "You're a lawyer, I suppose."

He looked over at her. "I guess," he said.

It made her laugh. She said, "Is it that bad?"

"No, it's not that bad. Are you a law student?"

"No. I'm still in college. I'll graduate this year."

"Hmmm."

She waited for him to ask what she would do next. But he didn't.
And she thought, He doesn't know. He doesn't know that I don't
have to think about a career or work or money. Sometimes you'd
let people know to keep things straight. She remembered seeing an
old Tom Hanks movie on cable. Tom Hanks when he was young
and thin, playing a recent college graduate from an aristocratic
family, telling the Long Island girl that he came from "that kind of
money" and then asking her to forget about it. She liked him in that
film because he played a pretty ratty guy and wasn't so serious. She
could tell this man, *I don't have to work. You see, I'm a Penmark.*
Maybe throw in a little Katharine Hepburn accent, see if it would
make him laugh. But maybe he wouldn't see that she was trying to
be funny. And she would hear him say "oh" in that way people
tended to say "oh" when they heard the name . . . well, maybe you

couldn't blame them for it. Maybe she would react the same way in their place, though she liked to think she wouldn't.

Cordelia said, "So ..."

"So?" the man said.

"You're going through a midlife crisis or something?"

"Right. The Corvette's down the street."

She smiled. "Corvette? Isn't that a little, uh, Arkansas for a serious lawyer?"

"That's not nice."

"I'm not a nice girl."

"Hey, don't tease a lonely man."

Cordelia laughed.

The man said, "Oh, here he comes."

It was Tom. Cordelia saw that he was uncomfortable. She looked from the middle-aged man to Tom. Tom said, "Hey, Ross. I see you've met my girl."

"Not formally," Ross said.

"My name is Cordelia."

The man called Ross gave her a tilt of his head.

Tom said, "Ross is our chief litigator. We call him the Terminator."

"Oh, God," Ross said, the intended flattery actually insulting him.

Cordelia said, "Do they now?"

"Not for a long time."

"You should see this guy at trial," Tom said. "He's the best."

And just like that, the mood was ruined. Cordelia, who was a little wise beyond her years, could see that both men now had to act in character. The middle-aged litigator had to hide his disenchantment with law and his cynicism from the young associate, and the young associate had to kiss up to the litigator. Ross was shaking his head now, saying, "It's just a job." He seemed embarrassed.

Cordelia thought, If Tom wasn't here, we could have fun. Not fun like dirty, shameful fun. But a good conversation. Jokes, some naughtiness, something to salvage this boring night. But we play different roles for different people and these two would not mix. She wondered if the man named Ross was aware of it.

She realized that he was when he said, "It was nice chatting with you." He started back to the house.

Tom was looking after him, not quite sure what to make of it. Finally, he said, "That Ross," like he really knew him. He turned to Cordelia and said, "You ready to leave?"

"Yeah," Cordelia said.

•

They were walking in the grass alongside parked cars, Cordelia keeping her thoughts to herself. Telling herself that it wasn't really Tom's fault. He was who he was. She had agreed to come to the party with him. She would have to do it soon: have to break it off with him. Maybe after Christmas. Maybe after New Years' Day. January was a bleak time anyway; he would be better off without her.

Tom walked ahead of her. The grass was still moist and she could feel wetness in her toes. The car was parked almost three houses down and she began to feel the chill. The noise of the party drifted off behind them.

They got to Tom's car, a new BMW 5 series he had bought a

month ago. Part of the lawyer's uniform, he told her. The cars were parked close together, so Tom had to squeeze between the car in front of his to get to the driver's side. Cordelia remained on the passenger side, watching him as he bent down to put the key in the lock.

Cordelia felt her heart jump before she realized that she was seeing the men. It surprised her because she hadn't heard anything. All in the same instant, she saw the first man on Tom's side of the car and another man on her side, to her left. She was frightened already and her jaw dropped as she saw the man on Tom's side raise a pistol. Tom said, "Hey," almost like he was starting a conversation, before the man shot him twice and he dropped out of sight.

Cordelia started to scream but then was grabbed from behind by the man on her side of the car. She smelled him, smelled his body odor, as an arm and hand encircled her throat and she felt something on her mouth and nose.

It was like a dream. Vague, black, hideous. Her vision blurring as she saw the man on the other side of the car, a man in a green jacket, pointing his arm down toward the ground. Tom, who she couldn't see now. Then the man pulled the trigger again.

That was all she remembered.

TWO

Terrill was pretty sure the guy had died with the second shot. He didn't scream or cry out. Just a short grunt and the guy was down. Then Terrill shot him in the head just to be sure. After that, he looked across the roof of the car. Ray had the girl unconscious now.

Lee drove up then in the Nissan Maxima. Ray put the girl in the trunk and shut it down. Terrill moved the guy's body behind the car so that he couldn't be seen from the road. His hope was that they were far enough from the house that no one had heard the shots. Terrill got on his knees to roll the guy's body under the back of the car. You would have to be right up close to the car to notice him. It would give them some time. He got into the Maxima and Lee drove them out of there.

Lee said, "Is it her?"

"No," Ray said, "we grabbed someone else."

"I'm just asking."

"Calm down," Terrill said. "Both of you. It's her, Lee. Just keep it under the speed limit."

"I am."

Lee Ensler had stolen the car the day before. The plates had been switched. Still, they would switch the car with another one about two miles away. Terrill had taught Lee to steal cars. Prior to meeting Terrill, Lee had never committed a felony in her life. She had been a journalist. Several of her pieces had been about Terrill.

Only one had been written after she interviewed him. Then she had gone underground. She was twenty-nine years old.

From the backseat, Terrill reached up and put a hand on her shoulder. "You're doing fine, babe."

They came to an intersection and stopped. A car made a right turn in front of them and then they went through.

Lee said, "I finished writing it, Terrill."

"You did?"

"Yeah. I think it's good. Maybe you can take a look at it when we get back."

"All right, Lee. Everything in time."

"But you said we need to have it ready for tomorrow's news. We—"

"We will, babe. Everything in time."

THREE

Hastings was standing on the porch, speaking on his cell phone. It was cold outside, but he didn't want his daughter to hear the conversation.

Hastings said, "This was not what we planned."

Eileen said, "You wanted to be with her for Christmas anyway. You said that."

"I know I said that. That's not the point."

"Then what?"

"You told her you wanted to spend Christmas with her. That you and her would go to your parents. She's expecting that."

"George—"

"Eileen, you told her that."

"She can still go."

"Go to your parents without you?"

"Why not? You can go too."

"Are you nuts? Spend Christmas day with my ex-in-laws who can't stand me?"

Eileen paused. Then offered: "Dad thinks you're okay."

Hastings sighed. Eileen's father didn't seem to feel one way or another about people. When he and Eileen had been married, Eileen's father would give him a handshake without eye contact and then retreat to his office or the television. He didn't seem to have much to say to Eileen either. Which might explain a few things. Eileen's mother, in contrast, had taken an active dislike to

Hastings from the start. And it hadn't taken Hastings long to figure out that the old lady resented Eileen for her youthful beauty. All in all, there were more pleasant households to pass time in.

"Eileen, listen to what you're saying: Amy and I should spend Christmas Day at your parents, while you're in Jamaica with your husband. Do you think Amy's going to want to do that?"

"I don't know."

The offhand tone Eileen used when she said that was something he had heard before. Before and after their divorce. He had never quite gotten used to it.

Hastings said, "She's your daughter."

"I know she's my daughter." She sounded almost confused. She said, "Are you giving me attitude?"

"Jesus, Ei— listen, I don't want to have a fight with you. I really don't. But I'm really furious right now."

"Look, do you want me to explain it to her? I don't mind doing that."

Christ, Hastings thought. She actually believes she's being generous right now. She actually believes it.

Hastings closed his eyes, opened them. He told himself to slow it down and he tried to do it. In a controlled voice he said, "No, that's all right. I'll take care of it."

"You sure?"

"Yeah, I'm sure. I'll talk to you later, Eileen."

In the house, Amy was doing her homework. Twelve years old now, and mature beyond her years. Smart like her mother, but different in other respects. More mature, as Eileen herself would tell you. Hastings sometimes wondered if Amy was competing with

Eileen; trying to show everyone that she was responsible and had her stuff together and they didn't need to worry about her too. But it didn't seem likely that that was her motive. She just seemed to have figured things out. Or the little bats that had chosen to fly around inside Eileen's head had decided to leave her alone. Eileen, in her thirties now, had a restless nature. She always had to be moving. As if she was afraid that if she sat still, she might have to answer some questions she didn't want to answer. It was one of her ways of hiding things, from herself as much as anyone else. Years ago, Hastings had been vain enough to think he could change her. It seemed to happen a lot in movies, but not so much in real life. His Holly Golightly took off again and probably dumped the cat in Tower Grove Park.

Amy was five when George met Eileen. Eileen had had her unwed. A smart girl from a moderately wealthy family, maybe looking for a husband, maybe not. Good-looking and clever. George fell in love with her when he met her. They married a few months later and he formally adopted Amy a few months after that.

He had wanted to have more children with Eileen, but it wasn't what she wanted. Whatever else could be said about her, she had never deceived him about that. And when she'd left George a few years into their marriage, she had taken steps to make sure that he would have joint custody of the girl he had quickly come to think of as his own. Even when he got angry at Eileen, Hastings would remind himself of that.

George kept their condo in St. Louis Hills. Eileen moved into her next husband's house. A rich personal-injury lawyer, living in West County. Harmless enough guy, though Hastings was relieved that Amy had never taken to him.

Amy was looking at Hastings now, as he walked back in the door.

She said, "Was that Mom on the phone?"

"Yes."

"She's bailing on me, isn't she?"

She always had been a smart girl.

"She's not bailing on you," Hastings said. "She just—"

"Got a better offer?"

"She's going to Jamaica with Ted. You can go with them, if you like. But she didn't think you'd want to."

She was looking at him now. Her lip didn't tremble; perhaps she'd grown used to this.

Finally she said, "She's right, I don't want to go with them. I just think it's shitty, that's all."

"All right, let's not use language like—"

"Well, it is. She doesn't even tell me herself."

Hastings said, "Well, we'll figure out something to do."

A lovely holiday season. Depression, anger, and now anxiety over what to do. Hastings had never cooked a big turkey dinner in his life. Pasta and simple meat dishes were the most he'd ever undertaken. Apart from Eileen's parents, there was no family for either of them. Not in St. Louis. Both of Hastings's parents had passed away. And he had never really gotten along with his father anyway. He had some cousins in Nebraska, where he had been raised, but they were relative strangers to him. His father hadn't been too popular with his siblings, either.

Amy said, "Dad, don't worry about it. I don't mind spending Christmas here. Really, I don't."

So now they were both lying. Hastings fabricating that thing about Eileen saying Amy could come with her to Jamaica, Amy saying she didn't mind spending Christmas in what would suddenly become a very small, very empty condominium. Gifts of the Magi.

Hastings looked at his cell phone.

Shit. He'd missed a call. It was from Karen Brady, the captain of detectives.

He walked into the kitchen as he pressed her number.

She answered before the second ring.

"George?"

"Yeah, Karen. What's up?"

"We've got a murder and an abduction. In Ladue."

"Ladue?"

"Yes. Happened a few minutes ago. Or, the body was found a few minutes ago. George, it was right outside this lawyer's house during his Christmas party. There were judges and some city leaders there."

"Happened at the party?"

"No. Outside. About a hundred yards away. Chief wants you there."

"Have you called Joe?"

"No. The chief said to call you."

"All right. I'll call him."

When he got off the telephone, he looked at Amy with an apologetic expression.

Amy said, "Do you have to go?"

"Yeah. It could be all night."

She sighed and stood up. "I'll call Randi."

Randi McGregor was a friend who lived down the street. They went to St. Gabriel School together. When Hastings had a call, it was understood that Amy could stay the night at Randi's house. In exchange, Hastings had cooked many dinners for Randi—her parents were lousy cooks—and there was the small payment of having to listen to Randi's dad talk about Cardinal baseball and whatever else came to his mouth whenever they ran into him at Francis Park. A fair trade.

Hastings was off the phone with Joe when Amy came out of her bedroom with her overnight bag.

FOUR

Sergeant Joe Klosterman was a few years younger than Hastings. He was bigger and heavier and, with the mustache he had worn most of his adult life, looked more like a policeman. Hastings, a lieutenant, was senior to Klosterman. But they were friends. Neither one of them abused his rank.

Earlier in the year, Klosterman had had a cancer scare. The tumor had been successfully removed and he was back at work now and liking it. While he'd been sick, he'd been replaced by Sergeant Bobby Cain. Cain had been an unlikable man but a good detective. Cain was dead now. Murdered.

If Klosterman thought there was anything ironic about it—his replacement dying of gunshot wounds while he had feared dying of cancer—he had not said so.

Hastings arrived at the Fisher house in a brown 1987 Jaguar XJ6. It was his police unit, the product of a seizure made pursuant to the RICO Act, which the department had given to his homicide team. The previous owner had replaced the stock engine with a Corvette V-8. It was a fast car and it made a beautiful burble when it idled.

There was a police tag in his windshield and they let him drive through the front gate and up the driveway. When Hastings got out of the car, he had a sense of being early. Not that there was a lack of people. In fact, there were too many. Civilians, that is. Too many civilians. Goddamn party. He saw a middle-aged man talking to a couple of uniformed police officers. He went up and identified himself.

The man extended his hand and Hastings found himself shaking it.

"Sam Fisher," he said. "And you are?" Asserting authority to civil service.

Christ, Hastings thought. He said, "Lieutenant Hastings. Sir, is this your home?"

"Yes." Fisher seemed almost taken aback by the tone.

Hastings said, "Would you help us out, please? If these people haven't witnessed anything, would you please get them out of here? Now."

"Well, sure."

"Thank you."

Hastings said, "I'll want to talk to you later. Is that all right with you?"

"Well, sure."

He went on his way, his ego a little less bruised by Hastings's parting deference. Hastings turned to the patrol officers.

"Where's the sergeant in command?"

"Over there, Lieutenant."

With the patrol sergeant's help, they got the area thinned out and cordoned off. Yellow tape went up and the medical examiners and technicians relaxed. Somewhat.

By the time Hastings got to the body, Klosterman was already there.

On the ground was a corpse of a young man. White male, midtwenties, good clothes. Most of his face was gone. The police photographer was walking around the body, snapping shots of visible wounds, bloodstains, stepping near him for the close-ups.

Klosterman said, "Shot three times. Once in the face."

Hastings looked up and down the road. Different-colored mansions on both sides of the street. Ladue. Some of the most high-dollar real estate in the Midwest.

Hastings said, "Out here?"

"Yeah," Klosterman said. "It's strange. It doesn't seem like a domestic assault or drug feud. We don't know ... there was a girl with him."

"Who?"

"Young lady. Name is Cordelia Penmark. Recognize that name?"

"No."

"Her father is Eugene Penmark. That's what I've been told anyway."

"By?"

"A couple of the guests. Attorneys who knew this young man."

"Who is he?"

"His name was Tom Myers. Young attorney, starting out his career." Klosterman paused. Then said, "It's a fragile thing, isn't it?" He had a son of his own, in high school.

"Yeah," Hastings said. They were neither one of them given to being maudlin. The nature of the work made that impossible. But looking at the young man, Hastings thought of his own age. Forty now. Not old enough to have a son of that age, but old enough to have a grown son. Hastings said, "Shit." He turned to Klosterman. "You said something about a girl?"

"Yeah. People saw him leave with a girl. Cordelia—"

"Penmark. Yeah, I got that. You asked if I recognized the name, though."

"Well, the thing is, she's rich."

"So?"

"No, I mean rich. Her father's one of the Forbes 400."

"I don't read that magazine."

"He owns some sort of software company. I don't know the name. He's a billionaire."

"Oh."

"So, what I'm thinking is, she left with someone else. Or she killed him and took off. Or..."

"Or she was abducted."

"It seems likely," Klosterman said.

"For ransom?"

"That, or it's a coincidence."

Hastings said, "Man."

He saw a news-channel van parked in front of the house, a handsome young man positioning himself in front of the camera, lights outlining him and throwing a long shadow across the lawn.

Hastings said, "Has the girl's family been notified?"

Klosterman turned to a patrol officer. The patrol officer said, "Yes. Delaney called them."

To Klosterman, Hastings said, "There'll be a lot of people to interview. Will you call Howard and Murph for me?"

"Yeah."

Hastings went back to the patrol sergeant, whose name was John Baumann. Each was vaguely familiar with the other, though they had never worked the same detail before. Sergeant Baumann was a younger sergeant; in his twenties, he'd had his stripes less than a year. Hastings believed that Baumann had screwed up this crime scene already by not taking adequate charge, but he still needed the man's help. There was a certain way to discuss this sort of police procedure. Diplomacy, nuance, tact.

"John," Hastings said, "This is becoming a clusterfuck. Half the guys here don't know where the crime scene sign-in sheet is. Please make sure every cop knows where it is and that they sign it. As for the rest of these people who aren't witnesses and are just rubbernecking, we need to get them the fuck out of here. Now. Also, get barricades set up on the road so we don't have media guys tromping all over the place. The guy that owns this house is some sort of big wheel, so more than likely the chief or deputy chief is going to show up here. If they see this, I'm going to get my ass chewed off. So help me out, okay?"

"Sure, Lieutenant."

Hastings patted him on the shoulder as he left. "Thanks, John."

Hastings walked back to the front of the house. Sam Fisher was still talking to the two men he had been talking to earlier. Fisher turned to acknowledge him.

Hastings said, "I need to speak with you."

Fisher hesitated, but the two men moved away from him.

"Okay," Fisher said.

"You're aware that the young man is dead?"

"I know," Fisher said. "It's just a terrible thing. A terrible thing."

"Did you know him?"

"Yes. He worked for the firm."

"An attorney?"

"Yes."

"What did you know about him?"

"He was an exceptional young man. A good lawyer, a hard worker."

"No trouble that you're aware of?"

"Like what, sir?"

"Drugs, gambling . . . that sort of thing."

"No. Not him. He had everything going for him."

"Did he bring a date here?"

"Yes."

"Who?"

"He brought a young lady named Cordelia Penmark. She's Gene Penmark's daughter."

"Do you know where she is?"

"I thought she left with him."

"Did you see them leave together?"

"No, but I'm sure someone did. They came here together and she was gone when he was gone."

"Had you met the girl before?"

"No. I met her for the first time tonight."

"Did he or she have an argument with anyone here tonight?"

"No. In fact, I don't think he had more than one drink the entire night."

"Excuse me, Officer?"

Hastings turned to see another man who had just walked up.

"Yes?"

"My name is Ross Kaufman. I was talking with them both, shortly before they left. Is the girl dead?"

"Excuse me?"

"The young lady, is she ..."

"We don't know. We think she's been abducted."

The man seemed shaken.

Hastings said, "Did you know her?"

"No. I just met her tonight."

"You did?"

"She was in the back, smoking a cigarette. And I went out there to have a smoke and started talking with her. I'm a lawyer at Sam's firm."

"Anything unusual?"

"No. We probably only talked a couple of minutes. And Tom came up and said he was ready to go."

"Any sort of anger between them, then?"

"Anger? No, I don't think so. I think she'd've rather stayed. But that's speculation." Kaufman added, "Is she okay?"

"We don't know yet. Would you mind giving me a card, in case I want to ask you some more questions?"

Kauffman handed Hastings a card. A middle-aged man looking distressed, missing the smile of young girl.

Klosterman came over. Hastings turned his back to the attorneys.

"George, we checked the young man's body. His wallet, his money are still on him. He wasn't robbed."

"Oh."

"Also, the girl's mother is here now."

FIVE

The woman was in her late forties. She wore glasses and her hair was long and gray and unfashionable. She did not look like the sort of woman who sat on a billion dollars. She looked like she worked at a library.

This is what Hastings thought, anyway. Like most detectives, he'd take a generalized guess if nothing else was available, and right now there wasn't.

When Hastings was a young patrol cop, he responded to a call reporting an auto collision on I-64 near the Kingshighway exit. It was one of those bad ones involving an eighteen-wheel semi and a car. The car's roof was completely sheared off; the sort of crumpled, twisted thing you see and you know that the odds of the occupant surviving the crash are slim. As he suspected, the woman driving the car had died upon impact, and the only positive thing you could think was that it had happened instantly without the person being burned first.

A few minutes later, a man drove up to the wreck and got out of his car and ran toward the carnage. It was Hastings who stopped him before he could see anything. The man said, "My wife's in there. My wife—is she . . . ?"

"Sir," Hastings had said, "please step back."

And the man said, his voice shaking, "She didn't make it, did she?" Knowing in the way people seem to know.

Hastings paused for only a moment, wondering in that moment

if someone else could do this, but knowing that he was there and he would have to. And he said, "No, sir, she didn't. I'm sorry."

It was a nasty, necessary part of this business. Passing on tragedy and watching some poor man collapse with grief. But it had to be done.

Hastings led the woman into Sam Fisher's study, so they could talk alone. They were still standing when he said, "Are you Mrs. Penmark?"

"No, my name is Beckwith. Adele Beckwith. I took my maiden name after I divorced Cordelia's father." She said, "Where is my daughter, Detective?"

"We don't know, ma'am. She may not have been with the young man when—"

"When he was killed?"

"Yes. The good news is, there's no evidence as of yet that she's been harmed."

The woman stared at him. "No evidence? She's missing, isn't she?"

"Yes."

"Do you know where she is?"

"We don't. I'm sorry."

The woman sat down on the couch. She put her face in her hands. Hastings could see that she was trembling.

"Ma'am," he said, "please don't jump to conclusions."

She looked up at him, her face screwed up with grief.

Hastings said, "We're working on it."

"Work—there's a young man out there who's dead. And you don't know where she is. You don't know."

No, Hastings thought, I don't. Because it wasn't his daughter that was missing. He could empathize, but he couldn't know.

He said, "Can you talk to me?"

After a moment, she nodded her head.

"When is the last time you talked to her?"

"... Yesterday ... she called me yesterday."

"Did she seem okay?"

"Yes ... we talked about what we would do on Christmas. ..."

"Was she in any distress when you talked to her?"

She struggled and then shook her head.

"You sure?"

She nodded.

"Do you want to talk about this later?"

She nodded again.

"I'm sorry, Ms. Beckwith. We're going to do everything we can to get her back to you. Okay?"

"Okay."

"I'm going to bring an officer back here to sit with you. All right? She's going to sit with you for a while. Okay?"

"Okay."

He went out to the front of the house and pulled Officer Annie Soames aside. To him, it was not a chauvinistic thing to ask a woman officer to comfort a woman. He knew from experience that it worked, and few cops, men or women, would dispute it. He had just escorted Annie inside when he saw Murph running up to him.

Detective Tim Murphy—Murph the Surf—had a build that was almost slight. But he possessed the air of fearlessness and menace that is inherent in Irish-cop DNA. Hastings had once seen him crook a finger at a man twice his size and say, "Come here," and the man did. Quivering while he did so. In such circumstances, self-doubt was not an issue for Murph.

In front of the house, Murph said, "George. We've got the girl's father on the phone. I think you need to talk to him."

Hastings followed Murph to the command post that had been set up after Hastings delivered his lecture to the young sergeant. Murph handed him a telephone.

"This is Lieutenant Hastings."

"Lieutenant? You're the one in charge there?"

"Yes, sir. For the time being."

"This is Gene Penmark. I'm Cordelia's father."

"Yes, sir."

"I've received a telephone call from a man who says he has my daughter."

SIX

Before he hooked up with Lexie, Gene Penmark had never attended a society event in his life. He did not own a tuxedo. Indeed, he thought he may have worn one to his high school prom, but that had been a long time ago. Gene was like that: brilliant in so many ways, ignorant in others. His had been a world of semiconductors and software, microchips and processors, not art or wine or people. For Lexie, he was a work in progress.

Gene Penmark was married to a woman named Adele when he'd met Lexie Lacquere. Lexie had called him to set up an interview for Channel 9. They had talked for no more than an hour. But in that time, something had been awakened in Gene Penmark. He was not an experienced man. Adele had been his first lover and women had never taken an interest in him. But Lexie Lacquere had taken an interest. At least, he thought so. She was the one who had taken the initiative. She was the one who had asked him out to dinner. Within a few months, he divorced Adele and, as soon as the law allowed, married Lexie Lacquere.

Eight years since and he owned a tuxedo now. An Armani. And he actually seemed to like mixing at the social events. He told Lexie he could not have done it without her.

Tonight they were at the Carpenter home in the Kingsbury section of St. Louis. A three-story mansion near the old Pulitzer house. Jo Carpenter and Lexie were cochairs of the Light Opera of St. Louis. They were a contrast: Jo, fifty-five and looking it, wearing a conservative gray dress with a black satin wrap around her zaftig figure. Lexie, narrow at the waist, her high, artificial breasts flattered by the maroon strapless dress she wore, shoulders tanned and healthy-looking. Feeling good at forty-one, she was. Jo Carpenter was from that social set people called "old money," such as it existed in St. Louis these days. Old money was not in Lexie Penmark's pedigree. Not by a sight.

But she was learning. Indeed, she was not surprised when a guest tipped her off that Jo's toast earlier in the evening—"Let's be frivolous tonight"—had been stolen from someone else. Lexie refrained from saying *I'm not surprised* or something else damaging. Her satisfied smile said enough, she thought.

The party was pleasant, though. The wine was sipped, the catered food nibbled. Guests stood and talked and mingled and behaved more or less as they were expected to. The Glenns were the Glenns. The Harrises were the Harrises. The Carlsons were the Carlsons. Congressman Hirsch hit on a doctor's wife who was roughly half his age. Pam Willits drank too much and started telling people her first husband was gay, so she knew what she was talking about. Ray Wharton was becoming irritated because none of the conservatives at the party would take his "impeach Bush" bait and give him a fight.

Lexie Penmark enjoyed it all. It was a world she felt comfortable in. People smiling, laughing, talking. She did not think of it as work.

She looked across the room at her husband. He was standing with three other men and a woman. He almost seemed comfortable talking with them. That was good. When she had first married him, he would follow her around at parties. Or expect her to remain with him at all times. As if he was afraid of being alone. She eventually taught him that he would be okay on his own. That if he remained in one place, people would come up to him. It was the way things worked.

He was laughing now. Ugh, Lexie thought. His teeth. Or rather, the set of his jaw. It never looked good when he laughed. It was not flattering to him. And it was probably not something you could have fixed; not a goofy jaw set. Perhaps, Lexie thought, it was better not to think about it.

She saw the smile on his face distracted. His glance down now, as he reached into the pocket of his jacket.

Oh, Jesus, he was answering his cell phone.

Lexie had told him not to bring the phone to events like this. *It's not like you're an ER physician,* she had said. *You're not on call.*

But it was no use talking to him about things like that. Clichéd as it was, his first love was technology. Gadgets. *Things.* He was never really comfortable without them.

His cell phone was next to his ear now. The people around him lowering their voices as he answered the call.

Lexie saw his expression change.

•

"Mr. Penmark?"

"Yes. Who is this?"

"Gene Penmark?"

"Yes," Gene said, his expression hardening now. "How did you get this number?"

"I got it from your daughter, Mr. Penmark. She's here with me."

"My daughter? Who is this?"

Gene was aware of his wife standing next to him now.

The voice was that of a younger man. Not much older than thirty, if that. He said, "Don't worry about my name. The important thing is, you believe that I have her. Here. I'll let you speak to her. Briefly."

There was a pause. Gene Penmark looked at his wife as he heard a shuffle. Waited for the joke to end. A prank. Like the time someone had tried to throw a pie in his face when he gave a commencement speech at Ohio State.

Then he heard her.

"Dad, it's me."

"Cordelia?"

"Yes."

The voice was hers. But it was strained. Not necessarily anguished; it was too, well, slow for that.

"Dad . . . they . . . they've got me."

"Cordy? *Cordy.*"

Another pause.

Then the young man on the phone again: "Okay, Gene, that's enough for now. Notice a little slur in her speech? We've given her a little something to help calm her down. Nothing too harsh, just a little tranquilizer. She's been through a lot, you see. Have you seen the news?"

"The news?"

"Oh, well, I guess you haven't. Well, when you do, you'll understand what I mean. But for now, you understand that we have her."

"I don't believe you."

"You don't—? Gene, what is the matter with you? Are you so enmeshed in your technology, you can't believe your own ears? That was your daughter you just spoke to."

"Maybe."

There was a silence.

Gene said, "Hello?"

"Yes, I'm still here, Gene. You're making things harder."

"I don't understand."

"You will," the man said.

SEVEN

Penmark told Hastings about the conversation he'd had with the young man on the telephone. He told Hastings that he hadn't taken it very seriously until he got home and saw on the news that Tom Myers had been murdered. Penmark said, "I remember meeting him."

Hastings said, "You're home now?"

"Yes," Penmark said. "I'm here with my wife."

Hastings looked at his watch. After midnight now. They weren't done with investigating this scene yet. Rhodes and others were still interviewing witnesses and the young man's body was still on the ground. Hastings estimated that they would be here when the sun came up. But then, this call changed things.

Hastings said, "You think it's someone trying to be funny?"

"Well, I'm not sure. I may or may not have heard my daughter."

"You mean, on the phone?"

"Yes."

Christ, Hastings thought. The man seemed awful nonchalant about it. Hastings said, "I think we need to talk about this."

"Okay."

"No, I mean, in person."

Hastings heard the man sigh. "Well, it's late and I'm not sure what else I can tell you."

"Well, Mr. Penmark, I'm afraid I'm going to have to insist. This is a homicide investigation. Perhaps your daughter's been abducted as well."

"Oh. Well, all right. Do you know my address?"

Now how the hell would I know that? Hastings thought. He said, "No, sir, I don't. Could you tell me?"

•

Klosterman gestured to the forensic investigators behind them, picking at things with their tools and tagging items for evidence. The St. Louis *CSI* guys. Klosterman had said before that if it were like the TV show, the detectives could just go home and rest once the technicians showed up to solve the crime, watch slow-motion film later on how the pieces explained precisely what happened. Would that it were so easy. They could match DNA with a donor, if an individual was suspected. But there was no O.J. to suspect here and the only bloodstains they'd found belonged to the young lawyer.

What they didn't have, Klosterman said, was witnesses. No one who saw people shoot the poor kid and drag away the girl. They had no description of a vehicle. They had very little.

Hastings stood in the dark with Murph as Klosterman summed things up as best he could. Murph had gotten a cup of coffee somewhere and there was steam coming out of the top.

Murph said to Hastings, "What about the girl's father?"

"It's a lead," Hastings said. "He got a call from someone claiming to have her. I have to go talk to him."

Klosterman said, "So it is a kidnapping?"

"It may be." Hastings said, "Can you take over here?"

"Sure."

"I'm going to take Murph with me, if you can spare him."

"Yeah, I've got Howard here. And some county guys to help out."

Hastings looked out amid all the emergency vehicles until he found his Jaguar.

"Shit," he said, "I'm blocked in." He said to Murph, "I guess we're taking your car."

•

They were going west on Litzinger Road. The road twisting and narrow; at times, Murph had to slow the Chevy to twenty to make right-angle turns.

Murph said, "You know, this is the only road through this area."

Hastings said, "Yeah?"

"So . . . after the shooter killed Myers, they had to go down this. One way or the other."

"Yeah. It's something to think about."

"It's something," Murph said. Though he didn't seem optimistic about it. If nothing came about, they would canvass the homeowners along the street and ask them if they'd seen someone driving a car that, what, "looked suspicious"? In the dark on an unlighted street, through the trees. Shit.

Murph said, "This is unusual."

"What?" Hastings said. "A murder in Ladue?"

"Yeah."

Ladue, Scarsdale, Beverly Hills. Places where people didn't have to think about gangsters, street corner drug feuds, prostitutes, pimps, or Saturday-night-special gunfire interfering with cable television.

Clean, well-kept places with grounds as opposed to front and back yards.

Detective Tim Murphy had grown up a million miles away, in a part of St. Louis known as Dogtown. Though he was conscious that his circumstances had been limited, it had never occurred to him that his childhood was deprived or even that rough. He remembered seeing some movie with Susan Sarandon playing a Dogtown hoosier who has an affair with a James Spader character who was supposed to have been West County rich. He thought the movie was ridiculous and he made a point of telling his wife, a Chicago girl, that he'd spent his entire childhood in Dogtown and had never once heard any woman or man say "cotton-pickin'." His wife responded that St. Louis did seem to cling to its class distinctions though, didn't it? And Murph rolled his eyes in reply.

Lieutenant George Hastings had grown up in a small town in Nebraska. From early adolescence, he had been more or less wanting to get out. He did not consider himself much of a scholar or a thinking person. But he was a good athlete and his hope was that baseball would move him out of the heartland.

He was a good first baseman. Not good enough to get a scholarship to either of the Oklahoma teams or the many in Texas, but good enough to get one out of Saint Louis University. He arrived in St. Louis in the early 1980s driving a '72 Buick Skylark. One of his earliest memories was viewing the Checkerboard Dome off Highway 40 and thinking it was the biggest sale barn he'd ever seen. A farm boy back then, but anxious to leave rural America behind. He had a good feeling then. A good feeling about living in a big city for the first time.

Injuries in his second year of college pretty much sidelined any realistic expectations of a career in baseball. But he stayed in St. Louis anyway and enjoyed watching the Cardinals play in the World Series in 1985 and '87. Graduated and tended bar for a year or so before enrolling in the police academy, giving it little thought at the time. A moderately successful career followed, with a failed marriage thrown in.

Joe Klosterman was Hastings's best friend. He thought Hastings was the best detective and the best overall law-enforcement officer he had ever worked with. When Hastings was passed over for the rank of captain in the last round of promotions, it angered Klosterman more than it did Hastings. It was the same way when Eileen left Hastings. Klosterman was a man who did not hate easily, but Eileen Hastings gave him pause. While Hastings seemed to accept her abandonment of him and her daughter with a certain understanding, Klosterman would spend perhaps too much time trashing the woman to his own wife.

Anne Klosterman, a smart and wise woman, said to her husband, "He knew what he was doing when he married her. It was what he wanted."

"She lied to him."

"How do you know that? You don't know him apart from the work."

"She left him for a guy with more money."

"Well, that was just a matter of time. Beyond being a babe, was there ever much to her? He knew what he was getting into."

Had George Hastings been privy to that conversation, he would have been inclined to agree with Anne. Though theirs was hardly an open arrangement, he had known that Eileen was hardly a safe bet for a stable marriage. But he had not thought her to be a shallow woman. They had shared an intimacy, a friendship that he could never quite explain to others. Not that he cared to. Eileen was selfish and unreliable, but she understood Hastings in a way few people did. She could make him laugh, too; open up a side of him that not many knew was there. It was easy to say that Eileen didn't deserve his love. But then deserving had little to do with it.

When Eileen left him, she told him that within a year he'd be grateful to her. Whether she meant it or was just performing was not something Hastings had spent a lot of time thinking about. It was what it was.

But he wasn't feeling very grateful tonight. He was thinking about the hurt on a little girl's face when she realized that her mother was bailing on her. I hate Christmas, Hastings thought.

"George?"

Hastings acknowledged Murph.

"Yeah?"

"You look pretty beat. Do you want to stop at a convenience store, get a cup of coffee?"

"No, that's all right. Let's just finish this."

"Do you really think it's an abduction?"

They were on I-64 now, heading west toward Chesterfield. The streets were still wet from yesterday's snowfall.

Hastings had let his mind drift from the kidnapped girl to his own domestic situation. Shitty, but he knew all cops did it. He said, "Yeah, I'm afraid it is."

"Do you know how much Penmark is worth?"

"No. Do you?"

"No. Not exactly. I know he's one of the richest people in the country, though." Murph said, "It must be nice."

"To be rich?"

"Not to be rich, so much. But not to have to worry. About money, I mean."

If he's the least bit human, Hastings thought, he's worrying to-night.

The twin green truss bridges came into view, looming over the Missouri River. They crossed over. Fifteen minutes later they were on a twisting rural road. Murph used the brights when there was no oncoming traffic.

They took another, smaller road off that one, which eventually led them to a security gate.

An armed guard came out of a small booth. His uniform was green.

Hastings leaned over to the driver's side window.

"Lieutenant Hastings. I've an appointment with Mr. Penmark."

The guard looked over the unmarked police car, going through a motion probably out of boredom as much as habit. Then he waved them through.

Murph said, "God, you'd think we were going to NORAD."

Hastings was looking out the windows and not seeing anything but forest and road. He said, "Where does this guy live?"

"I guess we just keep following the road."

Which they did. It twisted up, the bright lights of the car illuminating dark forest and dead leaves. Thick woods, though they were only a forty-minute drive from downtown.

The trees cut away and the view changed to one of grounds and open sky. And then they saw the mansion. A massive, beige brick thing. Obviously built within the last few years, but a traditional design. They could see only the front. But they knew it was perched on a bluff overlooking the Missouri. In back, there were two Olympic-size pools put together to form a T, a screened eating pavilion, a gazebo, his and hers cabanas, and three guest bungalows.

"Wow," Murph said.

EIGHT

Lexie Penmark was telling them that she had met Chief Grassino before. At a fund-raiser earlier in the year. She told them that she thought he was doing a great job.

The detectives nodded.

They were sitting on a couch in the study. Lexie sat across from them on a smaller sofa. There were a lot of hardback books on the shelves in the room, their covers still on them. Hastings didn't think they had been cracked.

There was a large-screen television built into the wall. Not against it, but in it. He'd seen one that size in a sports bar. There were no lamps in the room. Not one.

They had been led through the house by Gene Penmark. Through something that looked more like a hotel lobby than a foyer. From the outside, the building had resembled the Overlook Hotel from *The Shining*...a kid inside riding his Big Wheel through the hallways, trying to dodge the little girl ghosts. But they got inside and realized it wasn't like that. Not even close. Inside, it didn't seem to resemble a home or even a hotel. It seemed more like a corporation, and not a very warm, cozy one at that. Glass, steel, screens. Lots of screens.

Sitting in the room they called the study, Gene Penmark said, "I couldn't trace the call."

Hastings said, "Excuse me?"

"The call," Penmark said. "I couldn't identify the number of the caller."

"Well," Hastings said, "we'll look into that."

Murph said, "Did you recognize the man's voice?"

"No. Never heard him before."

Hastings said, "About how many people do you employ?"

"Oh, gosh." Penmark looked at his wife. "Well over two thousand. Why?"

"Well, possible disgruntled employee, perhaps. Someone who knows who you are. Who your family is."

Lexie said, "Well, that could be anybody."

Hastings said, "You said that you didn't believe the man when he told you he had your daughter?"

"That's right."

"But he put your daughter on the phone, didn't he?"

"I think so," Penmark said. "I'm not too sure, though."

"But you'd recognize her voice, wouldn't you?"

"Well, I believe I would."

Hastings said, "Does your daughter live here?"

"No." It was Lexie speaking now. "She has a condo in the loft area."

Hastings said, "What does she do?"

Penmark said, "She's a student at Washington University."

"How often do you see her?"

"Oh . . ." Penmark looked at his wife for an answer.

Lexie said, "I'd say about once a week."

"Sunday dinner?" Murph said.

"No," Lexie said. "It's not formal, like that. What I mean is, she drops by here and there."

Hastings said, "When was the last time you saw her?" directing the question to Penmark again.

Which made him look at his wife again.

Lexie said, "We saw her last Tuesday, right?"

"Yes," Penmark said, "I think that's right."

Hastings said, "Do you have other children?"

"Yes. I have another daughter. Her name is Edith. She's called Edie."

"How old is she?"

"She's about twenty-five, I think. She was going to school in Pennsylvania. Penn. But that didn't work out and she was married for some time. They divorced about a year ago."

"Where is she now?"

"She lives here now."

"Here in this house?"

"Not in the house. She stays in one of the bungalows. Outside."

"Are she and Cordelia close?"

Gene Penmark seemed to snort. He was a man of power and authority and he was not used to blunt questions.

"I don't know, Lieutenant."

"How about you? Would you say you and your daughter have a close relationship?"

"I don't see what that has to do with anything."

Hastings made a shrugging gesture with his hands. Like, *Maybe it does, maybe it doesn't, but work with me here.* "It might help me, Mr. Penmark."

"Well, we don't talk all the time. But my daughters . . . my children know that . . . I'm . . ." He was looking at his wife again.

Lexie said, "They've grown up, Mr. Hastings. You know how that is."

Actually, Hastings thought, he didn't know. His only daughter was twelve and she'd never had to live in a glass box.

Hastings said, "Mr. Penmark, is your daughter . . . wild?"

"Which one?"

Hastings paused for a moment, looking at the man they said was a genius. "Cordelia," Hastings said.

"Wild? No, I don't think so. She's never . . . been in trouble. Used drugs . . . not that I'm aware of."

"Who does she hang out with?"

"I really don't know."

"But you met Tom Myers before?"

"Yes. I remember him."

"You know he's been killed?"

"I know that now."

"So, knowing that, do you think this is a prank?"

"I don't know. Before, I did. But now—well, now I just I don't know."

Murph said, "His name was Tom Myers."

Hastings gave Murph a look. Hastings had not been unaware of Penmark's tone himself. He was a cold fucking piece of work. But he was not a suspect.

Tim Murphy had been on the receiving end of gunfire. Delivered from another, much colder piece of work. Still, when he saw Hastings look his way, he shut it down.

Penmark was aware of something between the two policemen, but he didn't know what it was. He said, "Pardon?"

"Nothing," Hastings said. "You told me before that the man said they had given your daughter a tranquilizer."

"Yes."

"He used that word—*tranquilizer*?"

"Yes."

Hastings said, "Well, sir. It may well be a kidnapping. In cases like this, the FBI is notified."

"The FBI? Is that really necessary?"

The detectives were looking at him again.

"I mean, at this point?"

Murph said, "Please understand, Mr. Penmark, it's not a question of us trying to pass it off. This is part of their mission. They have resources and manpower unavailable to us."

Lexie said, "Would you still be involved then?"

It took Hastings a moment to realize that she was directing the question to him.

He said, "Us?"

"Well, you."

"I don't know, ma'am. It's not my call. But I'll try to do everything I can."

Gene Penmark said, "But what will they do?"

"To start, they'll come here and set up tape-recording equipment on all your phones."

"I already have that."

"Excuse me?"

"I already have that," Penmark said. "On all my phones."

"Including your cell phone?"

"Well, not on that one. My homes and office."

There was a pause. And Lexie Penmark said, "His lawyer told him it was okay. As long as he's one of the people on the phone."

Murph glanced about the room. He wondered if they were being videotaped.

•

Driving down the road, Murph said, "What now?"

Hastings said, "We wait."

Murph said, "We're in the dark, man. And that guy didn't help one fucking bit."

"Yeah," Hastings said, "he's a strange bird."

Murph said, "Makes me wonder if she was trying to upset him. If such a thing was possible."

The guard waved at them as they drove past his booth.

Later, Murph said, "His wife."

"Yeah?"

"Do you know who she is?"

"No."

"She used to be Lexie Lacquere. Sexy Lexie?" Murph said. "She used to be on Channel 9 before she became Lexie Penmark."

"Oh, yeah," Hastings said. "Vaguely."

"Real cute thing with the fake boobs. Remember?"

"Yeah."

"Sexy Lexie. She's aged a little, but she still looks good."

Hastings said, "I usually watch the news on the other channel."

"Which one?"

"I don't remember."

Murph said, "I remember she was married to some other guy. A firefighter, in fact. And then all of a sudden she wasn't married to the firefighter and was married to this guy. Just like that."

"Yeah, well, her funeral."

The car was on the interstate again, the twin green bridges coming back into view.

Murph said, "You want me to take you home or back to the crime scene?"

"Crime scene."

NINE

She answered on the third ring.

"Hello?"

Hastings said, "Hi, it's me. Are you up?"

"Yeah. I just got out of the shower. What's up?"

"I've got some time. I just wanted to see if you'd like to meet for a cup of coffee."

"You mean before work?"

"Yeah, if you can."

It was a little after seven in the morning. Hastings knew that Carol usually set her alarm at 6:15 A.M. during the week. Her reading glasses were always by the bed.

"I can," she said. "I'll see you in about fifteen minutes?"

•

Carol McGuire was an attorney whose primary clientele were criminals. She used to be a public defender, providing legal representation to those who could not afford an attorney. She was a good lawyer, tough and bright. When she met Hastings, they were both, so to speak, on the clock. He was trying to get information out of a witness while she was trying to protect the witness's rights, and maybe something more. Voices were raised, fronts were presented, neither of them faking things or getting self-righteous. A couple of days later they had dinner together and confirmed that they shared a strong, mutual attraction. So they tentatively began working out something they never quite gave a name to. A long-term affair or a courtship or simply seeing each other. Being fairly wise people in this modern age, neither of them tried to define the relationship. Hastings was recently divorced and, in his way, relatively inexperienced at this sort of thing. He had hardly been monastic before he married Eileen, but things had been different then. Before his marriage, there had been no complications with children.

He had been involved with Carol McGuire for only a few months. They were around the same age and they appeared normal, as far as couples can appear normal. They were similar and different. In some ways they acknowledged their differences, and in some ways they did not. Hastings was, like most cops, of a fairly right-wing sensibility, while Carol could not contemplate ever voting Republican and had trouble understanding why anyone would. But they both had a healthy interest in sex and their conversation was rarely uncomfortable or forced. Carol McGuire was also divorced. She had no children. So far, she had not said much about having children.

•

A delivery truck rolled by on the cobblestoned road, a small noise of hammering wheels and stretching springs. Then it was gone and they could hear the murmur of people chatting while they stood in line to order their morning lattes. The coffee shop was on a corner in the Central West End, near Carol's apartment.

Carol was dressed conservatively in a blue skirt and jacket and white blouse. Hastings imagined she had court today. She was not a sexy dresser, not a glamour dresser. But Hastings realized, with some comfort at this age, that that didn't matter much to him. She was undoubtedly feminine and the garments beneath the business attire were more often than not lace. This morning, her hair was pulled back and she was wearing her glasses.

Hastings did not want to discuss the murder of Tom Myers or the abduction of Cordelia Penmark with her this morning. Not now. And without giving it much thought, he told her about his frustration with matters pertaining to his home life. In particular, his frustration with Eileen. He did not stop to ask himself if Carol wanted to hear about it. He did not think about that. It was with him and he needed to let it out.

Carol said, "Well, are you really surprised?"

"No, I suppose not."

"This is not the first time you've told me something like this."

"I know." Hastings looked up, aware of her now. "I'm sorry. Is it getting old?"

"Well, yeah, a little."

"I'm sorry."

"You keep saying you're sorry. But..."

"Well, what do you want me to do? She's the mother of my daughter."

"Divorce her."

"I did divorce her."

"I mean, divorce yourself from her."

Hastings sighed. "Not this again," he said.

Carol gave him a balanced smile. "I'm not accusing you, okay? I'm not accusing you of carrying a torch for Eileen. But it seems like every couple of weeks, I have to hear a bad Eileen story. Can you understand that I would be—well, I'm not going to say jealous, but, well, tired of it."

"You have nothing to be jealous about. You know that."

"I do know that. I know she's not your lover. I do, George. But there's an intimacy there."

"No—"

"There's—"

"No. There's not."

"There's something there, George. A connection."

"Yes, there is a connection. Her name is Amy. There's nothing I can do about that."

"Okay."

"She's our daughter. We have to—"

"*Okay.*"

Carol leaned back in her seat. A silence between them. Before it could stretch, she said, "You'll work it out."

"I know," Hastings said. He took comfort in the contrast between her blouse and her neck. "This is my fault. I'm dumping my domestic squabbles on you."

"It's not your fault. Forget it." She smiled. "I'm glad to see you." Saying it and meaning it.

"I'm glad to see you too."

"You've been up all night, haven't you?"

"Yeah."

Carol shook her head. "Shit," she said, feeling bad now. "Why didn't you tell me?"

"I don't know."

"Oh, George. It's a homicide?"

"Yeah."

"Oh, shit. I'm sorry."

"What are you sorry for?"

"You've been up all night and you take time out to see me and then I give you heat about . . . I'm sorry."

"Don't worry about it."

"You should've just come straight over this morning. We could have at least made love."

"But you were already out of the shower when I called."

She smiled almost sadly and gave a small shrug. "Maybe tonight," she said.

"That'd be nice." He said, "When do you leave for Chicago?" She was spending Christmas there with a sister.

"The day after tomorrow. My sister's first Christmas with her second husband. It should be interesting."

"Yeah," Hastings said, "I imagine it will be."

And he left it at that.

It could be weird, this business of dating. There was as much focus placed on what was not said as what was said. Hastings had never told Carol that he loved her. Nor had she said such a thing to him. He liked her very much and knew that she was not wily or adolescent in her dealings with him. He knew that when she had brought up her sister's second marriage, she had not been angling for a marriage proposal herself. They never discussed marriage. Never had an occasion to. But she was a perceptive woman, and after she had let out the reference to her sister's second husband, she was well aware of the effect it had. They were both of them cautious, always cautious. As if sensing the discomfort she had caused, Carol McGuire said, "I'll miss you."

Hastings said, "I'll miss you too."

"But we'll see each other before that. Tonight?"

"Tonight sounds great."

•

Matt Lauer was standing next to a young black man wearing baggy pants and thick black shoes, cap worn backward. Matt in a suit, the other guy in his uniform. Matt asking him a question about his refusal to change his shoes for the television show where celebrities waltzed around with professional dancers, the guy responding that his refusal to change his shoes somehow put him on the same level as Rosa Parks.

The interview was drowned out as a woman in her late thirties turned on the kitchen sink and rinsed milk and orange juice out of cups. She set the cups upside down on a towel, close to the small television set.

The woman was wearing sweats and a white T-shirt. She had blond hair, cut short, and she had an athletic build. Her name was Terry McGregor.

Outside, a Jaguar XJ6 rumbled to a stop. The rumbling cut off and Hastings got out. He walked to the front door of the house and knocked.

He was holding a bag of coffee. Terry McGregor came to the door and let him in.

"Hi," Hastings said. "I brought this for you."

"Oh," Terry said. "You didn't need to do that."

"Well, I appreciated you taking Amy in. Especially on such short notice."

"Forget about it. Anytime you need to drop her off, she's welcome."

Come on in and have a cup of coffee. The girls are upstairs getting ready."

He followed her back to the kitchen and took a seat at the table. Terry said, "You take anything in it?"

"A little milk."

She poured enough milk in the bottom of his cup to cover the bottom. Then poured the coffee on top of it. She set the cup of coffee on the table in front of him.

Terry and Chet McGregor had moved to St. Louis a few months ago. They were from Knoxville, Tennessee. Chet was a big fellow, military-looking with his hair cut high and tight. Talked big too, and often. He was a sales engineer. Hastings did not like Chet much, when he gave it any thought. But he liked Terry well enough. She had been a teacher and a girls' basketball coach for some time, but had given that up when she had Randi.

She went back to the kitchen sink, turning to George as she conversed with him.

"Were you out all night?" she said.

"Yes."

"You must be exhausted."

Hastings shrugged. "I'll get a nap later today. Chet gone already?"

"Yes," Terry said. She still had her Tennessee accent. Hastings thought it was pleasant. "He left at six thirty. He's flying to Cleveland today. He should be back late tonight."

Hastings felt some relief. Chet McGregor made more money than Hastings, had a sweet wife and a lovely daughter, and was not a bad-looking dude. But he was one of those guys who always had a need to compete with other men. He would speak often of his days as a champion football player. Not pro or college, but high school. And when Randi told him that Amy's dad had played baseball for the college team, he had looked at Hastings and said, "Really?" Finding it funny that Hastings had never mentioned it. The close friendship between the men's daughters made social contact unavoidable. Hastings found himself being very quiet when he was around Chet McGregor. Hastings found Chet not irritating so much as tiresome. Chet liked to talk a lot.

But Chet's being a bore was a small thing to Hastings. Chet's wife after all had been a great help to him and Amy. Her offer to put Amy up at any time had been entirely sincere. And the generosity had been extended without a moment's thought as to whether it would inconvenience her. It was what people like Terry McGregor did.

Had the McGregors moved to St. Louis, say, one year earlier, a friendship with them would probably not have come about. Eileen was an unregenerate snob and the likelihood of her taking up a friendship with the McGregors would have been slim indeed. She would have found Chet an unbearable oaf and would have dismissed his wife as a southern sorority yokel. And this conclusion would likely have been based on a five-minute encounter. Or a quick look at the woman's clothes.

Hastings himself was a bit of a snob. Indeed, that trait had in part drawn Eileen to him in the first place. But as Eileen would learn after marrying him, his snobbishness was of a different kind.

Terry McGregor said, "Amy says you have a girlfriend now?"

Hastings smiled. "Does she."

"You been seeing the woman long?" Her tone was pitched just about right. Curious and friendly, though not prying.

"A few months."

"That's good," Terry said.

That could have meant anything. Perhaps Amy had worried aloud that he was lonely. Or that it meant that he had stopped thinking, even in small ways, that Eileen would undergo a full-scale character change and come back to him. Maybe the woman was glad to know he had a lover and companion. She wouldn't be the only one.

Hastings said, "I can drop the girls off at school."

"You have time?" Terry said.

"Sure."

•

A half hour later, Hastings was motoring down I-64 toward the police department, Forest Park on his right, downtown and the Arch coming into view in front of him. It was catching up with him now, the lack of sleep, and he decided that he would go to the cot room and get a quick nap as soon as he got in. It was that or set his head on his desk, because he could only fight it for so long.

But then his cell phone rang and he answered it, and it was Klosterman on the line, canceling that nap stat.

Klosterman said, "Now it's official."

Hastings said, "You mean an official kidnapping?"

"Yeah, we got a ransom note."

"How?"

"It's on television. The Internet, too."

"I don't understand."

"The kidnappers gave a tape to a local news channel."

"So the media got it before us?"

"Yeah."

"Oh, shit," Hastings said. Feeling really tired now. "Have you contacted the feds?"

"Yeah. Their ASAC—Assistant Special Agent in Charge—is coming here with a couple of special agents. Show us how this shit works."

"Great," Hastings said. He'd known it would come to this. FBI moving in, trying to take over, talking to all the metro cops as if they were shaved bears. *You see this thing here? This is what we call a "recording device." Can you say that?* That sort of bullshit. Only this time, there would be additional axes to grind. Unless they had forgotten about what Hastings did. And feds aren't high on forgetting. Few law enforcement officers are.

Hastings said, "What about the ransom note? Or message?"

"I gotta say," Klosterman said, "it's pretty well done."

TEN

The terrain flattens as one crosses the Mississippi River west to east. Gone are the steep hills of the Ozarks and the bluffs of eastern Missouri. The land remains even all the way up I-55 to Chicago. Ronald Reagan was a native of Quincy, Illinois, and being a natural politician, he was adept at exploiting his rural roots for those "It's Morning in America" campaigns. But privately, he was a man content to live the rest of his days in California, presuming he could not be president. Privately, he would express pity for those who had never managed to escape the Quincys of this world. "There's nothing to *do* in those places."

It could make you anxious, out there in the heartland. A place where your mailbox might be a good mile away from your house. Long dirt roads that stemmed off cracked roads that could go for miles before hooking up with State Highway 9. The nearest place to buy cigarettes and milk was White Hall. It *was* isolated. Even though St. Louis was only an hour's drive away.

At the end of one of those long dirt roads sat an old white clapboard two-story house. There were two rusted vehicles, skeletal remains, sitting in the unkempt front yard. Behind the main house was a barn, rusted red now and leaning forward like the prow of a ship. Propane tanks were off to the side of the house. They were filled for the winter.

The house had belonged to Ray Muller's grandfather, the descendant of the original German immigrant who had come to southern Illinois before the First World War. The grandfather had died two years ago.

There were about a half-dozen people there now, including Ray and Terrill and Lee. Some of them had to share rooms. Privacy was discouraged. So were monogamous relationships.

Their new guest had her own room though. For now. She was locked in a room in the basement.

•

By the time they finished preparing the videotape, the sun was coming up. Jan and Toby were in the kitchen preparing breakfast for all of them. The others were attending to their daily chores. There was a television in the living room, among the sparse and run-down furnishings. The television was off. If you wanted to watch television, you had to have Terrill's or Maggie's permission. The same went for listening to the radio. Even if you were in the car just driving to town. Music was okay, though. But no news or talk radio.

Terrill and Maggie sat at the table in the dining room. The table was covered with papers. On top of the papers were assorted weapons: a couple of automatic rifles and handguns. On the wall behind the table hung a poster that had a picture of an arm holding a rifle and the caption "PIECE NOW!"

Also on the table was a videotape. It was a copy of the master, which was now upstairs in a cabinet next to Maggie's bed.

Maggie and Terrill knew the effectiveness of video. The Western powers—America and their kowtowing British—had viewed videotapes of the capitalist simps being murdered by Al Qaeda. Pleas for mercy delivered from a grainy background, poor sound quality . . . "Please . . . please . . ." All of it stupid and weak, virtually ignored by that war criminal Bush and his poodle Tony Blair.

But the effect it had on the masses. At least in England. After Kenneth Bigley was decapitated, his family blamed not the Arabs but Tony Blair, going so far as to say that Blair had blood on his hands.

Terrill sat listening to Maggie as she explained all this, nodding his head at the appropriate times. But he was unsure of something. He said, "Are you saying we should decapitate her?"

Maggie looked at him, briefly, before shaking her head. She was only three years older than Terrill, but she felt much older. Which was what Terrill needed.

Terrill was a beautiful boy. Maggie had thought so from the time she first met him. With his thick, dark shaggy hair and his sensitive, almost feminine mouth and eyes that hypnotized. He was a panther made man. A beautiful, beautiful boy. But he needed guidance.

"No," Maggie said. "We won't do that. We'll kill her if need be. But not that way."

"Okay."

A boy, Maggie thought. She said, "The objective here is to expose. Expose Gene Penmark for what he is. Him and his kind. We're not out to horrify people."

Terrill said, "Okay." Like he'd understood that from the beginning.

"But," Maggie said, "it helps. The way things are, people have already been conditioned to *expect* a decapitation. If they expect it, if they fear it will happen, we'll get results."

After a moment, Terrill said, "Right." He said, "You've read Lee's statement?"

"Yeah, I read it."

"And?"

"I worry about her," Maggie said. "She reminds me too much of those coffeehouse liberals."

"She's one of us now," Terrill said. "And she knows it."

"How was she last night?"

"She was fine. Didn't bat an eye."

"She's a schoolgirl."

"She's of value to us. She knows how to turn a phrase. And she's loyal."

"To what?" Maggie said. "You, or us?"

Had it been someone other than Maggie, he might have said, *What difference does it make?* But it was Maggie he was sitting with. And without Maggie, he would be nothing. He said, "It's us. I just helped her understand her priorities, that's all." Terrill got a little back then. "Are you sorry that I recruited her?" he said.

"No," Maggie said. "I'm not sorry. If we are to grow, we'll need people as well as money. It's not a social club. It's not camp. Make sure she knows that."

"She knows it," Terrill said. "So you're okay with the statement."

"Yes," Maggie said. "Have Ray and Mickey drop the tape off in town this morning."

"Why don't we let Ray stay here," Terrill said. "I'll go with Mickey."

Maggie lifted her hand in conciliation. *Suit yourself.* She had to give Terrill something once in a while.

•

Judy Chen was not a native St. Louisan. She had come to Missouri from Boston to go the state university's journalism school in Columbia. As cow town a place as ever they made, but it was the right place to start if you wanted this sort of career. She got out of there at the age of twenty-one and took a job in Amarillo, Texas. Which was a dump, but it was a job and it put her in front of the camera. She was there when Oprah came down with all her minions because the cattle ranchers had sued her for libel. Covered the trial to the degree her station would let her, hoping that national exposure would move her onward and upward.

After Oprah won the trial, Judy put out feelers to the major networks and CNN and MSNBC, but none of them gave her any positive feedback. Nor did any of the major eastern cities express interest. But she did get word back from a St. Louis affiliate who asked if she could overnight a résumé and some professional photos.

That got her out of Amarillo.

St. Louis wasn't too bad. But Judy Chen was as ambitious as she was cute, and she had no long-term plans to stay.

On this morning, she got out of bed when her alarm told her to and packed her stuff to go to the gym. She'd had the same trim waist she'd had when she graduated high school, but it didn't come easy. She would ride the exercise bike for one hour before showering and changing into her professional clothes.

She lived in a high-rise apartment on Lindell Boulevard, near the St. Louis Cathedral.

She stepped out of the elevator. The doorman opened the door and she walked out of the lobby and down the street.

Her Land Rover was parked around the block. After she'd unlocked it and gotten inside she heard her cell phone ring.

She answered it quickly. "Hello?"

"Judy?"

"Yes?"

Judy Chen had been asked out by football players, baseball players, men of power and wealth, most of them not caring anything about who she was or what she thought, but very much interested in screwing the cute little Asian chick they'd seen on television. Usually, she said no. Very rarely did she give out her private cell number. She said, "Who is this?"

"Well, for purposes of this conversation, my name is Carl."

"What can I do for you, Carl?"

Terrill said, "Boy, you are tough. Well, today is your lucky day."

"Why's that?"

"You know about Gene Penmark's daughter being kidnapped, don't you?"

Judy looked at the screen on her cell phone. The number was not identified. She took her hand off the ignition key.

"Who is this?"

"I told you: my name is Carl. Or Bill. Whatever you like."

"You said something about Penmark's daughter."

"Yes. I also said that today is your lucky day."

"Yes, you did."

"Do you know why?"

"Why?" She had already asked him this, but she knew that he wanted to control the pace of the conversation.

The voice said, "Turn around."

Judy turned around. On her backseat was a brown paper bag, the top folded over.

"You see a brown paper bag?"

"Yes."

"Inside that bag is a videotape. On that videotape is Cordelia Penmark. She was kidnapped last night by some very serious, very determined people. Cordelia is alive, you understand. She is very much alive. But she has been abducted."

"I—"

"Ah, Ms. Chen, I'm talking now. Take that tape to your station and play it. It's going to be the story of the day. Oh, and don't bother thanking me."

The man hung up.

A few seconds passed before Judy Chen looked in the bag and removed a videotape. She drove straight to the station and didn't stop to change out of her gym clothes.

ELEVEN

Most of the men on his team were in the detectives' squad room when he got there. Klosterman, Murph, Rhodes. They had the television set up and they replayed the tape. Not the original, Klosterman pointed out, but a tape of the news that had run a few minutes earlier.

News reporter Judy Chen was on the screen, saying that this was a News 9 special report. There were some graphics and then another woman's voice could be heard. The voice said, "Gene Penmark is a billionaire. His net worth is approximately two-point-four billion dollars. He is the owner of Penmark Industries. Last month, he floated his microchip company to Entech Company. As a result, Gene Penmark made a personal profit of forty-six million dollars. That figure does not include the net worth of his remaining businesses. That figure does not include the fifteen-million-dollar yacht he keeps on the French Riviera. That figure does not include the twelve-million-dollar jet he keeps at Lambert Airport. Out of that forty-six-million-dollar pure profit, Gene Penmark is being asked to give up two million dollars in exchange for the safe return of his daughter. We believe the decision is an easy one."

The screen changed and there was a young girl wearing a dress. She was holding a copy of the day's early edition of the *St. Louis Post-Dispatch*. She said, in a strange tone, "Please do as they ask, Dad. I want to come home. Please."

The picture changed and went back to Judy Chen at her desk. She said, "The police are continuing their investigation."

Hastings said, "Has anyone here spoken to that fucking woman?"

Klosterman knew he was referring to the news reporter, not the kidnapping victim. He was angry about it too and he said, "We have no record of her calling the Department."

"Goddammit," Hastings said. "God *damn* it."

Rhodes walked up on shells to him. "George," he said, "Captain Brady says the assistant chief wants to see you."

No doubt he would, Hastings thought.

•

Assistant Chief Fenton Murray's relationship with Hastings was not entirely settled. To start with, Murray had never worked as a detective; his entire career had been in either patrol or administration. When he was a patrol lieutenant, he generally took home less money than the average detective, who was technically lower in rank. The reason was, detectives worked a lot of overtime. The detectives did not openly speak of being an elite group. But they were a different tribe. A tribe within the greater tribe of the Metropolitan Police Department. Fenton Murray was black, but had been a policeman long enough that he was probably more Irish than anything.

Hastings, for his part, did not believe that he had any quarrel with Murray. He thought Murray was a bit full of himself and something of a blowhard, but he was more or less honest and a straight shooter. Whatever else could be said of him, Murray was not the sort of man who would glad-hand you in person, then push you off a cliff when your back was turned.

Fenton Murray had been with the St. Louis PD his entire law-enforcement career. In contrast, Chief Mark Grassino had been brought in from Atlanta to run the Department. Grassino had been assistant chief in Atlanta and had been in St. Louis a relatively short time. Hastings's contact with Grassino had been limited but positive.

Hastings was thinking about that now—wondering just how much of the chief's goodwill he had expended—though he wished he weren't, as Murray's secretary led him through the anteroom to Fenton Murray's office.

Murray was on the phone when he walked in, saying, "Yes, sir. Yes." Gesturing for Hastings to take a seat in front of his desk. "Yes, sir. Lieutenant Hastings is here now. . . . Yes, sir. Okay."

He hung up the phone and made a face. Mock curiosity.

Hastings said, "You've seen the news, sir?"

"Yes, I have. How did that happen?"

"I'm waiting to ask her."

"That was the chief on the phone. He's not happy."

"I don't blame him."

Fenton Murray went on as if he hadn't heard the acknowledgment. "It's a matter of perspective, Lieutenant. Perspective. One of the richest men in this city, perhaps the richest, his daughter's kidnapped . . . people want to believe we're doing something about it. And some television news reporter is one step ahead of us. We can't very well solve this by watching television, can we?"

"No, sir."

"Have you talked with this television reporter yet?"

"No, sir. I was planning to, but—well, sir, you called me in for this discussion."

He was pushing it, just. But then he'd just told the man he was waiting to talk to her about it. A police department is like any other organization: something bad happens, and everyone scrambles to avoid taking responsibility for it. *Well, there had been a message, but my secretary forgot to tell me about it.* And so forth. Hastings hated that sort of thing, and he was particularly hard on his own people when they tried it with him. But in this case, what had happened was legitimately beyond his control. He was getting irritated now because he believed Fenton Murray had to know that. And Hastings was fairly sure that Murray had gotten a full night's sleep, while he and his men had not.

Maybe the man sensed this, because the next thing he said was, "Did you get any sleep last night?"

"No, sir," Hastings said.

Assistant Chief Murray sighed. And Hastings realized it was as close to an apology as he was going to get that day. In a different tone, Murray said, "Well now it's officially a kidnapping. So FBI's in. We can work alongside, but it's their game. The chief's been on the phone with the local SAC. The ASAC and two of his agents are in the conference room."

"Okay," Hastings said. He had been expecting it. Indeed, he had even warned the Penmarks that it would happen. But it had happened sooner than he expected. The videotape on the news had accelerated things. It had upset people and made them frightened and anxious. It had reminded the authorities that they were not the ones in control.

Murray said, "Get as much of the file as you can, and meet us there as soon as possible."

"Yes, sir." Hastings stood up.

"George?"

"Yes, sir?"

Murray hesitated for a moment. "Have you had any dealings with the FBI since the Cahalin thing?"

The Cahalin thing.

Hastings told himself he should not be surprised that Fenton had brought it up. In fact, now that it was out, he was surprised he hadn't thought of it himself. Once they suspected that the Penmark girl had been kidnapped, it was just a matter of time before the FBI got involved. Frank Cahalin had been the former SAC for the FBI field office. He was dead now, having committed suicide. He had probably been aware that he would lose his trial. Hastings was not vain enough to be haunted by this. He was actually angry at Cahalin for doing it. By killing himself, Cahalin had deprived Hastings and others of the satisfaction of seeing him convicted in court. And Hastings had no doubt that he would have been.

Now Hastings said, "No, sir. I have not had any business with the FBI since then." His tone was a little hard then. He said, "Is the chief concerned about it?"

Fenton Murray said, "He didn't say anything to me about it."

After a moment, Hastings said, "And you, sir. Are you concerned about it?"

Murray flashed him a fierce look. "I think Frank Cahalin was a piece of shit," he said. "I'm not bothered in the slightest about him. But these feds may not see it that way."

"So what."

"So they may be a little chilly to you."

"I can handle it."

"You sure?"

Hastings wasn't bothering to hide his anger anymore. "Are you pulling me off the case?"

Murray's tone matched his. "No, Lieutenant, I am not. What I'm telling you is, the primary goal is to get this girl returned to her parents safely. *That's* the mission. You say you'll conduct yourself professionally, I believe you. But if they refuse to cooperate with us—directly or indirectly—because of you, then yes, sir, you *will* have to be replaced. If that happens it won't be fair, but fairness to you is not what's important here. Understand?"

Hastings straightened. "I understand," he said. "If that's all..."

"That's all. Go on."

Hastings walked out.

TWELVE

They didn't hesitate to bring up the fact that the television station had gotten a videotape of the victim before the police had. The agents wouldn't try to bawl him out or anything else direct like that. Just, "So you saw it on television?" followed by pitiful shakes of the head.

Hastings said, "We can't control the movements of the kidnapper. Or kidnappers."

There were three agents in the conference room with Hastings and Fenton Murray. Murray had done Hastings the kindness of sitting on his side of the table. The feds were on the other side. Dressed in full suits, as opposed to the herringbone jacket Hastings wore with dark slacks. Two of the feds had American flag pins on their lapels.

The ASAC wore a What Would Jesus Do bracelet. He was a tall, slender man in his fifties. He looked like a runner. His name was Jim Shellow.

The two other agents were in their thirties. Early to midthirties, clean shaven, and well groomed. Their names were Craig Kubiak and Curtis Gabler.

Hastings remembered watching a football game between Nebraska and Stanford University. A year when Stanford had a moderately competitive team. The contrast between the Stanford and Nebraska sidelines had been an added amusement to the game: on one side, clean-cut guys, blond with stylish haircuts, could have been models for *GQ*. On the other side, milling around Saint Tom Osborne, a bunch of mullet-haired two-by-fours in red jerseys who looked like they just got done changing a tractor tire . . . Stanford did well, but didn't win the game.

Hastings said, "My sergeant is arranging an interview with her right now."

Agent Shellow said, "Is that all?"

Hastings's voice was civil. He said, "What do you mean?"

"Well," Agent Shellow said, "it seems to me that we should be doing more than that, don't you think?"

"You mean," Hastings said, "threatening her with obstructing an investigation. Something like that?"

Agent Shellow was a bit taken aback: the Metro lieutenant had already thought of it. "Yes," Agent Shellow said, "that's exactly what I mean."

"I'd thought of that," Hastings said. "But that's only a misdemeanor. And it presumes that our DA would want to file on it. And I doubt he would. But even if he would, I don't think it's a good idea."

"Why not?" It was Agent Kubiak speaking now. His tone was not one of a man seeking input, but one of conducting an interrogation.

"Because we might need her," Hastings said. "Maybe the kidnapper feels comfortable talking to her. We go to her threatening charges, the first thing she'll do is refer us to the station's attorney. And we'll be stuck. And . . . we'll have lost the opportunity to work with her."

There was a silence then. Agent Gabler was taking notes and he stopped to look briefly at the ASAC. The ASAC looked over to Assistant Chief Murray, who wasn't going to give him any help on this one. Agent Kubiak continued to look at Hastings, appraising him. Hastings thought, *He knows.* He knows about Cahalin, but he's not going to say anything about it now.

"Listen," Hastings said, "for what it's worth, I'm not very happy about it either. Either she's pretty stupid or she just wanted to break a story and make a name for herself. Either way, she should have contacted the police first. And for whatever reason, she chose not to. But it's already happened and we can't change it."

"All right, Lieutenant," Shellow said. "Thank you for your recommendation. We'll take it from here."

Hastings said, "Where are you going?"

Agent Kubiak said, "Well, first we're going to interview the reporter. We'll keep you posted."

Hastings said, "I'm going with you."

Agent Kubiak smiled and shook his head. He looked over to Shellow as if to say, *I told you. I told you he was going to be this way.*

Agent Shellow said, "It's FBI's case now, Lieutenant. You can observe, and we'll call you if we need you. But it's a kidnapping and that makes it our ball game. You know how it works."

"Yes, sir, I do. But there's a homicide too. We can safely presume that the kidnappers killed Tom Myers. And that's my case."

There was another silence and exchange of glances around the table. Hastings kept a patient expression, resting a casual eye on Shellow. He'd decided that Kubiak wasn't worth eyeballing.

ASAC Jim Shellow turned to Fenton Murray.

Murray raised a hand, like there was nothing he could do about it. He said, "The lieutenant's right. It's our murder case. I've already discussed this with Chief Grassino. We all want the same thing here, really. We can joint-task it. And there's no point in the police and your boys interviewing the same witnesses separately. We can agree, can we not, that it's a waste of manpower. But the danger is that it gives the witness an opportunity to change his story on the second round. Best to do it all at once, don't you think, Jim?"

•

The meeting wrapped up shortly after that. Hastings got Fenton Murray alone and said, "Did the chief really say that?"

Fenton Murray said, "Don't talk to me." And then walked away. He was in a foul mood, obviously, and Hastings was wise enough to let him be.

THIRTEEN

Hastings remembered one time a copy of *St. Louis Magazine* being passed around the Department because it had an article titled "Single in the City" in it and there was a thirty-year-old patrolman who had been dumb enough to let himself be featured as one of the city's prime catches. The article said something like, "Get to know some of the metro area's most successful singles and find out what makes them tick, what they like to do when they're not hard at work."

The patrolman's name was Nick Pesavento, and he must have been something of a masochist because alongside a photo of him leaning up against a brick wall with his arms folded and wearing a ridiculous, self-satisfied smile with his tight black T-shirt, there was a profile of his "personal" details. Such as: *Ideal first date*: A long conversation over coffee; *First thing I notice about someone I'm attracted to*: Smile; *My secret talent/skill*: I'm good with people. *Celebrity dream date*: Cameron Diaz. And perhaps one of the best, *The celebrity who would play me in a movie*: George Clooney.

It was too much to resist. George Clooney? Long conversations over coffee? The guy was fucking asking for it. And homophobic comedy long being a staple of the law enforcement community, it was just a matter of time before a couple of cops with a computer put together a flyer and hung it on Department walls and cafeterias and locker space. The flyer had the same photo of Nick as the one in the magazine and the personal details included but were not limited to:

Ideal first date: Shopping for new boots at the Galleria.

Celebrity dream date: Nicholas Cage.

First thing I notice about someone I'm attracted to: His package.

The celebrity who would play me in a movie: Ricky Martin.

And so forth.

Joe Klosterman, who was known for instigating these sorts of things, swore he had nothing to do with it. But he made sure that Hastings and everyone else on the squad saw both the flyer and the magazine article.

Hastings read the magazine and, though he would never admit it, read the profiles of the other "hot" singles as well, men and women. He was then recently divorced and it was before he'd gotten involved with Carol, so he was curious about the singles scene, such as it was. The article wasn't promising. Many of the women seemed to answer their questionnaires with exclamation points. E.g., "*First thing I notice about someone I'm attracted to*: Personality! If you like to laugh and have a great time, you're a hit in my book!" Women wanting to take hot-air-balloon rides and saying that Selma Blair should play them in a movie. Ay-yi-yi.

He remembered Judy Chen being one of the singles profiled. Attractive girl still in her twenties. And Hastings had thought then that she was posing in the magazine not because of lack of dates, but more to gain publicity for the news network. And herself. Cute little thing. Had her arms been folded too . . . ?

•

He rode with the FBI agents to the news station. Kubiak and Gabler sat in the front. Hastings sat in the back. The agents didn't say much and when they did speak it was to each other, as if Hastings were not there. Hastings thought about asking them how long they intended to keep this up, but he doubted it would do any good.

When they got to the lobby of the station, he stood in the background as the feds presented their credentials to the front desk and said they were here to speak with Judy Chen and the station manager as well. Minutes later they were seated at a conference-room table in a room that had little more than a chamber of commerce seal as decoration.

Judy Chen and the station manager were seated opposite the law enforcement officers. The station manager was named Kelly Ingle and one of the first things he did was put a videotape on the table and slide it across.

Agent Craig Kubiak said, "Is that the original?"

Kelly Ingle said, "Yes."

"But you made a copy?"

"Yes, sir."

To Judy Chen, Kubiak said, "And when did you get this?"

"This morning."

Kubiak said, "Tell us about that."

She said, "Well, I was getting into my car—I had just gotten into my car and my cell phone rang. I answered it. And this guy said his name was Carl."

"Carl what?"

"He didn't give a last name. He just said Carl." She said, "I think he said something like, 'for purposes of this conversation.' Meaning, Carl wasn't his real name."

Kubiak nodded.

Judy Chen said, "So he asked me if I knew about Gene Penmark's daughter being kidnapped."

Kubiak said, "Did you?"

"I don't think I did, then."

"Did you tell him that?"

She seemed to think about that for a moment. Then she said, "No. I don't think I did. I think I said, 'Who is this?'"

"And he said?"

"And he said he'd already told me his name was Carl. Then he said, 'Turn around.'"

"Turn around?"

"Yes. Turn around. So I did, and there was the videotape."

"Where?"

"On my backseat. Well, in a brown bag on my backseat."

"Where is that bag now?"

The lady looked at the station manager and gave him a shrug. "It's in my car, I guess," she said.

Agent Gabler said, "We're going to need that too, ma'am."

Kubiak said, "Then what?"

Judy Chen said, "Then he said that they had kidnapped Cordelia Penmark. He said that she was alive and he told me to take the tape to the station and play it over the air."

Kubiak said, "And that's what you did?"

"Yes."

"Before contacting the police?"

Hastings noticed the station manager shift in his seat.

Judy Chen said, "Yes."

Kubiak said, "Do you think that was smart?"

"I don't know what the law is," Judy Chen said. "But I don't regret doing that."

Gabler said, "Why not?"

Hastings was listening a little closer now. He expected the woman to excuse it by saying she didn't want to risk the Penmark girl's life by not following their instructions. It would be a rational excuse, though Hastings probably wouldn't have bought it.

But Judy Chen didn't say that. What she said was, "Because I had a feeling that whoever was calling me was watching me too."

For a moment, no one said anything. Kubiak looked briefly at Gabler and even at Hastings before he turned his attention back to the woman.

Kubiak said, "Why do you think that?"

"I don't know. The way he said 'turn around' and then seemed to know that I had."

"Did you see anyone?"

"No. But I was parked near my apartment. I mean, he could have been anywhere."

"But you didn't—"

"I just felt someone was watching me."

Hastings said, "Did it frighten you?"

She looked down at the table at Hastings, her weighted expression not the one she wore in the magazine photo.

"Yes," she said. "Very much."

"And yet," Kubiak said, "you still didn't call the authorities."

Her expression changed again. Hardened. She said, "Sir, the man knew where I lived and what I drove. Knew who I am. Knows. I'm cooperating with you now and I haven't broken any laws."

"That's debatable, Ms. Chen," Kubiak said. "And how are we to know that this fear you're describing isn't just an act?"

"Because I'm telling you the truth."

Craig Kubiak smiled at the woman then. It was the sort of cold, superior smile that drives people to hate cops and managers and lawyers. It was working on Hastings now too, because he could see that the woman was seething and there was now a real danger that she would clam up on them.

Hastings could also see that she was no pushover. And that she would not hesitate at all to get a lawyer and make things difficult. Which would be a hardship for him and the feds. Unnecessary, but inevitable if this clod weren't so intent on pushing her. Kubiak was probably attracted to the woman and blaming her for it. Or he was just a fool. In any event, the woman was about one step away from ending the interview.

Hastings leaned forward, his body language conciliatory. He said to Judy Chen, "We believe you are telling the truth. I'm sorry if we've been misunderstood."

From the corner of his eye, Hastings detected a scowl on Agent Kubiak's face. Hastings said, "Our beef is not with you. I know you understand that."

Hastings waited for her to give him a nod. Which she did. Good.

Hastings said, "The goal for everybody involved is to get the girl back safe. That's what Agent Kubiak wants."

"Of course," the station manager said. He seemed a little relieved now. Judy Chen was looking wary, but it was an improvement over cold fury.

Hastings said, "Your car, where is it now?"

Judy Chen said, "It's in the parking garage."

"Has anyone touched it since you drove here this morning?"

"No."

"We're going to have to have some technicians go over it. Obviously, the man or men who planted that tape got into your vehicle, and we're going to have to look for prints and hairs and, you know, technical stuff. Now, we'll be glad to get you home by cab or police escort while we're using your car. Would that be okay with you?"

"Yes."

Hastings knew that if it wasn't, they could still seize it. At least temporarily. But she could make things difficult if she was of a mind to.

Hastings said, "Now, the man you spoke to. What did he sound like?"

Judy Chen seemed to have mentally unfolded her arms. She said, "Uh, youngish. Maybe thirty. I mean, twenties, early thirties." She shrugged in a way that was not unkind. "If that helps," she said.

"It does," Hastings said.

"He sounded white. He didn't sound like a country guy. He didn't sound like a redneck. I would say that his accent was midwestern."

"You mean midwestern like around here?"

"Yes. He didn't sound like a Chicagoan. Or a Michigander. He sounded like he was from around here."

"Okay," Hastings said, "And did you hear anything in the background? Traffic, music, anything."

"I can't remember hearing anything."

"All right," Hastings said. "Now, your car. When you're at home, where do you park it?"

"In the street. I have a permit."

"It's not parked in a garage?"

"No."

"You lock it?"

"Always."

"Any cameras around where you park?"

"On the street?" she said. "I don't think so. Sorry."

"That's all right." Hastings said, "Did he say he would contact you again?"

"No."

"Do you think he will?"

She said, "I don't know."

"Did you encourage him to?" Hastings believed it was a necessary question.

She paused for a moment, but did not seem offended. She said, "No. I don't believe I did."

"Okay," Hastings said. "I believe that. But I want to tell you that we're going to have to set up recording devices on your home phone and cell phone in case he tries it again. No one's interested in your private life, but this will be necessary. Do you understand that?"

"I understand it."

"Having said that, I want you to know that I don't *want* this man to contact you again. It may be a great news story, but this man is a killer. He murdered a young man who was Cordelia Penmark's escort. You know that, don't you?"

"I know it."

"And the physical evidence that we have so far seems to suggest that the young man gave them no struggle. In other words, they killed him in cold blood."

The woman didn't say anything.

Hastings said, "So he's not someone you want a relationship with. A man like this Carl, people are just objects to him. He used you and, if necessary, he'd kill you."

"Okay," she said.

"I don't think I'm telling you something you didn't already know." Hastings said this, though he didn't fully believe it. He said, "Am I right?"

Judy Chen said, "You're right."

"Also," Hastings said, "we have a duty to advise you that what you did technically constitutes obstructing an investigation." Hastings raised a hand and said, "Don't worry about it. No one's charging you with anything. But in the future, please notify us before doing anything. Okay?"

"Okay."

•

When they left, the station manager and Judy Chen both shook Hastings's hand. They shook the agents' hands too. Hastings had had enough experience dealing with people to know that this gesture was done more out of relief in settling a tense situation than out of friendship. He remembered when he was on patrol a belligerent drunk had wanted to shake his hand a few minutes after Hastings had thrown him against a car. But that was okay. They got the woman's cooperation and that of the station in less than an hour with minimal head butting and, better, no attorneys.

Still, when they were walking back to the car, Agent Gabler gave him a look that was pretty hard to read and said, "Man, you can be quite the charmer, huh?"

"I have moments," Hastings said. He didn't make eye contact when he said it.

FOURTEEN

There was little, if any, discussion on the ride back to the station. Agent Kubiak continued to talk about the case with Agent Gabler as if Hastings were not in the car. When they pulled up to sally port, Kubiak stopped the car and didn't say anything. Gabler turned around and said, "What are you going to do now?"

Hastings did not detect any sarcasm in the question. He said, "I'll check in with forensics. See what they got from the crime scene."

Kubiak shook his head without turning around. He said, "I'm not sure if it's theirs anymore."

Hastings said, "They're going to complete their report."

Kubiak didn't respond to that.

Hastings said to Agent Gabler, "I'll let you know if we turn up anything."

"Thanks," Gabler said.

Hastings got out of the car. The feds drove off and Hastings thought, Fuck it. It's not a time to be angry.

•

Andy Kustura was the lead field evidence technician (FET) on the Myers murder. He was a short, stocky man of around fifty with a gentle disposition. He dressed unfashionably—dated boat shoes and golf shirts buttoned to the top—and people often mistook him for a high school science teacher. Like many top people in forensics, he was a graduate of the University of California, Berkeley. He was quiet and studious by nature, but there were stories of him once doing a flawless David Caruso impersonation at a Christmas party, using sunglasses as a prop. It was said that he could be funny and animated once in a blue moon, given enough alcohol.

He met Hastings at the anteroom next to the tech lab. Andy Kustura had already been told that the feds were taking over.

He said, "We should probably have a preliminary report ready tomorrow. The crime occurred at night and we still haven't completed our daylight follow-up." All major scenes had to be redone in daylight.

Hastings said, "Can you give me a rough summary of what you got now?"

Andy brought Hastings to a table and showed him the crime-scene sketch. A street with rectangles marking cars and positions of bodies and bloodstains. He spoke as he indicated objects on the sketch.

Andy said, "Here's what it looks like. The victim's car, a BMW, was parked facing west. He and the girl walked through the grass. She's wearing high heels, he's wearing a pair of Allen-Edmonds. They both walk in the grass, single file, until they get to the car. Victim comes off the grass and around to the driver's side of the BMW. Here. And that's when two other people appear." Andy gestured to the other side of the BMW rectangle. He said, "We've got footprints on the passenger side, impressions in the soft ground. Behind the girl. A pair of Rockport boots. This guy grabs the girl from behind. On the driver's side, assailant one walks up to Myers. Bam, bam. Myers goes down, assailant leans over and shoots him again. See. The bloodstain is there, by the driver's door. They keep the girl and a car pulls up and they put her in the car. Then, they move Myers's body behind the BMW. Now, we were hoping to get something off the car. Because it appears like the assailants wanted to put him sort of under the car. Put him out of sight. But he must have been wearing gloves, because we don't see a print impression on the back of the car."

Hastings said, "You mean, the assailant crouched down to shove the body?"

"Yeah. He would have had to do that to shove the body. But he didn't crouch. See, he left knee impressions."

"In the grass."

"Yeah. We got those. But, see, this is what we were hoping for. We hoped when the guy got back up, he would put his hands on the car to steady himself. Help lift himself up."

"Well, I would," Hastings said.

"Yeah, but you're a middle-aged man. I would too," Andy said. "This guy didn't use the car to steady himself. Just stood back up."

"A younger man, then."

"Perhaps," Andy said. "That's what I would think. He pushes or rolls Myers's body sort of underneath the back of the car and then he gets in another car and leaves." Andy said, "I think the guy on the passenger side would have had his hands full with the girl, so this guy would have had to drag the victim's body by himself. He was strong enough to do that. And then they both got into another vehicle and left. My speculation—my reasonable speculation—is that there was a third person involved here. One driving the get-away vehicle. They kept the car out of sight until they killed the victim and had the girl subdued. You know Isaac?"

"Yeah."

"He was one of the first criminalists on the scene. He thinks they used chloroform to subdue the girl. He said he smelled it."

"You find traces of that?"

"No. Not on the vehicle. And . . . no, we didn't."

"Okay. What's the word from the coroner?"

"The victim was killed with a .357 revolver."

"That's a loud gun. I think someone would have heard it."

Andy Kustura shrugged. "There was a party going on. And they were a ways from the house."

Hastings said, "Would you say this was a planned abduction?"

"Oh yeah. They could have killed the girl easy. As to the victim, we haven't found any fiber evidence, et cetera, that he struggled with his assailant. Again, just looks like the assailant walked up and shot him." Andy said, "Now, George, I just look at things, you know. I'm not a people guy like you. But my guess is that they planned to kill him all along. Or decided to kill him once they saw him."

"Why do you think that, Andy?"

Andy shrugged. "Savages, like most murderers, I guess. He was at the wrong place at the wrong time and they wanted to get him out of the way. Dispose of him. But maybe something else too, if this was a planned abduction."

"You mean, like a demonstration."

"Yeah. We killed this guy, we can kill your daughter too."

"Right."

"I'll call you if something else comes up, George."

"Thanks, Andy."

FIFTEEN

Adele Beckwith's house was in Clayton, off Wydown Boulevard. It was a modest two-story home perched among lush, green grass and hedges and old-money trees. Maybe twenty-five hundred square feet to it and you wouldn't be able to touch it for less than three-quarters of a million. Hastings remembered a few years back Eileen pointing to a house in this neighborhood and suggesting that maybe they could make an offer. Hastings had said, "Are you nuts?" Not seeing the problems back then.

Hastings parked the Jag in the driveway and rang the doorbell.

Adele Beckwith answered. She seemed to hesitate for a moment.

Hastings said, "Ms. Beckwith, I'm Lieutenant Hastings. I called you a half hour ago."

"Oh. Yes, come in."

The house was less appealing inside. It smelled old and looked unkempt. There were books on the coffee table and dinner table and a lot of other places. Adele Beckwith led him into the living room, where there was a little black pug on the couch. The pug growled at Hastings.

"Now, William," Adele said, "you behave." She made no attempt to move the dog off the furniture.

She turned to the policeman and said, "Have you heard anything?"

"No, ma'am. Not yet."

For a moment she did not say anything. The silence discomfited him and he found himself saying, "We're working on it. And we think—we believe she's alive."

"How do you know that?"

"Well, it's a kidnapping. And they need her alive so they can ransom her."

The woman took a seat on the couch. The dog remained where he was.

Adele said, "A kidnapping?"

"Yes, ma'am."

"Who would do that?"

"I don't know. We're trying to find out."

"A kidnapping. For money."

"Yes."

"His money."

"You mean, your ex-husband's."

"Well, I haven't got it. Who else would it be?"

"Right," Hastings said.

It didn't look like she was going to ask him to sit down. So he asked if she minded if he did. She gestured to a chair.

"I'm sorry," Hastings said.

The woman shrugged.

Hastings said, "Do you have—do you have someone you could stay with?"

She shook her head.

"Any family . . . ?"

She shook her head again.

Hastings said, "Ms. Beckwith, do you mind if I ask you a few things?"

"No."

"Do you mind talking with me?"

"No."

"Your husband. Your ex-husband—are you aware of any enemies he had? People who would target him?"

She snorted, a bitter near laugh. "Gene? Enemies?"

"Well, I'm not sure what you mean by that."

"He's not the sort to have enemies. He's weak."

"Do you have much of a relationship with him anymore?"

"No. I've been discarded, you see. His past. He bought me off. Gave me this house, an annual stipend. He was generous, really. With money. He's got plenty of that. He just wanted me to go away."

"You didn't want to be divorced?"

"I don't know. I don't think so. I guess I became an embarrassment to him."

"Well…"

"This is supposed to keep me happy. This house. This… prison. This isolation. Would it keep you happy?"

"I don't know."

"He seemed to think so. Him and that—that beast he married. I was bought off. Paid to stay away from my own children."

"And that angers you?"

"Of course! What, does that make me a suspect? Sir?"

"No. I doubt it."

She put her face in her hands and sobbed. The sobs turned to shrieks. Hastings walked over and sat next to her.

"What's going to happen?" she said. "What's going to happen to her?"

"We'll get her back," Hastings said. He didn't have the strength to tell her he didn't know.

SIXTEEN

A few hours later, Hastings was in his office with Klosterman. It was close to end of watch and Klosterman was sitting in front of Hastings's desk.

Klosterman said, "What does she do?"

"She reads a lot," Hastings said. "She goes to coffee shops. She watches a lot of television. She buys things on eBay. He gave her enough money in the divorce that she doesn't have to work. I think it'd be better for her if she had something to do."

"You mean, during this?"

"No, I mean in general. I got the feeling she's pretty well educated. That at one time she had genuine feelings for Penmark. She said that when they married, she had no idea he'd get rich. She doesn't think he did either."

"But he did."

"And bought himself another wife."

"She hate the new wife?"

"Oh yeah. But . . . if it hadn't been Lexie Lacquere, it would have been someone else. He found a new life and Adele didn't fit into it."

"Would that make her vengeful?"

"Sure. But not enough to hire someone to kidnap her own daughter. If that's what you're suggesting."

Klosterman shrugged.

Hastings said, "God. She can't even control her own dog. It was heartbreaking."

"A house off Wydown, yeah, that's heartbreaking."

"Christ, Joe, show some fucking compassion. Her daughter's been abducted."

"Sorry."

"That's all right. Jesus, she told me she feels like she's a prisoner in that house. It sounds silly if you're outside of it. But if you're there, you understand what she means."

"How?"

"Well, she's . . . she's a misfit. Yeah, she's got the money. Enough money not to have to worry about living. But those groups—those society groups—they're not going to let someone like her in. They invent clubs like that to keep people like her out."

"Evolution at work, Georgie."

"I thought you Catholic types didn't believe in that."

"Yeah. Well, police work makes it hard for us mackerel snappers to cling to all our traditions. She couldn't make it in Penmark's new life, so he cut her out of it. Survival of the fittest and all that . . . shit. Now he's rich, and on top of being abandoned by him, her daughter's been kidnapped. Does she like the girl?"

"Her daughter?"

"Yeah."

"Yeah. Loves her. I don't think the daughter's cut her out. I don't think."

"Are you worried about her?"

"Yeah, I am. I think if Cordelia's killed, her mother won't survive it."

Klosterman said, "You think she'd . . ."

"Yeah."

Hastings had checked Adele Beckwith's bathrooms for sleeping pills. Had even asked her if she kept firearms in the house. (She didn't.) After that, he gave her the number of a counselor and told her to call the woman if she felt like she was in trouble. He gave her his own number as well and told her she could call him anytime she wanted to talk. Did all that and hoped it would help, though he didn't feel too secure about it.

Klosterman left it alone. It wasn't something they could do much about. Klosterman sighed and said, "They check out Judy Chen's vehicle?"

"Yeah."

"So nothing?"

"No," Hastings said. "We found a lot of her prints on the video-tape and car, but nothing else. They tried."

The FBI had brought in their Evidence Response Team (ERT). They had nicer vehicles than Metro and more personnel. Well trained and well equipped, they went over everything, but they were no closer to knowing who kidnapped Cordelia Penmark than they had been before.

Klosterman said, "And the phone?"

Hastings said, "That part's interesting. We did trace a number. The owner of the number lives in Sunset Hills. But it's a duplicate number."

"A duplicate?"

"Yeah. They duplicated a SIM card. And we triangulated it, but all we found out was that the call was made near Judy Chen's apartment."

"So maybe she was right," Klosterman said. "Maybe they were watching her when they called her."

"I think they were. As to the kidnappers, we seem to be dealing with someone who knows electronics. And telecommunications."

"What did you think of the feds?"

"Gabler, I don't know. Kubiak's an asshole. He almost ran the witness off."

"Kubiak . . . is he a blond-haired guy with glasses?"

"Yeah."

"I think I know who he is."

"Yeah?"

Klosterman said, "You know Fred Krafft?"

"Yeah, I worked evening shift with him about five years ago. He's a good guy."

"He's a shift sergeant now, on patrol. Last year, he arrested some crankhead turd, brings him down to the station. The guy's cuffed and Fred sets him on the bench in the booking room. Now you know Fred, right? Not an abusive guy. Never even talks smack to suspects. Well, this turd, he starts kicking and shouting, saying I'm gonna fuck your wife and your kids, and he's getting the other detainees riled up. They're still in the booking room, so Fred tells the guy to be quiet. Doesn't do any good. Fred tells him again, be quiet or I'm gonna O.C. spray you. The guy keeps going, shouting and kicking, and so Fred walks over and sprays him in the face. Well, the spray hits the guy and *it doesn't even fucking faze him.* So now Fred thinks the guy's on fucking PCP or something; O.C. spray isn't fucking working on the guy. Fred's eyes go wide open and the turd launches out of the chair onto Fred. They roll around on the ground for a while, Fred gets his fucking wrist broken, the turd, he gets his lip cut. Some other guys join in, they subdue him and get him off to a cell. After that, Fred leaves and goes to the emergency room to get his wrist splint. End of story, right? No. The guy's lawyer files a tort claim against the city for excessive force against Fred—"

Hastings said, "I heard about this."

"Yeah, Fred's captain, who wasn't even there, he tells the prosecutor that he's always had 'concerns' about Fred. Which is bullshit if you know Fred. But Lew Goodgame, that's the captain, he's always hated Fred. So the prosecutor dismisses the criminal case against the turd. They do an internal affairs investigation on Fred. He gets cleared. Because Fred was just following the standard use-of-force continuum."

Both Hastings and Klosterman were aware of the common misperception, outside of law enforcement, about the use of O.C. or pepper spray. That misperception is that the use of pepper spray is unnecessarily cruel or extreme and that thuggish police officers are all too quick to use it. But actually, pepper spray rates somewhere near the bottom of the use-of-force continuum. In other words, the officers are typically trained to use pepper spray *before* escalating to physical force such as closed fists, nightsticks, expandable batons, and firearms. The purpose of pepper spray is not to injure but to subdue. While it is, for a short duration, a pretty nasty thing to experience, it does not bruise or cause physical injury as a fist or a baton or a trained attack dog or a firearm would. To many civilian observers, the sight of a police officer pepper spraying a person in the face (the only place where it is effective) seems sadistic. But officers are encouraged to use it if it is reasonably believed that its use will prevent the use of a more serious force.

Hastings said, "So he was cleared?"

"Yeah, he was cleared on the IA investigation, but then the FBI did its own *criminal* investigation. And Craig Kubiak headed that up. From what I heard, he was just a prick. He'd haul officers in for what he called an 'investigatory interview.' The minute any one of them said Fred was clean, he'd start threatening them with criminal perjury charges. The guy was just fucking abusive. The lawyer for the police union showed Kubiak the policy manual on O.C. spray, showed him the report clearing Fred, showed him that everything Fred did was legit. But he could give a shit. He wanted Fred's scalp."

"Yeah, but Fred Krafft was cleared."

"Yeah, after about a year. A very long fucking year for Fred. And Agent Kubiak did everything he could to get the grand jury to indict Fred. It was the U.S. attorney that dropped it. So for a year Fred, his wife, they were just waiting for agents to show up and arrest him. That's not fun. The point is, Kubiak wasn't doing an investigation; he was witch-hunting."

Hastings shrugged. Craig Kubiak would hardly be the first witch-hunter in law enforcement.

"Well, yeah," Hastings said, "but would there have been an investigation if not for Captain Goodgame?"

Klosterman tried to wave that away. He wanted to hold on to the black-and-white notion. Feds bad, Metro good.

Hastings said, "It's not just feds that go after city cops. We do it to each other too." It was one of the more depressing aspects of the job, Hastings knew. Cops testifying against other cops in internal affairs hearings, sometimes stretching truth, sometimes just downright fabricating. The "blue code of silence" civilians believed existed was an illusion; truth was more often than not trampled over by fear and ambition.

Klosterman said, "You never have."

SEVENTEEN

In the videotape they gave to Judy Chen, the kidnappers had not specified when or how they would contact Gene Penmark. The FBI agents did not believe this was an oversight. They thought that the kidnappers would contact Penmark somehow. Or that maybe they would try to use a third party again, like Judy Chen.

When the FBI got involved, they immediately dispatched a team to the Penmark's home to set up recording devices on his phones. They sent another team to his office to do the same thing. Klosterman said to Hastings, "I don't know if it'll do any good. Didn't they contact him on his cell phone last time?"

Hastings didn't argue the point. He left the station after his conversation with Klosterman and drove out to the Penmark's home. The guard checked his identification at the gate and Hastings drove the Jaguar up the winding hill to the mansion.

There were a couple of Crown Vics out front and a shiny blue van, FBI vehicles. Hastings stopped the car, cut the engine, and got out. Late evening now and the sound of the city was behind him. It was quiet. Hastings stood still and looked up at the mansion. He decided it wasn't looking down at him and he moved to the front door.

He was surprised that it was Lexie Penmark who let him in.

She was wearing black capri pants and a black top. It made him think of early Mary Tyler Moore, when she was playing Dick Van Dyke's wife. A slim, attractive lady.

"Hello," she said, her voice warmer than he'd expected. "Won't you come in?" It was a little strange, that. Like he was here to help plan a fund-raiser.

"Sure," Hastings said.

She led him to a room that was almost human. It had a desk and some antique French furnishings. There were some pictures on the walls—Lexie with the mayor; Lexie reading a speech, looking cerebral and serious in her glasses; Lexie with a black child at a Boys and Girls Club Awards Dinner.

She said, "This is my office. Gene allowed me to decorate it. Notice it doesn't quite fit in with the rest of the house."

"Yes," Hastings said.

Lexie said, "Would you like some coffee or something to drink?"

"No, thank you."

Lexie was sitting behind her desk now. Hastings was aware of it, wondering what it was she wanted.

He said, "Where is your husband?"

"He's in his study. Waiting. Trying to work, I suppose."

Well, Hastings thought, it's good that he's not wasting his time. It's only his daughter. Hastings said, "They didn't specify when they would call."

Lexie said, "I know. We don't know much, do we?"

"No, not much. The waiting is difficult, I know."

For a moment she didn't say anything. Then she leaned forward and said, "I wanted to speak to you alone."

"Yes, ma'am."

"Please, you can call me Lexie."

Hastings was not one for undue familiarity. If someone he didn't know well used his first name, he always felt they were trying to sell him something. Still, it was a lady. He said, "Okay."

Lexie said, "I want you to be frank with me: how likely is it that Cordelia will survive this?"

Hastings said, "Well, we'll see. They haven't called yet, and . . ."

"You can tell me," she said.

Hastings was beginning to feel uncomfortable. He was thinking of Adele Beckwith, the girl's mother, though he wasn't sure why. He said, "Ma'am, I honestly don't know. The FBI is experienced with this sort of thing and they'll do the best they can do to bring her home safely."

"I'm sure they are. It's just that, . . . I feel more comfortable with you."

Now Hastings was irritated. Vain woman, probably shooting for attention more than anything. He could ask her to meet him at a hotel room and that might get her to knock it off. He said in a businesslike tone, "Well, thank you, but I assure you they know what they're doing."

It pushed her back, but for only a second. She said, "You don't remember me, do you?"

"No. I'm sorry."

"I used to be a reporter on Channel 9."

Sexy Lexie, Hastings thought. Not seeing it himself, though. "Yes," he said, "I remember."

She said, "I covered the Sullivan trial. You testified."

"Yes, I remember," Hastings said. Though there had been a lot of media at the trial.

Cal Sullivan, M.D., had murdered a man because he had tried to blackmail Sullivan for a murder Sullivan had committed in college. Just before beginning medical school, circa 1980, a coed of dubious reputation had threatened to turn young Cal in for date rape. Cal went to her and apologized for any misunderstanding and then threw her off a tenth-story balcony. He went on to become a successful surgeon. Twenty years later, Hastings put the pieces together and tracked him down. It was while he was working the case that he found out Eileen was having an affair with her boss. Eileen left him before the trial. He remembered coming home one night, before she left, and talking about the frustration he was having over the case. In spite of everything, it was Eileen who had comforted him then. When Hastings worried that he would never catch Cal Sullivan, it was Eileen who said, "Of course you will."

"How do you know that?"

"Because whoever he is, he thinks he's smarter than you. And you're not going to allow him to get away with that."

Smart, maybe. Lucky for sure. Cal Sullivan shot a police officer in a mall after a blown sting, and as Hastings chased him on foot, Sullivan drove his Mercedes into the path of an oncoming Chevy Suburban, and by the time he came to his senses, Hastings had a gun pointed at his head.

Sullivan was not so dumb as to try anything then. He was arrested and charged with three murders and one count of deadly assault for shooting a police officer. Sullivan's lawyer rejected all plea offers from the DA and the case went to trial. Hastings held his own against Sullivan's lawyer. And Sullivan's lawyer made the mistake of putting Sullivan on the stand to let him tell his side of the story. Sullivan testified the way doctors do, arrogant and self-assured, but overlooking the fact that he was on trial for murder, not medical malpractice. The jury concluded that Cal Sullivan, M.D., was a liar as well as a murderer and gave him three life sentences without the possibility of parole.

Lexie Penmark said, "I knew him, you know."

"You knew who?" Hastings said.

"Cal Sullivan."

After a moment, Hastings said, "Oh. A friend or something?"

Lexie made a throwaway gesture that made Hastings wonder if she'd slept with him. She said, "The federal agents have advised us to get the two million dollars together. For the ransom, that is."

Hastings nodded. "Yes, I understand they have."

"What do you think?"

Hastings said, "About what?"

"Do you think we should pay it?"

For a moment, Hastings had to look at the woman. He wasn't sure he understood her, but he was getting to like her less and less. He said, "Well, they're the ones in charge. But yes, I think you should pay it. If it gets your stepdaughter back alive."

"Oh, of course. But we have no way of knowing they'll keep her alive, do we?"

"No. No guarantees. But more often than not, kidnappers are caught."

"Right. But that's not the same thing as guaranteeing her safety, is it?"

"No, it's not, but ... you're just going to have to trust us." Hastings was using the word *us* now not because he was suddenly feeling a kinship with the feds. Far from it. But he sensed that this woman was playing some sort of game now that he didn't like one goddamn bit. She wanted him as an ally, for some reason. Perhaps against the feds, perhaps against her husband. She was making him ill.

He said, "Are agents Kubiak and Gabler here?"

"No," she said, "they left a while ago. But there are agents outside and in."

"Okay," Hastings said. He stood. "Well, I should get going. Someone will contact me if there's any activity."

She stood up and moved out the door without a word. Hastings followed her out and found himself looking briefly at her backside. She had a nice form, he thought, but not the sort you want to have behind you on a cliff.

In the hall, he said, "Excuse me, would you mind showing me the grounds out back?"

She turned to look at him.

"No, I don't mind. Why?"

He said, "I'm not sure, actually. I wanted to get a feel for this place."

"Why's that?"

"Well, it may be that the kidnappers may have seen this house. Or are familiar with your stepdaughter's schedule."

"Such as it is?"

"Such as it is."

She shrugged. "If you like. Let me get my coat."

She left him in the hall for a moment and soon came back with a gray, short mackintosh tied at the waist. It flattered her.

It was quiet outside. The pool was tranquil. There was a small pond nearby, next to a Japanese garden. They walked around the pool as Hastings took in the sights.

Hastings was not an unperceptive man. He was aware that the woman was attractive and vain and that she probably believed he was making some sort of play for her by asking this. It didn't matter to him though. He was not the sort to correct such misperceptions unless he thought it was necessary. The woman was quiet and he was quiet and they both seemed comfortable with the silence.

Lexie Penmark said, "Lieutenant?"

"Yes, ma'am."

"Please, don't call me ma'am. It makes me feel old."

"All right."

"Have you been a policeman long?"

"Yes."

"Do you like it?"

"Reasonably enough."

"Were you ever interested in doing something else?"

"Like what?"

"I don't know. Something in the private sector, perhaps."

Hastings shrugged. "Private sector" covered a lot of ground.

"You know," Lexie said, "my husband, he has a security office."

Hastings looked at her briefly.

And Lexie said, "I mean, he has an entire department."

"Hmmm."

"Maybe, when this is finished, I could talk to him about it."

"About what?"

"About giving you a job. Maybe even putting you in charge of security."

Hastings smiled. "I appreciate that, but, uh, I don't think so."

"Why not? It would pay very well. I don't mean to be forward, but, it would be a considerable increase in pay, I imagine."

"I imagine it would," Hastings said. He stopped and pointed at one of the bungalows. "You said that Gene's other daughter lives in one of those?"

"Yes. Edie."

"Is she there now?"

"I'm not sure, actually. Would you like to speak with her?"

"Yes. May we go check?"

"Okay," Lexie said.

EIGHTEEN

Lexie rang the doorbell. They could hear noise inside. Lexie rang it again and said, "Edie, it's Lexie. We need to talk to you."

There seemed to be a hesitation on the other side. And then the door was opened by a young blonde in her twenties. She wore jeans and a blue zip-up sweatshirt with an orange T-shirt underneath. She did not seem the type to smile, and there was a look of distrustfulness about her eyes. She looked tired and irritable.

She said, "What do you want?"

Lexie said, "Edie, this is Lieutenant Hastings with the St. Louis Police Department. He'd like to talk to you."

Hastings nodded at Edie Penmark. She looked at him and then over at Lexie and seemed to smile. A mirthless smile, suggesting to them that she suspected they were some sort of couple. Or planning to be. Hastings could see that she didn't think much of her stepmother.

Edie Penmark said, "Why?"

Hastings said, "I wanted to talk to you about your sister."

"My sister's been abducted. Haven't you heard?"

Hastings looked at her and wondered how much she'd had to drink. He could smell wine.

"I know," Hastings said. "But I just wanted to ask you a few things. It won't take long."

Edie Penmark pushed the door open with something of a flourish. "Suit yourself," she said.

They started to follow her in and Hastings stopped and placed a hand on Lexie's arm. He said, "Would you mind if I spoke to her alone?"

He detected a flicker of disappointment on Lexie Penmark's face. She said, "Oh. Well, if you—"

Hastings said, "Please."

"Okay," Lexie said. And walked back out the door.

Hastings closed the door behind her. Then he was alone in the bungalow with Edie Penmark.

The place was dirty. There was a large television built into the wall—as there was in the main house—but the couch and the coffee table in front of the television seemed out of place. As if Edie had added those things herself. The coffee table was covered with newspapers and magazines and other papers. There was an off-white ashtray on the coffee table half filled with cigarette butts.

Edie Penmark had resumed her seat on the couch and picked up the glass of wine she had left on the table. Her attention was supposed to be focused on the television. *Inside Edition.* Edie leaned forward to set the wineglass on the table, then leaned back with her lit cigarette.

Without looking at Hastings she said, "Cute, isn't she?"

"Who?" Hastings said.

"My stepmother. Fake tits, lifted chin, lifted ass. Holds together nicely, don't you think?"

Hastings shrugged. "Sure," he said.

The girl turned to acknowledge him. She said, "So what are you after?"

Hastings walked over to the coffee table and picked up the remote control and clicked the television off.

"Not much," he said. He sat in the chair at the end of the coffee table. She gave him her attention.

Hastings said, "Let's cut this out. Okay?"

She regarded him briefly. Her shoulders sagged and some of her defiance was gone. She said, "I already talked to one of you guys."

Hastings said, "Which one?"

"The one with the blond hair and glasses. Looks like James Spader?"

"Who's that?"

"Don't you watch television?"

"Not much," Hastings said. "Was it Agent Kubiak?"

"Yeah."

"Tell me about that interview."

"He asked me where I was last night, I said I was here. What I knew about Cordy's friends, I said not much. Had I seen anyone suspicious around here or around her, no I hadn't. Could I think of anything else, I doubt it." She said, "Okay?"

Hastings said, "That was it?"

"That was it."

"Well, that doesn't sound too comprehensive."

"It was to me."

"Edith. Let me ask you something: how long had Cordy been seeing Tom Myers?"

"Her boyfriend?"

"Yes."

"I don't know. A few months, maybe."

"Did she talk to you about him?"

"A little."

"Was she in love with him?"

Edie Penmark was looking at Hastings. She said, "What does that have to do with anything?"

"Work with me, Edie. I'm trying to help you."

"It's not my money they want."

"It's your sister they have."

"I know that," she said, her voice cracking at the end.

"I know you do," Hastings said. "Listen, I usually have reasons for my questions. All right?"

He was looking at her steadily now, acting on instinct perhaps. Interrogation was as much an art as it was anything else. Hastings had not yet figured out Edith Penmark. But he was hoping that there was more humanity in her than in her father or stepmother. He was asking this girl to trust him.

Finally, she said, "All right." She shrugged again. "We didn't talk that much. We're a little different, in case you haven't noticed. Well, how would you notice? You've never met her."

"No, I haven't."

She pulled on her cigarette, exhaled. "No," she said, "I don't think she loved him. He wanted to marry her, apparently. For her money. But she's not stupid. She's not lonely either. At least, I don't think she was." Edie put her head against the cushion of the couch. "Are you wondering if Tom Myers was in on her kidnapping?"

"I've thought about it," Hastings said. "I kind of doubt it, though."

"He was a little slick for my tastes. But, no, I'd doubt that too. Anyway, if you're wondering if she was so in love with him as to trust him with her life or some shit like that, no. Not her. She's not an idealist."

"Cordy's not?"

"No."

"How about you?"

She snorted. "Oh, God," she said. "Not hardly."

Hastings believed that. He said, "You're divorced now?"

"Yep."

"What happened there?"

She gave him a mild scowl. "What happened? It was a fucking disaster. It lasted, like, six months."

"Why was it a disaster?"

"Well, let's see. First, he was going to start a graphic design business. That took about forty thousand dollars of my money, and I don't think he ever left the house. There were always all these . . . people over. All these fucking people. I didn't know half of them."

"What were they there for?"

"Drugs. Bullshit. That's what he spent the money on: drugs and bullshit." She said, "My therapist said he was self-destructive. I was like, *No shit*. I don't even think he liked me."

"Why did you marry him?"

Edie Penmark sighed. "I had to do something. I mean, I didn't have a career and I wasn't going to school. I had to have something. . . ."

"Something to live for?"

She gave Hastings a glare. "Don't judge. I know how people like you are."

"What do you mean?"

"You need to pull people down so you feel better about yourselves."

Hastings nodded. He said, "What was this fellow's name?"

"Hap Melendy. He's in San Diego now."

"Doing what?"

"Shit, I don't know. Playing with himself, probably." She smiled bitterly. "Ain't it grand?"

"What?"

"The poor little rich girl. White trash living in her daddy's mansion. You could book me on Jerry Springer."

"I wasn't thinking that."

"Weren't you? I'll bet you feel a great satisfaction in it."

Hastings said, "Not hardly."

She was peering at him now and Hastings was thinking she was lost. Too much substance abuse, too many drugs, too much booze. Too much. A little girl not many years ago and now lost. He was not altogether surprised by what happened next.

Edie Penmark said, "Do you like me?"

"Sure." Hastings was calm.

Edie Penmark was still looking at him. She said, "Do you want to fuck me?"

"No, ma'am."

"No? Why not?" She was smiling at him now. A cold smile, which was not at all arousing.

Hastings said, "I have a girlfriend."

"So what? What does she do for you?"

"Well, that's private."

"Yeah? I'll bet she's pretty conventional in the sack. But you want something more, huh?"

Hastings was repelled by this. It was an invasion that was meant to arouse and interest him. It didn't. But he didn't want the girl to know how he was feeling. Not yet. He said, "Well, we do what we can."

Edie Penmark said, "I bet I know what you'd like."

Hastings made a gesture. "Well, who's to say?" He stood up. He put a card on the table. "If you think of anything, I want you to call me."

"Maybe I'll call you even if I don't."

Hastings was walking out the door when she said that.

•

The guard opened the gate and Hastings drove his Jag out onto the winding road. He looked at his watch. Then he called a number on his cell phone. She answered on the third ring.

Carol McGuire said, "George?"

"Hey," Hastings said. "What's going on?"

"Not much. Had a long day at work. How about you?"

Hastings said, "I kind of need a bath."

Carol laughed. "What happened?"

"Oh," he said, "it's a long story."

Carol said, "I understand you're working on the Penmark abduction?"

"Yeah. Lovely people, the Penmarks."

"Hmmm. You sound tired."

"I am," he said. "How was your day?"

"I pled out that assault case. So I won't have a trial next week."

"That's good. Was that the one with Sanderson?"

"Yes," she said, referring to a prosecutor they both knew. "I don't think he was crazy about trying it. Do you still want to come over?"

"Yeah."

•

When he got there, she asked if he had had dinner yet. He said he hadn't and she told him to sit down at the kitchen table and she would make him a sandwich. He did as he was told, glad to do so. A middle-aged man like most, happy to have a woman feed him like a mom. She could walk over and mop his hair with her hand and take the effect too far. But she wouldn't.

She set the sandwich in front of him. She said, "Do you want a beer?"

"Yeah. That'd be great."

She was smiling at him now. "You're enjoying this, aren't you?"

"What?"

"This little domestic scene."

"Sure."

"Don't get used to it. It's not really my style."

"I'll remember that."

She put the beer on the table and sat across from him.

She said, "How's it going?"

"You mean the Penmark thing?"

"Yes."

"It's pretty unpleasant."

"I imagine it would be."

"I mean, yeah, the murder of a young man and the abduction of a young girl. But it's not just that."

"Oh? What else?"

"The people involved . . ."

"You mean the Penmarks?"

"Yes."

"What about them?"

"They're creeps." Hastings stopped, considered. "Well, I don't want to judge. They've had their daughter kidnapped. Who knows how you'd deal with that situation if it were you."

"You mean if it were Amy?"

"I wasn't thinking that."

"You sure?"

"Yeah, I'm sure. I can't do things like that."

"What do you mean?"

"I think you know what I mean. The nature of this work requires you not to think that way. I would think you would understand that."

"What, because I defend criminals?"

"Sure. You can't afford to be bound up with sympathy or fear. Not for the victims. Not for your client either. Not too much, anyway."

"That's true," Carol said.

"It's the same here. I could say, *Gee, what if it was Amy that was kidnapped*? But that would lead to me having a breakdown and . . . that's not going to do anybody any good."

"Okay. Then why are you down?"

"I don't know. Well, I guess I do know. The girl's family . . ."

"They're not nice people."

"No."

"And you feel sorry for the girl?"

"Yeah."

"Beyond the kidnapping."

"Yes."

Carol was smiling at him. "What did you expect?"

"I don't know. I didn't expect anything."

"Yes, you did. You expected them to be nice people because they had money."

"No, Carol. Much as you'd like to believe otherwise, I'm not that predictable. I wasn't expecting Ozzie and Harriett."

"Well, I'm not surprised."

"That's good you're not surprised. But did it ever occur to you that you're predictable in your own way?"

"How so?"

"Someone's wealthy, you presume they got it by ill means. That they're corrupt."

"I do not. I don't envy the rich."

"I don't either."

"No one says you do. I just wonder if you presume nice things about them, that's all. Don't categorize me either."

"As what?"

"As the simplistic liberal."

Hastings smiled at her. "I don't do that. I don't think I do, anyway."

After a moment, she said, "No. You don't."

Hastings said, "Gene Penmark may not be a nice man. But he never killed anyone. I don't think he ever stole from anyone. And no one deserves to have their daughter abducted."

"I know that."

"I know you do. I just wanted to say it."

The sandwich was finished and for a few moments they looked into each other's eyes, their expressions simple, plain, and unsentimental.

Carol said, "Can you stay the night tonight?"

"No," he said. "I've got Amy. I'm sorry."

"It's okay," she said. "Can you stay a little while longer?"

They got up from the table and moved to the bedroom. Undressed on opposite sides of the bed and met in the middle.

NINETEEN

Amy was still up when he got home. He unlocked the door and came in and she was curled up on the couch with a blanket over her, watching television. Becoming a little lady now. He remembered when she was younger—five or six—and would sit in front of the television on a little reindeer beanbag, one leg crossed over the other. It all went by too fast.

"Hi," she said.

"Hi," Hastings said.

He turned to see what was on the television screen. A newscaster talking about Cordelia Penmark. Shit.

Hastings said, "Why are you watching this?"

She looked up at him, not hurt, but noticing his irritation. He was not often sharp with her. She said, "It's on all the news stations. What do you want me to do?"

"You can do your homework."

"I already did it."

Which was probably true, knowing her. Hastings checked his watch to see if she was up past her bedtime. Then realized she hadn't had a bedtime in a couple of years because she had been, since an early age, more or less self-disciplined. Shit.

Hastings said, "Okay."

He put his coat away and stored his gun. Then he got a Heineken out of the refrigerator and popped the top off. He came back to the living room and took a seat. He let out a sigh, then turned to his daughter.

"Sorry," he said.

"It's okay," Amy said.

"Did you have a good day at school?"

Amy shrugged. "It was all right." She said, "Is it your case? The kidnapping?"

"Sort of," he said.

"Oh." For a moment, she didn't say anything else. Amy Hastings had inherited her mother's intelligence, if not her character. And she had a partial understanding of why Hastings was in something of a black mood.

Amy said, "Would you rather we watch *South Park*?"

Hastings smiled wearily. "No," he said.

"*Friends?*"

"If you like."

"I was kidding. Jay Leno?"

"If we must."

"Or," Amy said, "I could go to bed if you'd rather be by yourself."

"No," Hastings said. "Why don't you stay up with me for a while? A half hour, then go to bed. Okay?"

"Okay, Dad."

•

She got up to go to bed while Leno was helping Russell Crowe laugh about something that wasn't that funny. From the hall she called out "love you" and Hastings said "love you too." After she was gone, Hastings clicked the television off and sat alone in the quiet living room.

Eileen had been a Catholic of sorts. During their marriage, he had attended mass with her a few times. He saw a side of her there that he never could quite reconcile with the one he knew at home. Kneeling, praying, reciting the prayers from memory, receiving the Eucharist. She knew her theology too. Made a point of it, in fact.

Hastings remembered a priest who was from England, visiting apparently, giving a homily about the sin of anger. He said he reserved his harshest penances for those parents who took their anger out on their children. The priest seemed to have a passion not seen too often in the American clergy. But, whatever. An elementary sermon not said often enough.

Hastings was aware that he had either done that or come close to doing that to his own daughter tonight. Irritable and depressed, he had spoken sharply to Amy. Over nothing, really. They were neither one of them emotive types, and her acceptance of his apology was expressed by staying up with him a half hour longer than usual. And like that it was fixed. They said their *I love you*s as usual without any additional melodrama or meaningful pauses.

He was thinking about the last time he had questioned Amy about her viewing choices. He remembered coming home and seeing a DVD on the coffee table titled *Grizzly Man*. Not being a man who read the entertainment pages, he thought it was in the same ballpark as, or a remake of, *Grizzly Adams,* a soft-touch show from the 1970s. Nice liberal fellow with a beard having adventures with his friend Ben, the warmhearted bear. But no, that's not what it was. It was about a young man named Timothy Treadwell who was more or less mentally ill and went to Alaska to commune with the grizzly bears.

Once Hastings figured out what the conclusion was likely to be, he turned to Amy and suggested that they turn it off. She asked him not to do that and pointed out that it was a documentary, not a dirty R-rated film. Which was true, he remembered. But it was ultimately going to conclude with poor Timothy Treadwell being eaten by a thousand-pound bear.

Fortunately, there was no video of that scene. Though it was on audiotape, the filmmaker had mercifully refrained from playing it. So Amy and, for that matter, Hastings were spared the anguish of that. And once he realized that neither one of them would have to see a man and his girlfriend being torn apart and then eaten, he enjoyed the film and was actually glad that he had seen it with his daughter.

Hastings had been a hunter since childhood. There hadn't been much else to do in Nebraska. He'd tracked and killed quail, deer, and duck, but had never shot a bear. When the movie was over, he explained, as best he could, certain realities of nature to Amy. That you could give cute names to grizzlies like Sergeant Brown and Mabel and Big Mama, but that wasn't going to change them into human beings any more than if you gave the names to sharks in the sea. That you could tell yourself that you understood the bears and that they understood you. But telling yourself didn't make it so. Timothy Treadwell was an idealist and he made those bears his religion. And he was dogmatic in his self-made faith to the bloody end.

Amy, being young, seemed to take more interest in the fact that Timothy's watch was still ticking when they found it inside the bear.

Hastings sipped his beer and wondered what would have happened to Timothy Treadwell if he had instead gone to live with the Penmarks. Mama bear, Papa bear, Lexie bear, Edie bear. Jesus. The mother he had not quite gotten a handle on. But as to the rest . . . well, was it fair to judge a family who had potentially had one of their own taken away from them? Perhaps forever? How would you know how you would react unless it happened to you?

He remembered watching a deposition of police officer who was sued for allegedly using excessive force when he shot and killed a man who had charged him with a knife. At the deposition were the brother and sister of the dead man. Hastings watched them during the deposition and saw not a trace of grief or sadness. And it was hard to avoid concluding that they were only using their brother's death as a means to sue the city for money.

Hastings had seen too much in his career by that time to be horrified by that scene. Yet, the events of this day were disturbing him. It was difficult to see in Gene Penmark any fear or terror over the fate of his daughter. It was impossible to see any in Cordelia's barracuda of a stepmother.

As to the sister, Hastings wasn't quite sure what to think. A relatively young woman who was a walking demonstration of why it was not only a sin to envy the rich but a waste of time as well. A miserable, deviant girl who may well have been corrupted by cynicism and nihilism. Angry at her father, contemptuous of her stepmother . . . perhaps justifiably so on both scores.

Though still, apparently, concerned for her sister.

When he had first questioned Edie Penmark, Hastings thought he detected a frightened, sad girl beneath the anger and bitterness.

He thought she was opening up to him. But then he had asked her about her divorce and what caused it and she started to get ugly with him. Perhaps he should not have asked her about her personal life, but he felt the questions were necessary at the time. He was thinking, vaguely, that a disgruntled ex-boyfriend or ex-husband of Edie's may have had something to do with her sister's abduction. Perhaps it was a long shot, but Hastings often went with his gut during investigations and discarded hurt feelings thereafter. In any event, the questions did not justify her asking him if he wanted to fuck her. She obviously had meant to shock him. Or debase him. Reduce the tough-talking cop to the level of a man fiddling with himself at a strip joint. It was an act he had seen many times before and it was hardly shocking to him. Nor would it have been to most experienced detectives. He remembered rolling his eyes at that scene in *Basic Instinct* when Sharon Stone opened her legs to reveal the sunshine state to a few detectives in the interrogation room and the detectives responded with dry throats and gulps like it was the first time they'd ever seen one. Silly.

Hastings looked at his watch. Late. It had been a long day and he wasn't sure he had the energy to analyze it anymore. They weren't one step closer to knowing who had kidnapped Cordelia Penmark.

TWENTY

Lee Ensler was one year out of Brown University when she started a Web site dedicated to the things that mattered to her. She was the daughter of a neurosurgeon in Chicago and she had no need for a steady income. This gave her the time and the opportunity to write about the things worth fighting for: animal rights, gender equality, antifascism, and eco-defense. She wrote long, earnest essays promoting the Zapatista cause in Mexico and denouncing Bush's criminal war in Iraq and Afghanistan, accusing the United States of plotting to kill Chavez in Venezuela and the Israeli Mossad of planning 9/11. She was a well-educated girl and she did not doubt herself often.

Between preparing essays for the Web site, she would travel. She spent a year in Europe, most of it in Germany, where she found plenty of young people sympathetic to her worldview. During that time, her belief that democracy was a joke was strengthened. Either consciously or unconsciously, she sought out people whose views were similar to hers. She labeled discussions with these people "interviews" and took their statements as confirmation that the United States was a sick society. A land not of the Bill of Rights and free spirit and opportunity but of gross individualism, decadence, and corporatism. In time, Lee Ensler became disenchanted with liberalism and, indeed, came to look upon that label with contempt.

In spite of that, some part of her knew that she would not be content living in Europe indefinitely. So she returned to the States. She did not inform her parents of her return.

She had been in Boston for a couple of months when she found out about a trial taking place in Portland, Oregon. Three people with an organization called the Liberation Front had been arrested for blowing up a meatpacking plant. A security guard was injured in the explosion and the three young men were charged with willful destruction of property and negligent assault.

The story was on the Internet. A photo of Terrill Colely appeared in the story.

The next day, Lee Ensler flew to Portland to cover the trial. She was a persistent young lady and it only took two meetings with Terrill's attorney to secure an interview with him.

She met with Terrill in a small room in the county jail. He was wearing the inmate orange jumpers and blue sandals. He stood up when she came in and smiled at her. Lee Ensler's immediate thought was, He's even better-looking in person. She thought he was the most beautiful man she'd ever seen. With his thick black hair and the eyes. Beautiful, hazel eyes.

The next two hours passed quickly for Lee Ensler. They talked about the exploitation of the Mexican employees at the meatpacking plant, the government's refusal to look into the violations of human rights, the barbaric treatment of animals, the endless assaults upon the environment. When Terrill said that the doctrine of nonviolence was not only self-deceiving but counterproductive, Lee quickly agreed. America was a cesspool, a nation built on murder and corruption and greed. And ignorance, so much fucking ignorance. In exchange for their bloated SUVs and tacky houses and manicured lawns and cheap gas, they gladly accepted the genocide of nonwhite people. And was it not the most despicable irony that dropping bombs on Iraqi children was somehow not criminal, but protesting it was. It took very little time for Terrill to persuade Lee Ensler that he and the two other codefendants were scapegoats for the real crimes. Indeed, he hardly had to persuade her at all.

"The worst thing about it," Terrill said, "is the arrogance of these pigs. They think that by putting me in jail for ten years, they won't be stopped. They're already building another plant. The insurance companies and the banks, they just rebuild and make more profit. To them, we're just a nuisance. They presume that they'll always win. And why not? They usually do. But," Terrill said as he rested his fingers on her hand, "they're wrong. We're not going be stopped. Not by them."

"But what can we do?" Lee said.

Terrill appraised her, giving her the full attention of his eyes. "It's funny," he said, "but I feel I know you. You're not a bullshit person."

"I don't think I am," said Lee.

"You're not. I have feelings about people. And I know you. I know you now. Do you feel it too?"

Lee said, "Yes."

"It's something, isn't it?"

"Yes, it is."

He leaned in and whispered in her ear, "I'm going to get out of here."

Lee felt electrically charged. His closeness, his beauty, his mystery. Confiding in *her*. "How?" she whispered back.

His voice still a whisper, he said, "Go to Wilson's Flat. A bar called Henry's. Ask for Moira. Tell her I sent you."

"Moira. But why will she trust me?"

"Say to her, 'What the hammer? What the chain?' Tell her I said that."

Lee repeated it. " 'What the hammer? What the chain? . . . In what furnace was thy brain?' Right?"

Terrill smiled. "You know it?"

"How could I not know Blake?" She was smitten now.

Terrill said. "I knew it. I should have known it." He smiled tenderly at her. "Go, Lee. Go right away. And when it's done, we'll be together."

•

A fine drizzle, coming down amid gray light, the green and white mountains in the background. In the northern part of Mount Hood National Forest. A semi hauling timber drives by, its wheels hissing on the blacktop. It passes a small wood bar and grill with two gas pumps in front. The name above the door reads HENRY'S.

The bartender flicked a thumb toward a table where a black-haired woman sat with two young men. The woman was dressed like a logger, her hair dark and cut short. Her skin was not smooth and her expression was hard. She could be attractive, perhaps, if she smiled, though she looked like she rarely did. Her name was Maggie Corbitt, though she had been using the name Moira Conners for the past few months.

She did not look up as Lee approached her table. Lee had to stand there for a few moments until Maggie acknowledged her.

"Yes?" Maggie said. Her voice had the hard, self-assured tone of a natural aristocrat. Her eyes drilled in such a way as to discourage small talk.

"Are you Moira?" Lee said.

"Who are you?"

"My name is Lee Ensler." After a moment, Lee said, "I'm a writer."

"Hmmm," Maggie said, unimpressed. She wasn't going to give Lee anything else. The young men with her smiled. They were Ray and Mickey.

Lee managed to focus her attention on the woman she believed was Moira. She said, "Terrill sent me. If you're Moira, I need to know."

Maggie said, "Who's Terrill?"

"He's the one that's in—are you Moira or not?"

"Sit down," Maggie said. "Lee." Saying her name the way one does to ridicule.

Lee Ensler took a chair and sat down. Once seated, she felt like she was being interviewed by a committee. Which she was. Lee Ensler was smart enough to have figured out by now that she had found "Moira" and that Moira was the one who ran things around here. She wondered if Moira was Terrill's chief lieutenant, then told herself that she was.

Maggie said, "What's a nice little Ivy League girl like you doing out in a place like this?"

"Terrill sent me."

"You said that already. But maybe you're an FBI agent. A spy."

"No," Lee said, trying to sound defiant and fierce. "No, I am not."

Ray Muller tittered.

Maggie said, "Ooh, Muffy's getting mad." And the young men had a chuckle over that too.

Lee felt her face burning. It took effort to prevent tears from welling. "He said you wouldn't believe me."

"Who said?"

Lee said, "Terrill said."

Maggie was smiling at this too. She had told Terrill that most women were predictable. Particularly liberals. But behind the mild torturing she was giving Lee, Maggie's instinct was leaning forward now, thinking that Terrill may have found a way to help himself out of this fix.

Maggie said, "What did he tell you?"

Lee said, " 'What the hammer? What the chain?' "

There was silence at the table then. Maggie looking at her two male associates as Lee began feeling redeemed. Maggie said, "When did you see him?"

"Yesterday."

But Maggie Corbitt was still shaking her head. "A few words of poetry," she said, "and you think you're in? You think it's that easy?"

Lee said what she had been waiting to say: "I'm committed. I'm in it now."

"We'll see," Maggie said. "You and I are going to the bathroom now and you're going to take off all your clothes. If I find one recording device, if I find any proof that you're a pig's spy, I'll kill you myself. Do you understand me?"

Lee nodded and said, "I'm ready when you are."

•

Terrill Colely had been patient. He believed with the certainty of a prophet that he was not meant to go to prison. He also believed that he would be convicted of the criminal charges he was now facing. Accordingly, he knew that his way out had to be an escape. Maggie Corbitt shared this view.

But he and Maggie were, in their way, realists. After a time, he had determined his best chance at an escape. Every day, between two and four in the afternoon, the county sheriff's office would allow him to meet with his attorney in the county courthouse law library. Terrill had not then been charged with a capital crime, had not been charged with murder, and he and his attorney had convinced the authorities that he needed access to the law books to adequately prepare his defense. Terrill also let the authorities know that he was preparing a book about the "false promise of the American system of justice." The local deputies exchanged some eye rolling over this, dismissing Terrill Colely as another punk. Terrill's claim as an intellectual also made the deputies underestimate him.

Still, when Terrill went to the library, he was always escorted by two of them. One deputy stood far enough away to give Terrill room to consult with his attorney and his books and the occasional journalist. The other checked the doors to ensure that they had not been tampered with. There were two exits, one being the door at the front, the second being the fire door at the back of the library, which could be opened only from the inside.

The day after Lee Ensler met with Maggie Corbitt, Lee obtained permission to meet with Terrill in the county law library. The day after that, she made her appointment to interview Terrill. She wore slacks and a nice shirt and a blazer, and her hair was pulled back in a studious ponytail, looking about as dangerous as a young Jane Pauley. Her purse and person were checked at the front door by one of the deputies. The deputy found nothing but a tape recorder, pens, and notebooks.

The deputy was an older man, in his late fifties. He was polite to Lee; in a way, she reminded him of his daughter. He pointed to the library shelves and said that Mr. Colely and his lawyer were seated at a table behind the last shelf. Neither that deputy nor Lee could see Terrill from the front door.

Lee walked down the length of that library section and found Terrill seated with his lawyer, whose name was Milton King. Seated against the wall, approximately fifteen yards away, was the second deputy. He sat in a slumped position with his hands on his legs. Lee made herself look at him only once.

Maggie Corbitt had not threatened her directly. She had only said, "I hope you understand the importance of not fucking this up." Lee remembered the intense look in Maggie's eyes when she had said this. But Maggie had followed it up with, "Terrill's trusting you. And he's very selective about who he trusts." It was said with the intent of making Lee feel that she was special to Terrill, and it did.

Lee took a seat at the table. She ignored the attorney, who stared at her boobs, and gave her attention to the new Clyde Barrow in her life, his dark hair and expressive eyes that told her now that he was very glad to see his new Bonnie. Lee spent ten minutes asking Terrill questions about his childhood, his experiences, and his political philosophy before she asked the attorney where the bathroom was.

But it was Terrill who answered her, telling her that it was on the other side of the library. For Milton King was not privy to their plans and he was as likely as not to tell her that the one in the general hall was cleaner than the one in the library, and that could have ruined everything.

Lee walked past the deputy on the chair, again telling herself not to look at him. She went down the aisle on the back side of the library. She got to a dogleg in the aisle, and there was the back door.

Her heart was pounding and she told herself, Don't think, just do it. Do it now or you're gutless, you're worthless, you're the simpleminded college dipshit they think you are. And she quietly unlocked the door and let Mickey and Ray inside.

Once they were in, they pulled ski masks over their faces.

Ray mouthed to her, "Stay *here.*"

Both Ray and Mickey were carrying 9-millimeter pistols. Mickey crept to the third set of bookshelves and crouched down in the middle of the row. Ray moved down the back aisle. He took a breath at the dogleg, then moved out.

The deputy on the chair saw a flash of movement to his left. He had just turned his head when Ray shot him in the shoulder. It knocked the deputy off the chair, and when he was on the ground Ray shot him two more times, the second time in the head.

The first deputy—the one who had been at the front door— rushed forward when he heard the shots, followed by the sounds of

Milton King screaming. The first deputy ran past several shelves, drawing his service weapon as he did so, and when he passed the third row, Mickey stepped out behind him and shot him twice in the back. The first deputy went to the ground.

Milton King could only say "Terrill" as his client went off with the masked killer around the back aisle. Terrill did not acknowledge him.

In less than twenty seconds, Terrill, Ray, Mickey, and Lee were in a Jeep Cherokee speeding away. Maggie was driving.

Within twenty-four hours, they were all out of Oregon, in separate vehicles, making their way back to the Midwest, where Ray Muller had grown up. They had their alpha male back along with their alpha female and they had plans to kidnap the daughter of a very wealthy man. To strike back at the profiteers and the cake eaters.

Two deputies had been murdered, and Ray Muller and Mickey Seften's identities were unknown to the Oregon state police. But charges were prepared against Terrill Colely and Lee Ensler for conspiracy to commit murder. And in that sense, Lee Ensler had gotten what she wanted. She had become a fugitive with the man she loved.

The county sheriff gave a press conference the evening two of his deputies were murdered. He held back tears of grief, rage, and frustration before the microphones and told the public what information they had and didn't have. A local reporter wrote the next day that the sheriff "vowed to catch these murderous jackal bins," the reporter thinking that term was another cop's way of labeling the criminal element. It wasn't until after that edition of the newspaper ran that another reporter suggested the sheriff might have

said "Jacobins" instead. The original reporter shrugged it off, saying "jackal bins" was what he had put in his notes.

•

Once in the St. Louis area, it became clear that Lee was not exactly
the Bonnie to Terrill's Clyde. In fact, it wasn't even all that clear that
Terrill was Clyde. He was the one with the most presence, the one
with the looks, but if one observed him closely, he would see that
Terrill cleared just about everything with Maggie. Though sometimes this was done indirectly. Short and compact in stature, Maggie
was like the border collie who stares down the cow that towers over
her. Smarter and more determined than any livestock, Maggie seemed
incapable of self-doubt. It was a dynamic that everyone more or less
was aware of and accepted. Even Terrill.

But, like most intellectuals, Lee Ensler was practiced in self-
deception. Maggie encouraged Terrill to screw Lee as soon as possible. "She's expecting it," Maggie said. But after that, Maggie had
Terrill explain to Lee that monogamy and individualism had no
place in the Liberation Front. Those were bourgeois attachments
and they had to be eliminated. They were all equal here. Part of
Lee's reconditioning required that she have sex with all the members of the Front, men and women. When she had intercourse with
Ray, Lee squeezed her eyes shut, waiting for it to be over, not giving in to human impulses like grief and anguish. And by the time
she was on her fourth partner, her expression had become not unlike that of a sex-show performer in a third world country, blank
and lifeless.

In addition to the sexual sharing, Lee was subjected to what they
called "the instruction." This exercise placed her in the center of a

room where all the members heaped verbal abuse on her, calling her names, "limousine liberal creep" and "poser" and much worse until she admitted her deep-seated feelings of "white supremacy." That Toby was the only nonwhite member of the group was not discussed.

Yet, through all this, Lee remained convinced that she was special to Terrill. After all, Terrill had quoted her poetry and made her feel special. For their parts, Maggie and Terrill had allowed Lee to retain this fantasy. Lee Ensler was underground now. She had made sacrifices to the group for Terrill, had undergone the brainwashing for Terrill. Her fealty to Terrill had become fealty to all of them. Fealty to the Liberation Front, whatever that was. She was too far gone now to think otherwise.

There were seven of them all together. Maggie, Terrill, Ray, Mickey, Toby, Jan, and now Lee. With the exception of Mickey and Maggie, they were generally from middle- to upper-class backgrounds. At least half of them had some college education. Their goals were vaguely defined. And when they were defined, it was usually done by Maggie and Terrill. Some of them were committed to destruction for its own sake. Some of them were committed to the disruption of what they called a sick society. What they all shared was an adolescent nihilism, a general laziness, and an attraction to hatred. When seeing any group of middle-class Americans on television, invariably one of them would say, "Look at those fucking people."

Unfortunately for Lee, their cruelty was not limited to those outside their circle. As leader, Maggie singled out Lee for abuse. Maggie's bullying engendered no sympathy for Lee from the others.

Rather, they took their cues from Maggie and sooner rather than later joined in. Such is the way among any canine pack. Lee was the best educated among them, probably the most accomplished. A scholar and a talented writer. It didn't matter. She was weak and unbalanced. They knew it and they exploited it.

·

It was cold in the basement. Damp too. They had given her a yellow blanket that seemed like it had been lying in a yard. It was crusty and dirty. She could wrap the blanket around her, but there was no carpet or anything else between her and the concrete floor. She was chained to a thick, rusty pipe. Chained. Cordelia could feel the chill coming up through her dress and coat. They had let her keep her coat. She had heard small rustles her first night there and screamed because she thought it might be a rat.

She had been in the basement for approximately forty-eight hours. But they had taken her watch and she was having trouble tracking time. She had spent that time trying to hold on to her sanity. The potential of rats being down here with her, the fear of being raped or worse. More than once she wondered and even hoped that they would just kill her. But the thoughts of suicide passed as some voice told her that it was wrong to think that way.

Cordelia Penmark had not been raised in a religious environment. Her father was a man of science and technology, not of faith. Her mother was a woman who had placed her faith in culture. Books, paintings, art, something called political science. No one had ever encouraged her to pray. Her childhood had lacked any discussion of life or death or the rightness or wrongness of wishing you could die.

They brought her food twice a day . . . she thought. Each time, it was a tall man with a soft voice. Two peanut butter sandwiches on a paper plate and a bottle of water. White Wonder Bread, which she had not eaten since early childhood. The second time the man came, she said to him, "What are you going to do to me?"

"That's up to your father," the man said.

"What do you mean?"

"He has to pay us before we'll give you back. It's up to him."

Then Cordelia said, "Is Tom alive?"

The man did not answer her.

And she knew. Tom, murdered. Just like that. She remembered the man in the green jacket, walking up and extending his arm and shooting Tom . . . Tom falling. Would that it had been a nightmare. But it was real.

How? How did such a thing befall a person easily? One minute, he's in a party in a house in Ladue that's warm and people are drinking and laughing, and then he walks to his car and is snuffed out like a . . . a light. On, then off. Just like that.

It couldn't be. Tom dead. Dead before he could raise an arm or fight or ask them what it is they wanted. Dead and then she was hauled away.

Tom wasn't stupid. He would have given them his wallet. He would have handed them the keys to his car. He would have told Cordelia to hand over her purse. And, as far as Cordelia was concerned, Tom would have tried to stop them when they took her away.

And knowing that, it was easy to put it together. A child could have put it together. They weren't interested in Tom's wallet or car.

What they were interested in was her. The daughter of Eugene Penmark. The bounty. The ransom.

So that was it. Tom Myers had died because he was with her. Tom—vain, ambitious, in love with her physical presence, her prettiness, her status, her family's money, the potential boost she brought to his career. In love with the girl he thought he knew. Or didn't care to know.

Cordelia sobbed at that thought. Here she was thinking critical things about Tom Myers. *He didn't really love me.* Didn't love you? For Christ's sake, bitch, the man is dead. Did he deserve to die for not appreciating the "real" Cordelia? And just who is that anyway? What about the boy's parents? His siblings? What do you think they're thinking about?

She believed that it was sometime during those feelings of re-morse and guilt that she determined, quietly, that she did not want to die. That it was not right for her to die this way. That there was no need for it. That there was no use in it. That any feeling she had that she "owed" Tom Myers a death was misplaced. Maybe even sinful. And it was this feeling, this determination, that kept her go-ing through her darkest fears and anxieties, that motivated her to kick away the snake of panic that approached her from time to time. She feared the snake, dreaded it, but maybe after so many kicks, it would come to fear her.

TWENTY-ONE

Gene Penmark received the call at five thirty that morning. He was in bed alone; Lexie had her own bedroom. She liked to get up early and use the exercise cycle while she watched her morning shows. So Gene was alone when he spoke with Terrill, his daughter's captor.

Terrill said, "Gene?"

Penmark recognized the voice. He remembered the FBI agents. They would be in a van in the driveway, awake, he hoped.

"Yes?" Penmark said, apprehensive.

"It's me. Today's your lucky day. You can save your daughter if you do exactly what I tell you."

"I'm listening."

"Good. Now I know there are probably FBI agents on the line with us, so I'll come to the point: if you do not follow all the instructions I give you today, your daughter will be killed. It's that simple. It's in your power to save her or cause her death. The law enforcement officers are more interested in catching me than they are in saving her. They're not your friends. Right now, I'm the best friend you have. So when it comes to deciding whether or not you want to please them or please me, you need to go with pleasing me every time. Your daughter's life depends on it."

"I understand that, but—"

"There's more than one of us. While you're on the phone with me, someone will be watching you. You'll never know who and you'll never know when, but it will be going on. If you lie to me, I'll know it. And your daughter will die. Try to outsmart me, and it's goodbye sister disco. You and I are working on this project, Gene, and the goal is saving Cordelia's life. To that end, I'm the one you're going to have to trust. Do we understand each other?"

"Yes."

"Now the first thing you do is drive to Lambert International Airport and rent a car. A white Ford. One that hasn't been bugged by FBI agents. After you rent the car, you drive straight downtown. Drive alone. No agents in the backseat or trunk, because if there are, I'll make you regret it."

"Okay," Gene said.

"Now," Terrill said, "have you got the money ready?"

"Yes."

"Now, Gene, marked bills, sequential bills, or ink bombs, those are a death warrant for your daughter. Understand?"

"I understand that. It's only money. I just want her back."

"Well, I'm glad to hear you say that, Gene. You put it in a backpack, a blue Lands' End backpack. Wear a ball cap too; I don't want people to recognize you. Got it?"

"Yes."

"Good. Keep your cell phone with you and I'll be calling you back soon. Remember, Gene, it's you and me here. Not them."

Terrill clicked off.

•

The red light on the dashboard flashed on and off, alternating with the headlights that had been rigged for the same purpose, as Hastings pressed his Jaguar through west-bound traffic on the interstate.

Cars pulled over to the right lane, some quicker than others, and Hastings averaged around eighty-five miles per hour to the airport.

He had received a call on his cell phone from Agent Gabler ten minutes earlier, saying that the kidnappers had contacted Penmark and it was going down now and he needed to be at the airport right away. Hastings said "thanks" to Gabler for some reason, expecting something in return, but Gabler had hung up already.

Gabler called him again fifteen minutes later and said they were at the National Car Rental agency. A few minutes after that, Hastings had parked his car there and was standing under a canopy with Gabler and Kubiak and another dozen or so other law enforcement officers.

There was another man there, tall and big shouldered and wearing a mustache. He wore a crisp white shirt, a tie, and red suspenders. Hastings had not seen him before and there was something about his bearing that suggested he was not an FBI agent. He was talking with Lexie Penmark.

Hastings said to Gabler, "Who's that?"

"That's Mr. Jeffrey Rook," Gabler said. "Do you know him?"

"No."

"He owns a private detective agency here in town."

"Oh," Hastings said.

"Apparently," Gabler said, "Mrs. Penmark thought his presence was necessary."

Hastings sighed.

"Yeah," Gabler said, "that's pretty much how I feel about it."

Hastings was halfway beginning to think Gabler was all right. Gabler could have gotten away with not calling him this morning.

Feelings would have been hurt, but there would not have been too much Hastings could have done about it. He didn't have time to give much thought to it, but his suspicion was that Gabler wasn't trying to be considerate to him, but that Gabler respected his ability and felt they would all be better off with Hastings assisting them than not.

Hastings said, "Is he waiting to be briefed?" referring to Lexie's new beau.

"You'd think so," Gabler said.

Hastings thought about his conversation with Lexie Penmark the night before. Perhaps hiring Rook had been her way of paying him back for not showing interest in her offer of employment. Perhaps not. It depressed him in any event. The order of importance that people like Lexie Penmark placed on things. As if controlling this "event" was more important to her than the safety of her stepdaughter.

Agent Kubiak came up to Gabler and Hastings and said, "There's a briefing session inside."

•

It was Agent Kubiak who led the briefing. Though he was younger than many of the other men in the office, he did not seem to notice it. Hastings leaned against the back wall with his hands in his pockets and was unpleasantly surprised to see that someone had let Jeffrey Rook into the room.

Kubiak played the tape of that morning's conversation between Gene Penmark and the kidnapper. Some of the agents took down a few notes.

When that was finished, Agent Kubiak said, "First off, I'll tell you that the kidnapper used another cell phone with a stolen SIM card. So we got nowhere with the phone identity. We triangulated the call and learned that he called within an eight-block area in the Central West End. But he was gone after that."

There was a pause, Kubiak getting the bad news out first. When that was done, he said, "If this man is to be believed, he is not acting alone. He is smart. I do not want any of you presuming otherwise. He killed one man already and we have no doubt that he would not hesitate to kill Cordelia Penmark."

Hastings glanced about the room to see if either Gene or Lexie Penmark was there. They were not.

Agent Kubiak said, "The kidnapper has expressly instructed Penmark to trust him and not us. As psychological tactics go, this is a clever one." For a moment, Hastings thought he saw Kubiak glance at Rook. "But, gentlemen, let me be clear: when he suggests that we are more interested in apprehending him than saving the life of Penmark's daughter, he could not be more wrong. Now. We haven't much time. Agent Gabler will brief us on how we're going to proceed."

Agent Gabler stood up. The room was small, and as time was short, he stayed where he was. He said, "There will be a helicopter in use. And there will be agents positioned as close to Penmark as safety will allow. No one is to move close until ordered by me. This is a difficult situation. If we get too close to Penmark, we risk exposing ourselves and breaking the terms laid out by the kidnappers. If we're too far away, Mr. Penmark himself may be at risk of getting abducted. Or worse. I've gone over this with Mr. Penmark." Gabler paused. Then said, "Lieutenant Hastings with St. Louis PD will be tailing as well as part of a joint task force. For those of you who aren't familiar with him, he's driving a brown Jaguar, so don't anybody shoot him accidentally." There were a few laughs. Men frightened and tense, wanting a release. They looked over at Hastings against the wall and he was acknowledged as one of them in a way he had not been before.

Jeffrey Rook raised his hand. He gave his face a bored look, like this was all old hat to him.

"Yes," Gabler said. Like Hastings, he was wondering who had let the man into the room.

"Am I correct," Jeffrey Rook said, "in assuming that you're going to leave Gene on his own?" There was insolence in his tone. Suggesting that the feds were fucking things up.

"No," Gabler said. "We will be as close to him as we can without getting the girl killed. It's the best we can do."

"Hmmm," Rook said, his voice a snort. He didn't lack for shame, this one. He said, "Then I'd like to ride with Gene."

There were a few muffled groans and sighs in the room.

"Negative," Gabler said. "You are a private citizen and you will stay out of it."

"I was a special agent with the Bureau for twenty-two years. Longer than you, Agent Gabler. And I'm working for Mr. Penmark now."

Hastings said, "Mr. Penmark is not running this, Mr. Rook. We respect your experience, but this is not your show."

Rook turned around and looked at Hastings. He said, "Who the hell are you?"

Hastings acknowledged him with a blank expression and turned back to Gabler. As if to say, *Anything else?* The man wasn't worth the drama. This, of course, irritated Rook further. He said, "Wait a minute, I asked you—"

Hastings said, "St. Louis PD, and if you interfere with this drop, I'll have you arrested."

"Is that right?"

"You can count on it."

Hastings had given this a modicum of thought. Rook had pulled FBI on them. Retired, but maybe a guy who had some stroke with the local FBI field supervisors. Which may or may not have made the FBI agents in the room reluctant to put him in his place. But it meant nothing to Hastings.

Rook was getting the hard-on now, giving Hastings a look like he was insubordinate or something. But to Hastings, there were few things sadder than seeing a man with lost power trying to recapture it.

Rook said, "Are you threatening me?"

"Yeah," Hastings said, his voice conversational. The man deserved nothing more than that.

Rook made something of a show of getting on his feet. He walked to the back door. Before he went out, he pointed a finger at Hastings and said, "You'll regret this."

Whatever, Hastings thought, deciding the man wasn't worth a smile either.

When he was gone, Gabler said, "Who let that fucking guy in here?"

•

Outside, Agent Kubiak had a few words with Gene Penmark. Penmark was sitting in a white Ford Taurus, while Kubiak stood at the window. Kubiak seemed in a hurry to get him out of there, partly because of the kidnapper's request, partly because he didn't want Penmark having any more consultations with his wife or Jeffrey Rook.

Then he stepped back and Penmark drove away. Kubiak trotted to a Dodge Ram pickup with Gabler behind the wheel. They went after Penmark's Ford and Hastings followed in his Jaguar.

They spread out when they reached I-64, going east to the city. Several car lengths separated the hunters and the quarry and the Jag alternated with the Dodge pickup for first tail.

Penmark passed the towering Amoco gas station sign at the Clayton exit and then his cell phone rang.

Penmark said, "Hello?"

Terrill said, "Hello, Gene. Well, we're off to a late start. But at least you're moving, huh?"

"Yes."

"Gene, have you been to the President Casino?"

"No, I haven't. I don't gamble."

"Good man. Well, it's on the Admiral, which is on the river. At Laclede's Landing. Okay?"

"Okay."

"Drive there right away. Park the car at the Riverfront Garage. Then go into the casino. Once inside, go to the blackjack tables. Table nine. Have you got that?"

"Yes. Table nine."

"Play a couple of hands there. Relax. We'll talk again soon."

Terrill clicked off.

———

They had Penmark's cell phone bugged and Terrill knew it. The agents and Hastings knew that the kidnapper knew it too. He would presume it, they thought, because nothing so far had given them any indication that he was stupid. It was common in their business, stupid behavior. People using their own cars to rob banks, leaving their driver's licenses at crime scenes, etc. Successful kidnapping could not be pulled off by someone who was dumb.

Hastings felt like he was on one side of a wall and the kidnappers were on the other. He couldn't see their faces, couldn't see where they were operating from. He'd heard a voice—one voice—and that was it. Yet he was trying to form an identity to this voice.

A young man, probably. White. Sure of himself, smooth, and clever. Hastings could figure out that much. He didn't want to waste too much time trying to form a profile beyond that. Hastings had never been a big fan of profiling. It had been a fad started by the FBI Behavioral Science Unit and strengthened by Jodie Foster and Scott Glenn in *The Silence of the Lambs*. Hastings, like other detectives, had attended the two-week course on profiling at the FBI school in Quantico, Virginia. But he had come away skeptical. First of all, it became apparent that most of the police officers had come to study the cult of the serial killer more than anything else. So right off, he suspected the course had more to do with satisfying the vanity of those teaching it than it did with an actual serial killer "epidemic." Yet a study of the statistics demonstrated that serial killers were responsible for about two hundred murders a year. A relatively low number on a national scale and a drop in the bucket compared to the old-fashioned occurrences of murders committed during robberies, over television sets, spree killing, petty disputes, dissing, turf wars and other gang-related mayhem, all of which was monstrous enough in Hastings's view. But then the commonplace killing didn't involve cannibalism or sexual deviance. Rank-and-file homicide cases didn't make national headlines. Hastings believed he had approached it with an open mind, but at the end of the course, he considered his years of experience in law enforcement and concluded that profiling was, at best, a pseudoscience. It could never serve as a substitute for evidence. The theory that one could study personality traits and habits and "see" a serial killer didn't quite hold up to scrutiny. You might find a Jeffrey Dahmer among the millions of Cliff Clavens, but it would more likely be luck than anything else. Besides, the only reason they caught the serial killer Dahmer was because one of his intended victims was lucky enough to escape and contact the police. That is, they had a witness. Profiling had nothing to do with Dahmer's capture. Plenty of people who claimed to be experts had profiled Dahmer *after* he had been arrested. But that was hardly a difficult thing to do after they'd found all the photos of corpses and body parts stored in the man's fridge.

After that, it became accepted theory in the law enforcement community that all serial killers were white males. And the law enforcement community—which was as susceptible to herd mentality as any other group—clung to that theory even after they found out that the Washington, D.C., serial killers who shot all those people at various gas stations were black.

Klosterman was a man of religious faith, unlike Hastings. Klosterman had said, "We all want simple answers and explanations for things. Cause and effect. But it's not always like that. Who knows what makes any of us tick?"

Still ... Hastings would have liked to know who the man on the phone was. What made him tick was of less concern to Hastings than who he was and where he was hiding.

After Penmark pulled the Ford into the Riverfront Garage on Sullivan Boulevard, Agent Gabler squawked Hastings on the walkie-talkie. They were using the walkie-talkies because they had decided to presume that the kidnappers had a police scanner and would be listening for them. Hastings picked up the communicator.

"Yeah?"

"George," Gabler said, "Penmark is going into the Riverfront Garage. Drive by. Go north a block and park and tail him into the casino. Don't get too close to him."

"Okay."

Hastings drove down the steep slope. The Eads Bridge loomed up to his right, the Mississippi River in front of him. He turned left on Sullivan and sped past the garage. The Jag passed under the Martin Luther King Bridge and he made a left on Biddle Street and parked the car there. He got out and ran until he got back to Sullivan Boulevard. He slowed when he was near the casino, not wanting to look like a cop tailing a man carrying two million dollars.

Hastings saw Penmark buy some chips and move over to a blackjack table. He seemed out of place there, with his glasses and ball cap. Gambling was obviously not his thing. But the dealer helped him out with the rules of betting and the first hand managed to get finished and his chips were swept off the table.

Hastings saw Penmark change his expression and reach into his pocket for his cell phone. Hastings could make out the dealer telling him something ... telling him he couldn't use a cell phone in here.

Penmark held up an irritated hand and moved back. She was telling him again, her voice raised slightly, "Sir—"

Penmark stood up. He grabbed the pack and strapped it to his back and walked away.

He walked across the casino floor, the sounds of the crowds, sighs, wins, losses, tinkling of ice in glasses, the dreary vibe of what they called gaming, legal as it was on the river and not on dry land. Penmark kept walking and then he was trotting toward the gift shop. Like he was in a hurry.

And they were away from the gaming tables and Hastings saw what it was that Penmark was rushing to.

The pay phones. One of the pay phones was ringing.

Penmark picked it up.

•

Terrill said, "Are you being tailed?"

"No," Gene said. "Not to my knowledge."

"Go to the men's room. The one about twenty yards behind you. In the second stall under the plumbing cover is a Nextel two-way phone. It's wrapped in plastic. That's the phone you're going to use from now on. Your regular cell phone, you're going to throw in the trash can in the bathroom. Do you understand that?"

"Yes."

"I'm going to call you on the new phone in three minutes. If you don't answer it, Cordelia will die. Do you understand that?"

"Yes."

Terrill hung up.

By this time, Hastings had walked past Penmark into the gift shop. He picked up a *USA Today* and was standing in line to pay for it. He looked at the front cover as he did so. The line moved forward and Hastings saw Penmark move away from the pay phone.

Hastings put the newspaper on the counter, cutting in front of a woman who was ahead of him. She said, "Excuse me," pissed, but Hastings left the newspaper there and walked out.

He rounded the corner and looked for Penmark. He didn't see him. Christ, there were too many people there. Where was Penmark? He scanned the crowd, men, women, white, black, Asian . . . there. Shit, it was Kubiak sitting at the bar, looking over his shoulder at Hastings, and Hastings decided that Kubiak didn't know either.

Then Hastings saw Penmark. On the other side of the place, moving into the men's room.

•

The door to the second stall was closed. Gene Penmark stood in front of it. He said, "Excuse me."

No answer.

Penmark raised a fist and rapped on the door.

The man inside said, "Just a minute."

I've only got three, Penmark thought.

"Hurry up. Please."

The man on the other side grunted.

Gene Penmark looked at his watch.

About fifty seconds later, he heard a flush of water. He expelled breath and the door opened and a man stepped out. Penmark stepped in and shut the door behind him.

He lifted the plumbing cover off and saw a Ziploc bag taped to the side. Water droplets on it, and something yellow inside. For Gene Penmark, it seemed to become more real then, for some reason. It could have been a bomb for all he knew. But it wasn't. It was a two-way phone and it validated the truth of what was happening and the seriousness of the people he was dealing with.

He took the phone out of the bag and put it in his coat pocket. Before he walked out of the bathroom, he dropped his personal cell phone into the trash receptacle.

When he was out of the washroom, he didn't quite know what to do. So he thought of what was familiar to him. An instinct told him to retreat to something he knew. The car. It was rented but it was his, temporarily at least.

When he got to the casino exit, the Nextel phone rang.

He answered it.

"Leaving already, Gene?"

God, they could see him. They knew he was walking out of the casino. How? Which one of these mass of people could see him? Where was the man on the other phone?

Penmark said, "You didn't tell me where to go. I got the phone, obviously."

"Good," Terrill said. "Now we don't have to worry about spies. Gene, walk out of the casino and go down to the MetroLink train depot. It's a short walk. Get on the train going west. Get on the second car from the front. Now get going."

•

Hastings heard his two-way squawk. He checked to see if anyone was looking before he answered it.

Gabler said, "Where is he?"

"He's walking out."

"He dumped his cell phone," Gabler said. "We don't have any audio on him."

"What?"

"He dumped the fucking cell phone. You got him?"

"Yeah, he's about forty yards out."

"Keep with him," Gabler said. "But not too close."

Hastings was about to move, but Gabler said, "*Wait.* Craig's got him. Stay there."

And there was Kubiak, moving out of the casino at a good pace, falling into line behind Penmark, who by this time had walked almost two blocks away.

It occurred to Hastings then that Gabler was making this up as he went along. They were in it now and there was only so much planning you could do and then the planning was useless and you had to move and think quickly. They had no communication with Penmark now. He was just a man they could see, but not talk with. They didn't know what the kidnappers had said to him or were saying to him. Things were confused and frenetic now and there was goddamn little they could do about it.

Hastings said into to his two-way, "What do you want me to do?" He would have felt more comfortable directing the thing himself. Not so much out of pride but because it's usually less stressful to be in the action than to have to watch it helplessly.

"Just stay there for a minute," Gabler said. For he wasn't sure himself. Gabler thought he should tell Hastings to get back to his own car and wait for a directive, but his gut told him to hold off on that and his gut was mostly what he was working on now.

———

Craig Kubiak would later say that he had handled the situation appropriately. Or, at a minimum, that he had done the best he could. The kidnapper had expressly warned Penmark that if he saw a federal agent around Penmark, he would kill his daughter. Yet everyone knew that they did not have the option of leaving Penmark entirely alone. That was not possible. So they had to be with him without being on him. With him without being seen. Besides, everyone involved knew that the thing had not gone as planned. As much as such things can be planned.

What Craig Kubiak would not admit to anyone was that he'd first felt a sense of doom when he saw Penmark move toward the MetroLink train depot at Laclede's Landing. Penmark had a good lead on him and right away, Kubiak felt his heart thud and his immediate thought was, Please, God, don't let him board that train without me.

Which is exactly what happened.

Craig Kubiak got to the turnstile and jumped it, bringing the attention of a couple of uniformed transit officers, in that moment Kubiak telling himself that being exposed was worth the risk, was better than letting Gene Penmark board that train without him, but it didn't matter, perhaps would not have mattered even if the transit cops hadn't gotten in his way, because the train was rolling away before he could even identify himself.

TWENTY-TWO

"George."

It was Gabler on the two-way.

"Yeah."

"Uh, Craig lost him. He's on the fucking train. It's going west."

"Oh, shit. He got on at Laclede's?"

"Yeah."

"Where are you?"

"I'm in the pickup. I'm right—"

Hastings saw the Dodge Ram pickup roaring toward him, Gabler getting frantic now.

Hastings jumped in the passenger side.

He said to Gabler, "The next stop is the Convention Center. *Go.*"

The truck screeched off, tires peeling on the cobblestone road. They raced up the inclines, accelerating and decelerating as traffic and obstacles would allow. And when they were out of Laclede's Landing, Gabler pushed the throttle almost to the floor and then they were in downtown traffic, both of them thinking, Christ, Gene Penmark is alone now, all alone, and God knows what could happen.

The MetroLink goes through an underground tunnel through most of downtown St. Louis. So they could not even see the train. It was a short drive from the Laclede's stop to the Convention Center station, but the train had gotten a good jump on them.

"There," Hastings said. And Gabler stepped on the brakes and brought the pickup to a stop just as Hastings jumped out, and then Hastings was running, closing the distance between the truck and the stairs, descending into the station.

The train was by the platform, but the horn sounded as Hastings reached the bottom stair. He sprinted and caught the doors of the last car and squeezed in before they shut tight. Then the train was moving out of the Convention Center station, continuing in underground tunnel.

Hastings kept his mouth closed, his heart pounding from the exhaustion of the run, which he didn't want to demonstrate to the other people on the train. So many. Fifty thousand riders a day on a normal day and this was the Christmas shopping season. He was in the last car. He reached out and grabbed a pole so he would look like an average person and not a policeman. And he moved closer to the pole so no one would be able to see the strap under his jacket, which held his .38 snub-nose revolver in place.

The train gathered speed, the black walls of the tunnel whizzed by in the windows, light and white.

Hastings saw a discarded newspaper lying on a seat. He picked it up, folded it, and started to move forward, looking for Gene Penmark and the people he might meet.

•

Gene Penmark had boarded the third car from the front, but remembering the man's instructions had moved up to the second. He took a seat in the center of that car. He felt lucky to find one. He was not a man to look at people and even now he did not look at the other passengers to see if one of them might be watching him.

Two of them were, however. At one end of the car was Mickey. He was wearing a black raincoat and he had a suit and white shirt and tie on underneath. He was of slim build, his cheekbones prominent, and he wore glasses and his hair was cut short. He did not look like a revolutionary or a terrorist. He looked like a young executive. In his hands was that day's *Wall Street Journal.*

Near the other end of the car was Toby Eagle. With his black hair pulled back in a ponytail, he almost looked more Cherokee than Kiowa, which was what he was. He wore jeans and a T-shirt and a black leather coat that came down over his waist.

Gene Penmark felt his Nextel phone thrum and heard it ring a moment later. He pulled it out of his pocket and answered it.

"Yes."

"Gene. Are you on the train?"

"Yes."

"You're where I told you to be?"

"Yes."

"Good. You can take the backpack off now. Put it under your seat."

Penmark undid the straps and slid the backpack under his seat.

Terrill said, "Have you done it?"

"Yes."

"Good. We're almost home now. Is the next stop Union Station?"

"Yes."

"I want you to get off there. And after that, I want you to walk to the Sunshine Café. The big one with all those tables. You will buy a coffee and take a seat at one of those tables. You are to stay there for thirty minutes. No telephoning, no communicating with anyone. You stay at that table for thirty minutes. If you don't, we'll know about it. Are we clear?"

"Yes, but what about my daughter?"

"If everything is in order, we'll release her in two hours."

"That's not right. You told me—"

"First things first, Gene. We can't take chances."

"But you have to hold up your part of the agreement."

"We will. If you don't comply with my instructions, you know what will happen. Is the stop coming up?"

"I think so."

"Good. Leave it, Gene."

And the voice was gone.

Gene Penmark felt very alone. He looked about the car, looked at faces that didn't look back at him. Strangers. He stood up.

•

Hastings walked through cars, looking at faces. He didn't see Penmark in the first four cars and he started to worry that Penmark might have gotten off at the Convention Center stop and taken another train west and was now in Illinois. But he kept going and then he was looking in the window of the second car from the front and he saw Gene Penmark sitting on the other side.

The train was slowing.

And Gene Penmark was standing up.

Hastings stepped back and pulled out his two-way.

"George?" Gabler said.

"Yeah," Hastings said, "he's here. We're coming up to the

Union Station stop. It looks like he's getting off." Hastings looked at Penmark's back and saw that he no longer had the money.

Hastings said, "He's dumped the ransom. If he gets off, I'm going to stay on to see if I can find who picks it up."

He hadn't asked Gabler if that would be all right. He knew that Gabler didn't know the right call any better than he did. Besides, Gabler wasn't here.

Gabler said, "Okay, George. I'm going to Union Station; I'll find Penmark. Good luck."

Hastings put the two-way back in his jacket pocket and opened the door to the car and moved in. The train was slowing now, coming to a stop. Gene Penmark was walking toward the doors. Hastings stayed where he was, did not go to him. He prayed in that moment that Penmark would not turn around and see him, would not turn around and acknowledge recognition with his eyes. That could get them both killed, if Hastings's instinct was correct. Hastings turned around, his back now to Penmark.

When he turned and looked over his shoulder, Penmark was stepping off the train. The doors closed behind him and the bell sounded. And then all Hastings could do was glance through the window at Penmark as the train left the station. Hastings thought, If I'm right, I'll know soon enough. He'd made a decision and he was stuck with it; Penmark was off the train and Hastings was still on it.

Hastings took a seat near the door through which he had come in. He cast a casual eye on the place where Penmark had been sitting. The seats on the train were arranged like those on an airplane, so Hastings could not see what, if anything, Penmark had left on his seat. Or under it. Hastings didn't know. And now Penmark was gone, so he couldn't ask him. Penmark was gone but the money was probably still here, probably still on the train. Which meant that the man who wanted that money was on the train as well.

But who? Which one of these people?

There were between twenty and thirty other passengers on the car. Women, children, students, workers...shoppers holding bright-colored shopping bags from St. Louis Centre with Christmas gifts in them. Clothes, toys, DVDs, and video games. Too many people. Too goddamn many.

Hastings unfolded his newspaper, thinking that if there was a man on this train to collect the money, he was probably looking out for someone like Hastings. Looking for a cop. Hastings was hunting for a man, but the quarry could turn around and shoot back if he was of a mind to. And if that quarry was here, he would no doubt be capable of doing it.

The train was out of the tunnel now, above ground, and gray light was changing the complexion of the passenger compartment. The people in the car became easier to consider and discern. A young guy in a Chicago Bears jacket and wearing one of those young-guy goatees took a pair of sunglasses out of his pocket and put them on. Hastings began to pick up snatches of conversation. Weather, sports, the shopping season, children's Christmas programs, work, family coming into town for the holidays, entertainment. Between cracking the pages of the newspaper, Hastings would look into the faces of the passengers and try to eliminate the ones who would be unlikely to pick up a bag stuffed with two million dollars. An old man wearing a homburg; a heavyset woman in her fifties wearing a jacket with Bugs Bunny on the back; a woman with two small children; two younger guys having an animated discussion about the point spreads on the upcoming college bowl games.

It was helping, but he couldn't eliminate everyone. And as Hastings discarded the obvious and impossible, he became more and more convinced that his man was on the train. He could not see the money, could not see the bag, but he knew he had seen Penmark step off the train without it. He had a sense of where Penmark had been sitting, where he could have left the money. There was no one sitting there now. Hastings knew he could confirm it for himself just by getting up and walking over there. But if he did that, he would expose himself to the other man—the man who was there to take the money. Maybe the man would shoot him then. Or maybe the man would just quietly get off the train and make a telephone call that would end the life of Cordelia Penmark. It was a tough thing, having to sit there quietly looking for someone who could be looking for him.

The train was bending around a turn now, and Hastings could see the car ahead angle into view, passengers on that one too. They were almost at the Grand Boulevard station. People were starting to gather their things and get ready to get off. And then some of them were on their feet, shuffling to the doors.

And that was when Hastings saw it. A man in a black raincoat, moving down the aisle, so casually, so nonchanlantly, so *normally*, that Hastings would later wonder if the man had been on some sort of sedative or had once been in the theater, and the man stopped and reached under the seat and picked up a blue backpack and then was carrying it as if he had owned it since childhood. Not a trace of guilt or embarrassment colored his expression. For a second, even Hastings thought the man in the raincoat owned the bag.

Hastings followed him off the train and into the station, Hastings falling in behind him. The man in the black raincoat neither slowing nor hurrying when he walked past the newspaper stand and Dr Pepper concession booth, and then that was behind them as the man in the black raincoat went into the men's room.

Hastings hesitated before entering the bathroom. Conscious of the two-way radio in his jacket pocket, but telling himself then, right then, that the man in the raincoat could be aware that he was being tailed and could be setting up a machine-gun turret if Hastings hesitated too long, so Hastings kept going, acting on gut instinct, wondering then if the man in the black raincoat was going to transfer the money from the bookbag to another container because that was what Hastings would have done in his place, and Hastings pushed the door open and then he was inside.

It was like most bathrooms at a metropolitan train station. Dirty white tile, beige doors on the stalls that had seen their share of kicks, the sort of metallike mirrors that are difficult to smash.

The man in the black raincoat was standing in front of one of the stalls, looking directly at Hastings. Not smiling, not frowning. Not looking surprised or alarmed either . . .

Which meant, *shit*, he had been expecting this.

And Hastings turned almost before he heard the door behind him crash open and then the big Indian was rushing him with a knife, quickly and silently, and there was no time for Hastings to reach for his gun because the Indian was right fucking on him, driving, and Hastings had to put both hands out to grab the guy's wrists, which he succeeded in doing, but the Indian was bigger and stronger and younger and faster and the bathroom was not a large one and Hastings anticipated being slammed back into the wall, but somehow he managed to turn and twist so that both he and his attacker smashed up against the wall, but Hastings taking most of the force, the Indian still quiet and determined to kill, and Hastings could see the man in the black raincoat smiling at him, as he placed the blue backpack and its contents into another, black backpack that he would sling over his shoulder. The man in the black raincoat walked out of the bathroom then, feeling it was over, tipping his brow at the dipshit cop who was about to be gutted.

Maybe the man was supposed to hang around until it was finished. Because the Indian sort of looked up, perhaps surprised himself at the other's cowardice, and Hastings shifted his weight again as a smaller man must do, and the Indian thrust forward at the right time, but Hastings had moved, pressing himself back to the side as the Indian pushed the knife into the sink. It didn't knock it out of his hand, but it loosened his grip, and in that moment Hastings took the Indian's hands and smashed them back onto the sink again.

This time, the Indian did drop the knife. It clattered to the ground, but right away the Indian grabbed Hastings by his jacket and hurled him back against the wall. Hastings felt his head bounce off the tiled wall and it did more than hurt. He was disoriented, seeing stars, as he slumped to the ground and watched with blurred vision as the Indian went to the ground to pick up his knife, which gave Hastings just enough time to draw his revolver and shoot the man three times.

The echoes of gunfire boomed out in that small room and the smoke seemed pungent to Hastings, who was trying to remain conscious. But the smoke cleared and he saw the Indian on the ground now, looking quite dead, though Hastings eventually crawled over to make sure. Yeah, dead.

Hastings reached for his two-way to call Gabler and let him know about the man in the black raincoat. He said Gabler's name once, then twice, then slumped over on the floor and passed out.

TWENTY-THREE

Mickey Seften did not slow his walk when he heard the shots echoing from the bathroom in the station. Rounds cracking out and people looking at one another with faces asking, *Is that what I think it is? Yeah, shots fired in a toilet.* Maybe by Toby, maybe by the cop who'd gotten the upper hand.

Mickey kept going.

If Toby had gotten killed, that was all right with him. He had never liked Toby all that much anyway. He wondered now why Terrill had sent Toby along to watch him. Mickey could have killed that cop himself. If he had had a gun, he could have. But Terrill had said he didn't want Mickey carrying a gun on this trip. He'd said he wanted Mickey clean in case anyone stopped and searched him before he picked up the money. So Mickey had gone unarmed and Toby had brought along his big Buck knife. Toby liked knives. He had met up with them when they were in Canada for a few months. Toby was exploiting his heritage even then, stepping in and out of it when the time was convenient. Toby used to kayak down backwoods rivers, smuggling marijuana across the border. Toby was getting by, until he got into a wage dispute with one of his dealer bosses and Toby stabbed him to death. Toby left Canada then and migrated south with the rest of the jackal bins.

Mickey kept his reservations about Toby to himself. He had never believed that Toby had bought into their mission. He believed that Toby was too independent, not one to be beholden to

much of anything. Not even his own culture. Yet Maggie and Terrill were quick to interpret any criticism of any culture apart from
the Judeo-Christian one as deep-seated white supremacy. And
maybe this discomfort with Toby stemmed from that. Mickey
Seften was from Shaker Heights, Ohio, the son of upper-middle-
class parents. His father was a successful patent lawyer, his mother
a judge. He had not seen them in years. He couldn't remember ever
having liked them. His mother had been remote and cool. His father shaking his head a lot, more than once muttering, "Loser."
Both of them relieved when he left home.

Mickey had to stand at the intersection of Grand and Laclede
for only a moment before Terrill pulled up in a Toyota Camry.
Mickey got in.

Terrill said, "Where's Toby?"

"He's still there. I heard shots." Mickey paused. "I think a cop
may have killed him."

Terrill had pulled away from the curb. He was driving west now
on Laclede. He slowed to make a left turn onto Spring Avenue.
Terrill was looking at him as they coasted down the hill.

They stopped at the traffic light at Spring and Forest Park Avenue. Sirens then, distant at first, then getting closer. They stayed at
the light as two police cars and an ambulance raced by them, heading to the Grand Boulevard railway station, and Terrill knew
Mickey was telling the truth.

Terrill said, "How did it happen?"

Mickey hesitated. Shrugged, and said, "The cop followed me
into the bathroom and Toby just went crazy. Jumped him with a
knife."

"What did you do?" Terrill said.

"I left him," Mickey said. He turned to Terrill, not wanting to hide his expressions now. He said, "Look, it's not my fault Toby didn't keep his cool. I had no weapon so there wasn't much I could do to help. Besides, you yourself told me the important thing was to bring the money back."

"Yeah, I told you that."

"It's not about the individual," Mickey said, repeating something else Maggie and Terrill had taught him.

"I know," Terrill said. He continued south on Spring Avenue until they got to I-64. He turned onto that and drove back east. Soon they were rising on the highway as the places they had used unfolded on their left: Union Station, downtown St. Louis. Then the Arch was in view and then behind them as they crossed over the Mississippi River and they were in Illinois.

It was when the city was behind them that Mickey felt the emotion. Two million dollars on them, *two million fucking dollars,* right there in the car with them. He had seen it in the bathroom, had touched it, had put his hands on it. It was there.

Mickey said, "Jesus, I can't believe we did it. Two million dollars. Can you believe it?"

"Yeah, it's a lot of money."

"You were right, Terrill. It wasn't that hard. They're not that bright."

"No, they're not. Hey, who was the cop that was in the bathroom?"

"What? Oh, I don't know. Just some guy in slacks and a jacket. He had dark hair."

"Would you recognize him if you saw him again?"

"Yeah, I guess I would."

Terrill said, "So you saw him long enough for that?"

Mickey shrugged. "Yeah, I guess. Why?"

"No reason."

TWENTY-FOUR

Jan said, "Maggie said only Terrill's supposed to bring her her food."

Ray said, "Maggie's upstairs." She was probably sleeping. Or getting baked.

"But Maggie said—"

"She's not here now." Ray looked at Jan and made a gesture. Like, *Are we supposed to check everything with Terrill and Maggie?* Ray said, "They should be back soon. If it goes well, he's not going to want to worry about whether or not the bitch has been fed."

Lee was standing behind them in the kitchen. She said, "I can bring it to her."

Jan and Ray had almost forgotten she was there. Lee was saying less and less these days.

Before Jan could say anything, Ray handed her the paper plate with the sandwiches. "Good," Ray said. "Do it."

After Lee left, Jan said, "They're not going to like it."

"Fuck 'em," Ray said. "I'm not a child."

Jan did not argue with him. She went to the kitchen sink and turned on the taps, adjusting the hot and cold. She said, "Do we know if they got it?" She was talking about the money.

Ray said, "They haven't told us. They'll tell us when they feel like telling us."

"So much money," Jan said. "What if they actually do it? Did you ever think we'd actually be able to do it?"

After a moment, Ray said, "I don't know."

He had had doubts. But they had told him that doubts were not allowed. They were to think only in terms of winning. They had been told not to think about bad outcomes. Negative thinking was not permitted. If you spoke of your concerns, of any reservations, they threatened to put you in the circle. They had said that you were either on the bus or you were off the bus. If you wanted to get off the bus, get off it now.

Ray Muller thought that he might have heard that bus thing somewhere else before. He couldn't quite remember where. But he thought Maggie had taken it from someone else. Maggie had said there was no place for bullshit people here. But what did it mean to get off the bus? Could you quit? Could you get an honorable discharge? Or did it mean that Terrill put a bullet in your brain?

Ray Muller was conscious now of being alone with Jan. He had brought her into this. He felt no guilt over that. Jan seemed as much a true believer as anyone. In fact, he sometimes thought she'd bought into it more than he had. She had not questioned Terrill or Maggie or the movement or anything they did. And even now, she was worrying about whether she was being insubordinate in having Lee take food to the girl.

Why was it not all right for the bitch to see Lee? What difference did it make? They had not spoken of it, but Ray knew they were going to kill the bitch. What was Terrill trying to sell them? They all knew. Why couldn't they all acknowledge it?

Was it a fear that not all of them would go along with it? That didn't make sense. Mickey, the little cocksucker, he'd do anything

Terrill wanted him to do. He'd shoot the bitch himself if Terrill ordered him to. If Terrill asked him to.

Lee? Yeah, Lee too. If not for her, Terrill would still be in jail. She'd known what she was getting into. And she hadn't batted an eye after Terrill plugged the bitch's boyfriend. Besides, she was so tweaked up these days . . . always pulling imaginary bits of lint from her shirt . . . checking for unseen parasites, always touching herself . . . twitching on uppers. She could probably shoot the girl herself. Even if Terrill didn't ask her to do it. And if Terrill did ask her, that would be that. Of course, Maggie would probably believe that Lee would be uneasy about it. To Maggie, Lee was still the dipshit Ivy League girl. The English major. Maggie believed that everything Maggie said was true. Was the way it was. She had such conviction, she made you think she had to be right. But more and more, Ray was wondering, What is it she actually *does*? What does Maggie do? What does she have that makes her so sure all the time?

As for Lee, Ray had already made up his mind about her. He had no sympathy for her. To him, she held the same value as a deer does to a wolf. Once or twice, he'd wanted to shoot her for being an irritant. This stemmed, mostly, from her silly worship of Terrill. He felt no jealousy, but he resented Lee for giving Terrill more credit than he deserved. Perhaps for empowering him and furthering his self-image as a god. This was something Ray had not given much thought to until they had come to this house.

It's this house, Ray thought. We've been cooped up here too long. It was better back when they were in the Northwest. Back when they were roaming and free. Unattached. It was better then.

Things would pick up when they got the money. Then they could roam again and get some distance from one another.

•

Cordelia started when she heard steps coming down the stairs. Light steps. A woman, not a man, now in front of her.

Lee placed the food before her, as if she were a dog. Lee stepped back.

"Hey," Cordelia said. It came out of her involuntarily. She wanted to communicate with someone. A sister, a person. Christ, something.

Lee moved back to the stairs.

"Hey," Cordelia said, "wait."

Lee said, "I have nothing to say to you." Her voice sounded hollow, even raspy.

Cordelia said, "Have they gotten the ransom?"

"I'm not talking to you."

"Please. *Please.* You have to give me something. You're not a bad person. You can't be."

"I'm not bad. You don't know what I am."

"I know you're not. I've done nothing to you guys. Whatever it is you want, we can get it for you."

"How generous of you."

Cordelia tried to discern the woman's figure in the darkness. She seemed younger than she had first thought. Educated, maybe. Cordelia said, "I have nothing against you."

"Why should you?" Lee said. "You don't even know me."

"Please let me go. Please? Can't you talk to them?"

"I could. If I wanted."

"Tell them. Tell *him.* Tell him I'm not going to tell anyone."

"Him?" Lee said. "You mean my husband?"

"Yes," Cordelia said, confused. The girl had to know who had been coming down there. It was her husband? Oh God, please let it be. Please give me something. "Yes," Cordelia said. "Tell him I won't tell anyone. My dad will pay you. He'll pay you to release me. You must believe me. You must tell him that. You must please tell him that when you talk to him."

"I talk to him all the time. I don't see why I should help you."

"Because you can. You *must*. Please, for the love of God, you must."

"Don't speak to me of God, piggie."

Lee walked back up the stairs, immune to the cries behind her.

TWENTY-FIVE

The television screen flickered colored images of two young guys with nice haircuts, earnestly discussing their feelings for a girl named Brooke, and the camera held on them for a moment, sustaining the drama, until they went to a commercial break. And as the commercials came on, the people in the emergency room of Cardinal Glennon hospital went back to their *US*es and *Entertainment Weekly*s.

Joe Klosterman had not taken a seat, but he had checked in with the administrative nurse and had been informed that George Hastings had received a minor contusion on the head and sustained a minor concussion but would be released at any minute.

This was what Klosterman was telling Murph on the cell phone when Hastings came down the hall into the waiting area. There was a goose egg on the back of his head that wasn't visible for his hair but was tender to the touch.

Klosterman said, "Here he is now. I'll call you back." Then to Hastings he said, "You all right?"

Hastings said, "Yeah, it's nothing."

"Murph's down at the train station, picking up what he can."

"Feds there?"

"Yeah," Klosterman said. "I guess they took you away before the feds got there."

"I wish they hadn't," Hastings said.

A couple of patrol officers had found him unconscious on the bathroom floor and called for an ambulance. The paramedics looked for a knife or gunshot wound and didn't find one and eventually located a moist spot of blood on his head where it had been knocked up against the wall. Hastings was coming to when they were putting him into the ambulance but was too weak to make much of a protest. Now, he was feeling better, though still a little unsteady on his feet as he and Klosterman walked out of the hospital into the cold afternoon air. Klosterman gestured to the felony car, which was parked down the hill about a block.

Klosterman said, "Murph said they have no identification on the man you killed."

Hastings said, "Shit. Well, I guess I'm not surprised."

"I presume you think it's related? That he wasn't just attempting to mug you?"

"No." Hastings was aware then that no one had yet questioned him about it. "He was with the other guy. A young man in his twenties wearing a black raincoat. Short dark hair, pale skinned, glasses. The John Lennon kind."

"The man in the raincoat?"

"Yes. He's the one that picked up the money. The Indian was with him. He led me into the bathroom and the Indian came in behind me. A trap, and I walked right into it."

"Indian Indian, or American Indian?"

"American Indian."

Klosterman said, "You don't say Native American?"

Hastings shrugged. He had played high school basketball with a couple of guys from the Osage tribe: Don Buffalohead and Amos Ribs . . . Don was okay, a funny guy, but Amos had been a bit of a prima donna who didn't pass the ball much. They called themselves Indians, not Native Americans. Last Hastings heard, Don Buffalohead was running a small insurance agency in Lincoln, which didn't surprise Hastings much as Don was a born salesman ... shit, thinking of Don Buffalohead now because he'd shot an Indian dead in a bathroom. Maybe he was a racist. Or maybe the conk on his head was messing up his thought process. Hastings said, "He had a Buck knife."

"I know," Klosterman said, "Murph told me about it. How close did he get?"

Hastings thought back to the cold nightmare of that bathroom, the knife about an inch away from his stomach. "Pretty close," he said.

"Well," Klosterman said, "if he's within twenty feet of you, it's a clean shoot."

"It was clean," Hastings said. "I'm not worried about that."

They were up to the car now, a blue Chevy Impala slick-back police unit. Hastings put his hands on the roof for a moment to steady himself.

Klosterman was looking across from the driver's side. "You okay?" he said.

"I'm fine," Hastings said. "I just need some coffee." He got into the car and Klosterman did the same.

Hastings said, "What happened to Gene Penmark?"

"He's fine. He's at home now."

And Hastings said, "Where's debrief?"

"FBI field office," Klosterman said. "There's a chair there with a lot of fingers pointed at it and I got a feeling it's waiting for you."

Klosterman drove fast, flashing the high beams on interrupting traffic when necessary to get them to pull to the right, and they were at the field office in less than ten minutes. Klosterman walked in with him and Hastings decided that was okay too.

Then they were seated in a conference room with ASAC Jim Shellow and Agents Kubiak and Gabler and some guy wearing a full suit who just took notes that Hastings believed would go straight to Shellow.

Kubiak and Gabler were still in their undercover clothes: plaid shirts and jeans that looked like they'd been purchased that morning from the Bass Pro Shop.

Kubiak told his part of the story and Hastings was glad to hear that it was mostly straight. Kubiak even acknowledged fault in allowing Penmark to board the train without him, saying that the responsibility had been his and his alone. He avoided the "mistakes were made" terminology common to most bureaucrats and politicians and Hastings started to wonder if the guy was perhaps tolerable on a good day.

Then Hastings told them what he remembered, Gabler questioning him here and there, though not in a hard fashion. Klosterman was asking him things too and none of the federal agents seemed to take issue with this.

And when it was done, Jim Shellow said, "Gentlemen, this sounds like it was poorly planned from the beginning. We have a man who escaped with two million dollars. We have a dead alleged assailant who we can't identify. And we have received no word that Cordelia Penmark has been released. Lieutenant, I do not hold you solely accountable for this. This was an FBI operation and it was not one for which you had been trained."

If this was supposed to make Hastings feel better, it did not. Hastings looked Jim Shellow up and down. A man, not much more or less, who was only a few years older than Hastings. He could accept Shellow's comments quietly and just wait for it to end. And if he'd been smarter, he probably would have.

Hastings said, "Pardon me, Mr. Shellow. Is this something you can train for?" He said it in a tone that you couldn't quite call insolent.

Jim Shellow said, "Excuse me?"

Klosterman said, "What the lieutenant means, sir, is that even the FBI can't draw up a plan for every contingency." Klosterman turned to Hastings as if to acknowledge the obvious. "Right?"

Hastings suppressed a smile. Few could do bogus respect like Klosterman. "Yes," Hastings said.

"That's not the point," Jim Shellow said. He wasn't going to have these two hicks twist him around. "In my view, you cowboyed this thing."

Hastings said, "How did I do that?"

Shellow said, "You shot and killed one witness and let the other one get away. And the one you killed wasn't even armed."

"He was armed, sir. He had a Buck knife."

"You don't just shoot someone with a knife," Shellow said. "You order him to drop the weapon."

"Sure, if there's time." Hastings paused, wondering if this jackass was for real. "Are you—"

"Jim," Gabler said, trying to head off this confrontation, "let's be fair to the man. We weren't there and he was. He said the assailant was charging him with a knife and I think we should take him at his word."

"Sure," Shellow said, "what else can we do? One witness dead and the other on the run with two million dollars." He was talking now the way a small man talks, petty and sarcastic.

Hastings took a breath and tried to think things through. Then he said, "If you want to blame me for what happened today, go ahead. I don't answer to you, so it makes no difference to me what you think. Every shooting in the line of duty is investigated by my Department. So I'll answer to them when the time comes. But I think we should move on now, if you don't mind."

Jim Shellow said, "You're not running this, Lieutenant."

"I'm not trying to. I want to find the girl. I do that and I'll find the murderer of Tom Myers."

Shellow said, "What were you doing there, anyway?"

For a few moments, nobody said anything. Hastings felt uncomfortable all of a sudden; he didn't want to name names or point fingers. But it was taken care of when Gabler spoke up and said, "I asked him to assist us, Jim. It's joint task."

For a second, it seemed like ASAC Jim Shellow didn't know what to say. He looked at Agent Kubiak, but Kubiak was not giving him anything back. Then he returned his attention to Gabler.

Shellow said, "You guys didn't clear that with me."

Gabler said, "You didn't indicate that we had to, Jim." His tone was respectful, almost soft.

Jim Shellow took another look around the room. An experienced bureaucrat, he knew when to quit, and no one in the room was really surprised when he stood up and walked out of the room.

After the door was shut, Klosterman said, "Well, that was pleasant."

"He's a good man," Gabler said, giving something of a sharp look to Klosterman, the outsider. He wasn't going to form alliances against one of his own. Not yet, anyway.

Klosterman gave Gabler one of his forgive-me gestures. Which helped, but Hastings was still uncomfortable.

Hastings said, "Look, I've been worrying about this for a while, so I'm just going to say it: are you guys hacked off at me over this thing with your old SAC?"

Gabler said, "What?" He was smiling now, genuinely surprised. "You mean Frank Cahalin?"

"Yes."

"You mean because you're the one that caught Frank Cahalin?"

"Well," Hastings said, self-conscious now, "yeah."

And Hastings heard Craig Kubiak laughing now, a sound he'd never heard before.

Gabler said, "You thought there were hard feelings over that?"

"Well, I—"

Kubiak was still laughing.

Gabler said, "George, no offense, but apart from a handful of candy-ass agents, just about everybody here hated Frank. We were only sorry that we didn't catch him." Gabler looked down the table at the other agent. He shared a smile with him and said, "I guess if we gave it any thought, we should probably thank you for it."

They were ribbing him now and the only thing Hastings could do was say, "Okay, okay," meaning, he got the point.

Kubiak said, "Let's get some coffee. This could be a long night."

After the agents had left the room, Hastings said, "Hmmm." He had been worried about it, flattering himself that they had an ax to grind against him all along. But they hadn't. He had imagined it all.

Klosterman put a consoling hand on his shoulder. "Cheer up, George," he said. "Maybe there's somebody out there who's mad about it."

•

They walked down the hall to a small office that Kubiak and Gabler shared with two other agents. The file was open on Kubiak's desk, photos of the dead man spread out. Shots taken close up and at distances, the slumped corpse on the bathroom floor. Clinical-looking and lifeless, even to Hastings, who had been there when it happened.

Kubiak said, "Well, Lieutenant, does he look familiar to you?"

"No," Hastings said. "I saw him for the first time today."

Kubiak said, "No identification on him. And we can't match his prints to anything we have in our database. You seem to have killed a ghost."

Hastings didn't respond.

Gabler riffled through the photos, the ones that were taken later at the medical examiner's office. He found what he was looking for and centered on the desk a photo of a tattoo on the man's back. It was a couple of triangles laid in a horizontal manner, the lower triangle forming a sort of fulcrum—like a seesaw, yet on the other side was a semicircle arcing over a dot.

Gabler said, "I did a little Internet search while you were napping and I believe this thing here is a bird. The symbol of a bird. If he was one of the southwestern tribes, this could mean that our man here was carefree and lighthearted."

"Hmmm," Hastings said, remembering the grim determination of the man with the knife.

"But that," Gabler said, "is a shot in the dark."

"It's not all we're doing," Kubiak said. "There'll be faxes and e-mails going out to all our field offices within an hour. Maybe someone's seen this guy before." Kubiak was looking at Hastings now. He seemed to hesitate, only for a moment, and then he said, "Do you want to look at the dispatch before I send it out?"

It was a small thing, but in a way not so small. The agent was acknowledging Hastings's role in this and perhaps something more, but there was never going to be anything more dramatic than that. And for that, it was important for Hastings not to dwell on it.

"Sure," Hastings said, as if it were routine.

Kubiak left them and then Klosterman drifted off for a cup of coffee.

It was then that Gabler turned to Hastings and spoke in a low voice.

"Listen," he said, "I'm sorry if I let you down earlier."

Hastings frowned. "What are you talking about?"

"The whole thing happened so fast," Gabler said. "We didn't know he'd get on that goddamn train and—well, we weren't ready for it."

"Well, that's what I was trying to explain to your boss. You can't be ready for everything."

"Yeah, but we're expected to be."

For a moment, Hastings wondered if the *we* meant law enforcement or if it meant FBI. He decided that Gabler had meant FBI and the local Metro guys were not included. You could interpret it any way you wanted, up to and including not being ready for 9/11. But doing that after the fact was an easy thing and all too often a convenient game for politicians.

"The point is," Gabler said, "we put you on that train by yourself. Between you and me, it's our bad."

"Forget it."

Gabler nodded. He was not comfortable with the conversation and it was obvious to Hastings that he wanted to end it as soon as possible. Yet something was still bothering him. Gabler said, "Still, I think you handled it pretty fucking well. Craig does too."

"Does he?"

"Yeah." Gabler gave him a look. "Don't write him off, George. He's a good agent."

"Okay," Hastings said.

Gabler said, "We'll catch these fuckers, George. They're smart, but they're not smarter than we are."

TWENTY-SIX

Hastings sat with the sketch artist from the FBI and together they put together a fairly good likeness of the white guy he had seen on the train and in the bathroom at the station. They couldn't put a name to it and Hastings said that he had not seen the man before. But the photo was submitted to other FBI field offices to see if it would spark anything. It was also released to the local media outlets.

That was how Terrill and Maggie realized that the thing had not gone as smoothly as they had thought.

They were watching the television alone, upstairs in Maggie's room, when the six o'clock news came on and there it was: Mickey Seften, sketched in charcoal, a nice little portrait of his hair, eyeglasses, and intense expression. Their rules prohibited people from watching television without permission. Maggie and Terrill controlled the flow of communication, the access to media.

Maggie sighed.

Terrill said, "I knew it."

Maggie said, "These runs to White Hall for food and cigarettes, has Mickey gone on those?"

"Yeah, he's gone."

"Then you know that it's just a matter of time before someone from White Hall calls the police."

"It's possible," Terrill said. "It doesn't mean it's probable."

"It's more than possible, Terrill. We have to move," Maggie

said. "Sooner than we planned. When did you tell Penmark we would release her?"

"I said within two hours."

"And that was how long ago?"

Terrill shrugged. "About six hours ago."

Maggie seemed to think it over. She said, "We can do the next one in Chicago. Maybe we ask for more next time."

And Terrill was thinking, More what? They had two million dollars with them now. It had just been a figure before, but now they had it. It was real and they had it. And now Terrill was finding that he was actually intimidated by it. What does a person do with two million dollars? If he wants a car, does he walk up to the car lot and just start counting it out? Well, no, because any exchange over ten thousand, the dealers were supposed to report. Laws intended to keep drug dealers in check, though the laws didn't seem to deter much. He and Maggie had drilled these people for so long with all their talk of revolution and pigs and anarchy and the Man and had said that they would use the proceeds of the kidnapping to finance their mission. But now the money was here and the mission no longer seemed that clear. They had *accomplished* the mission, hadn't they? They had gotten the fucking money. If that wasn't striking back at the establishment, it was hard to say what was.

Maggie was saying something to him now.

"... Terrill."

"Huh?"

"Terrill." Maggie spoke in a low voice now, scooting her chair closer to him. They were alone in the room, but Maggie was worried about people listening outside the door.

"What, Maggie?"

"I'm a little concerned."

"About what?"

"Did you notice what happened earlier?"

"What?"

"When you brought that money back, everyone was looking at it. Didn't you feel funny?"

"What do you mean?"

"All of them," Maggie said. She was referring to their comrades, eyeing the money as if it were scraps of food, eyeing it like wolves around a deer. "All of them wanting it. Except for that idiot, Lee."

Terrill said, "I think you're imagining things."

Maggie tried to maintain patience, wondering now if Terrill was starting to believe his own publicity. "Terrill," she said, "Ray and Mickey are going to want that fucking money now. Do you not see that?"

"Hey, Mickey had a chance to run off with it himself before, and he didn't."

"Okay, he didn't. But before, Toby was watching him, and while Toby was alive Mickey was watching him."

"Maggie, you're losing me."

"You know what I mean. Anyway, time's gone by and I assure you Mickey's not feeling the same way he did this afternoon. Listen to what we're doing now, Terrill, listen to the conversation we're having. Don't you think maybe Mickey and Ray are having a conversation of their own? Or Mickey and Jan? Or all three of them?"

"All right, then," Terrill said, getting upset now. "We split it up in the morning and then we don't have to think about it anymore."

Maggie Corbitt was experienced at hiding her thoughts. What she was thinking now was, *Evenly?* An even split? She said, "Baby, I know you mean well. But do you think that's right? After all the work you did?"

"I don't know."

"You're too generous, Terrill. You always think of others first, it's your nature. But, baby, we've got to be realistic about things. We've got big plans."

"I know that."

"I know you know. But if you split that money up with those guys like we're just a gang of thieves, they'll take it and run. They'll go blow it. And how long do you think it will be before they catch up with Mickey? A day? Maybe two or three days?"

"Mickey helped bust me out."

Maggie's face was a hard shell. She said, "He did that because I told him to." Her expression adding, *And don't you forget it.*

Terrill opened his mouth to defend himself, to say something back to her, but she was looking at him in that determined, reproachful way of hers and he was chastened. Finally, he said, "I don't know what you want me to do."

Her expression softened, just. She said, "Baby, you were beautiful today. Just beautiful. I don't know anyone who could have done what you did. Directing around Gene fucking Penmark like he was a toy soldier. You were stunning." She put a hand on his leg. "But this is just the beginning." She reached up to stroke his hair now. It could have been a lover's touch or a mother's. She said, "Splitting the money . . . we can talk about that later. But Mickey—Mickey's going to be a problem."

"I know," Terrill said, "I've been thinking about that since this afternoon." *Would you recognize the cop if you saw him again, Mickey? Yeah, I guess I would.* Well, great, dumb shit, that means he'd probably recognize you too.

Maggie said, "I don't like talking about these things. But he did run and leave Toby alone with the cop. If he had stayed, he could have helped Toby and killed that fucking pig and then we wouldn't have this problem."

"I've thought about that too," Terrill said.

"After all," Maggie said, "we have to think of what would be right for Toby too."

"Yes. We do."

"We owe him that," Maggie said. She took Terrill's hand and placed it on her breast. "Don't you think?"

Terrill was looking at her, stirring now. With Maggie, sex was always so intense, so purifying. She gave of herself sparingly—sometimes weeks would go by during the intervals—but when she did make herself available, it was like no other girl he'd ever been with and it was like the first time he'd been with her. A gift, an opportunity to fulfill himself that no other girl could offer him.

They embraced and kissed, but only for a moment. Briefly as young people do, and then she stood and led him by the hand to the bed.

•

When he and Maggie met, Terrill had been little more than a small-time criminal. He stole cars and stereo equipment and sold little bags of marijuana and lived off young girls who fell in love with him. And there were plenty of those. Terrill was a tall man with wide shoulders, yet the girls always talked about his eyes. Hazel eyes and dark hair, a black Irish beauty. Terrill was aware of his looks, aware of his presence. He was aware of his allure for men and women. Though heterosexual, he liked to tease and, ultimately, humiliate gay men. He had a hypnotic effect on them as well and he knew it. For him, seduction was an easy art.

Except when it came to Maggie. He had not seduced Maggie. Indeed, he had not even tried. When he first met Maggie, he thought her a little too boyish for his taste. With her short dark hair and her sharp face, she didn't seem worth the bother. But then he saw the weight in her face, the way she looked when someone said something stupid, the way she could reduce people to stammers, and it changed him. He approached her not with the goal of seducing her but rather to impress her. Impress her so that she would allow him to be with her while she spoke and he listened. She was three years older than he and he had never had a sister. Nor had he ever truly respected a woman. Certainly, he had never feared one. But no one had ever seemed as smart as Maggie, as powerful, as natural a leader. As their friendship developed, she began to teach him about politics and art and history. Things he thought he had thought about, but really hadn't. She told him that he had it in within himself not to be a bullshit person, that he had marvelous potential, that he was a natural disruptor of the bullshit scene, but he needed to learn to channel himself. She told him that when they met, she knew right away that they thought and felt alike. Maggie was smart and she did not tell Terrill all these things in one session. Rather, it was over a series of get-togethers. Usually when they were together, she would give him LSD to make him more suggestible. Maggie would take it too, but always in smaller doses. It left her with the control. Control was important to Maggie.

She grew up in relative poverty. The daughter of an Assembly of God minister, her formative years were in northwestern Arkansas. Her father and mother had to work full-time jobs apart from the church because the church was too small to pay a salary. Her mother was not cruel or mean-spirited, but she was stupid and weak, and by the time Maggie was a teenager she had come to despise her mother as she would most weak people. Maggie had a little brother named Bobby. By the time he was two, the parents realized he was autistic.

By all outward appearances, Maggie Corbitt was a good girl through her childhood and early adolescence. She read her Bible daily. She helped her mother with Bobby. She did well at school.

She was never a pretty girl. But she was an attractive one, with a cute figure. Even as a young teenager her face seemed more like a woman's than a girl's. And this was something that men noticed. When she was sixteen, she had her first sexual experience. It was with a local police officer who was assigned to the school. The young cop was in his early twenties and was married and had the maturity level of a sixteen-year-old himself. Consequently, it did not occur to him that having intercourse with Maggie was a crime or even a sin. As he saw it, he and Maggie were on the same wavelength.

Maggie Corbitt was by no means dumb. But the environment in which she was raised was not one that encouraged frank discussion about sex or its consequences. Still, when she missed her period, Maggie was vaguely aware that she was going to have a baby.

When she told her parents, her daddy slapped her and called her ugly names. At one point, he said, "I knew it." Like it was something he knew she'd do to him one day, and she did. Maggie remembered the sting of that. Her mother didn't defend her. She just sat stupidly in her chair, her hands shaking. Her lips were moving silently and Maggie realized that she was praying. Praying to the Lord and doing nothing while her husband called her little girl a slut and slapped her around.

They put her on a bus to Texas the next day to live with an aunt. Maggie presumed that she would stay with her aunt until she had the baby and then she would be allowed to come home. But her folks never called. Two months later, she had a miscarriage. She telephoned her parents to tell them that it was over. Her father would not speak to her. Her mother kept saying, "Well, I don't know." Even when Maggie asked her if they wanted her to come home.

When she was seventeen, Maggie hitched a ride with another girl to St. Louis. Life got rougher then, living in the underground. Drug-dealer boyfriends, roommates without last names, strippers calling themselves dancers, Internet pornography, and so forth. But Maggie had already developed a hard shell before she got there. And in the next few years she forged a persona quite separate from the one she had in northwestern Arkansas. Her accent became submerged, her clothes urban, her politics hard-edged and pitiless. It was as if somewhere along the way, she had decided that she would act like a certain kind of person and after playing that role long enough, she would become that person. In this, she succeeded. And by the time she met Terrill Colely, the preacher's daughter had long since been buried.

Now she lay in bed with Terrill. Terrill was sleeping, sleeping like a baby. He usually slept afterward. She slipped out of bed and sat on a chair and lighted a cigarette. She looked at him. He was beautiful, even in sleep.

Earlier, Terrill had defended Mickey by saying that Mickey hadn't run off with the money when he had the chance. Jesus. Of course he didn't, Terrill. Mickey's a faggot and he wouldn't do anything to displease his black prince. God, the things Terrill could forget. Maybe he'd smoked too much dope over the years. Well, what did it matter? Tomorrow, she'd direct Terrill to take care of Mickey and the Penmark girl and he would do it. And after that, she would figure out how to deal with the rest of them. Maybe starting with that idiot child Lee. Not that Maggie was jealous of Lee. Not by a long shot. But if she had to hear Lee say "Terrill" with her lovelorn eyes one more time, she'd throw the bitch down the stairs.

TWENTY-SEVEN

Klosterman pressed the buzzer at the A&W hamburger stand and a voice came back on the squawk box. Klosterman said he would take a deluxe cheeseburger value meal and a Coke. The voice said was Pepsi okay? Klosterman said no, but he would take a Dr Pepper. He turned to Hastings and said, "What do you want?"

Hastings's stomach had become sensitive over the years. He liked the taste of fast food, but his system wouldn't abide it. In contrast, Klosterman could eat anything.

"Just coffee," Hastings said.

"Come on," Klosterman said. "You've had an injury. You've gotta eat something."

"Just coffee. I'll get a sandwich later."

Klosterman sighed resignation and ordered coffee.

The food came and they stayed in the car, like the guys in the Sonic commercial, only older and a little less self-aware. Hastings sipped the coffee and felt the heat travel up to his head, jumpstarting the cortex. Wincing, but he would be okay.

Klosterman said, "It went okay, I think."

Hastings said, "Back there?"

"Yeah. The ASAC was being an asshole, but those other guys seemed okay."

"They probably are."

"You think they'll be able to get an ID on those guys?"

Hastings sighed. "I don't know. Maybe." He wasn't too optimistic though and it showed on his face. He said, "I've got to get back out to the Penmarks. Can you do something for me?"

"Sure."

"Talk to Rhodes and Murph and have them check out Edie Penmark. The sister."

Klosterman was holding the cheeseburger, some of it sticking out of the wrapper. "Why?" he said.

"I'm not sure yet," Hastings said. "Yesterday, I interviewed her and she came on to me."

"Really?" Klosterman was not smiling. He knew it was not an adolescent subject.

"Yeah. Kind of creepy, actually. She may be unstable."

"You think she had something to do with this?"

"No, not necessarily. But I wouldn't be surprised if she were into some pretty bad shit."

"Drugs?"

"Maybe."

"Did you ask her?"

"I didn't ask her that directly. If I had, she wouldn't have answered. I got the feeling she was hitting on me to throw me off. To distract me."

"The only worse thing than a bad girl is a bad girl with money."

"Well, what I'm wondering is, is this bad girl connected to bad people? Who are not rich?"

"If she's buying, she may be," Klosterman said. "Yeah, we can check her out."

"Thanks. Hey, will you drive me to Laclede's Landing? That's where I left my car."

"You think you can drive?"

"Yeah." Hastings gestured to his head. "Like hitting your head on the ceiling."

"If you say so."

•

The security guard let Hastings by and when he pulled up to the drive, he saw an unfamiliar Mercury Marauder there that he suspected belonged to Jeffrey Rook. Not an official police car, but resembling one enough to give the illusion of security and authority. Hastings saw that and sighed. He knew what waited for him inside, but his comfort was secondary.

And sure enough, there was Jeffrey Rook, waiting in the front hall, standing a few feet in front of Lexie Penmark, his patroness. Hastings felt his anger set on slow boil now, the fright of being nearly stabbed to death not quite out of him yet and now he had to tell himself not to deck this big piece of shit.

Jeffrey Rook, an authority figure in his own mind, had his hands on his hips like a school principal, but performing for Lexie Penmark, maybe hoping to get in her pants, and he said, "Would you mind explaining what happened?"

Hastings stopped and briefly looked the big man up and down, as if just noticing him. Then he walked past him to Lexie Penmark. Hastings said, "Where's your husband?"

Lexie Penmark looked back at Rook, surprised that he had been ignored. He had spent so much time and effort building himself up and the lieutenant had simply ignored him. She said to Hastings, "He's in his study."

Hastings nodded and walked off.

•

Gene Penmark sat behind his desk, his hand on his face. It stopped Hastings. He had never seen Penmark this way before. Vulnerable, frightened, human. Who could say what it was? All he had been through and still there was no word, no sign, that his daughter had been released. They had not let him know that they would keep their word or that they would not. He had done everything they had asked him. He had given them the money, unmarked, nonconsecutive bills. And yet he had no word about Cordelia. His wife was standing with another man in another part of his house, wanting to somehow control the situation. But she wasn't standing with him.

Gene Penmark did not wonder if he was the first man of power and wealth to trade in a wife. It was not his nature to think about things like that. He was, in his way, a brilliant man and an innovator and a huge success. But he was not worldly. Nor was he given to honest introspection. Lexie Lacquere was aware of these defects in his makeup and she did not hesitate to exploit them. Gene had an ego and it took little to assuage it. Compliments, flattery, self-deprecating remarks about her own ignorance. She timed these things and she did not overplay them. As a result, Gene Penmark never really asked himself whether Lexie loved him or his children. Indeed, he did not stop to ask himself if he was lucky or unlucky to have her in his life. The way he saw it, he was entitled to someone like her.

But sometimes the unconscious mulls over things even when the conscious does not. So when Hastings walked into his office, Penmark was sad without fully knowing why.

Penmark looked up at him and for a moment did not say anything.

Then he said, "They're going to kill her, aren't they?"

Hastings said, "We don't know that."

"I don't understand these people. They got their money. Why can't they let her go?"

"I don't know."

Penmark said, "I talked with her mother today. And that's what I said to her: 'I don't know.' She's—inconsolable. Taking medication. I don't know what to say to her. She was screaming at me and I didn't know what to say to her. I've always known what to do. I've always had control over things. And I have no control over this. Adele thinks it's my fault."

Hastings said, "Why is that?"

Penmark shrugged. "The money, the success. She told me today that it's all I've ever cared about. More than her, more than my children, more than Lexie. She told me that I don't give a shit about Cordelia."

"She's upset, Mr. Penmark."

"Yeah. Maybe. I don't know."

"Mr. Penmark, you spoke on a Nextel phone with the kidnapper. And those conversations were ones we couldn't hear."

Penmark was looking down at his desk, disoriented and alone. "I told Agent Kubiak about it," he said.

"I know. I read his report. But I want you to tell me about it too."

Gene Penmark shrugged. He said, "He told me to get on the train. And then to leave the money on the train. And then to get off at Union Station."

"When you were on the train, did you recognize anyone?"

Penmark shook his head.

Hastings took out a photograph of the man who had tried to kill him in the bathroom. He put it in front of Penmark.

"Did you see that man?"

"I saw him on the train, I think. I never saw him before that."

Hastings pulled out a copy of the charcoal sketch of the man in the black raincoat. He said, "And him?"

"I don't remember seeing him on the train. I don't think I do. I never saw him before. I know that."

"And you're sure you've told us everything?"

Gene Penmark lifted his head. "Yes," he said. His face was contorting now, pain and anger registering. "What do you mean? You think I'm hiding something?"

"I didn't say that."

"What are you saying?"

"Take it easy, Mr. Penmark. I'm not accusing you of anything."

"You guys, it's just a fucking job to you. But this is my family."

"I know. But I assure you that we're doing everything we can."

"Then where is she? Where the hell is my daughter? You don't even know. Lexie was right."

There was a pause.

Then Hastings said, "Right about what, Mr. Penmark?"

"She—she said that you guys don't know what you're doing."

Hastings sighed. "I think that's Mr. Rook talking."

"So what? He couldn't have done any worse than you guys."

"Mr. Penmark, I can't tell you that I know how you feel, because I don't. It's not my daughter that's been kidnapped. If it had been, I know I'd have trouble holding myself together. Respectfully, I don't know why your wife felt it was necessary to hire Mr. Rook. But I assure you, he is not helping anybody. Now if he had some experience with kidnapping, I'd be happy to listen to him. But he doesn't, so I'm not going to."

"He—"

"We all want answers and solutions, Mr. Penmark. But he's just second-guessing so he can look important. And it's not helping. This is not the sort of thing you can solve by hiring your own police department."

Penmark was looking at his desk again, his thumbs up to his mouth.

Hastings said, "Okay?"

"Okay," Penmark said.

"Now, as you know, we disseminated copies of the sketch of the man on the train to the news media. And Agent Kubiak has also given them a photo of the man who attacked me. We don't know their identities, but we're hopeful that someone in the greater St. Louis area has seen them."

"So we wait?"

"Well, partly." Hastings said, "Now, I've been thinking that the person who did this knows you. Or at least knew something about you. Did you get that feeling during your dialogue with the kidnapper?"

"Honestly? No."

"Hadn't heard his voice before?"

"No."

"You have staff at this house, yes?"

"Yes. Agent Kubiak went over that with us."

"And drew no suspects, correct?"

"Correct. Are you saying it was an inside job?"

Not for the first time, Hastings noted that civilians liked to use crime terminology. Inside job. Five hundred large. And so forth.

"Well," Hastings said, "not exactly. What I mean is, the people who abducted Cordelia knew where she would be, what party she would be going to. Maybe even who she would be going with."

"Or they could have just followed her there."

Hastings made a gesture. "Yeah, they could've."

Penmark said, "Do you want to speak to my wife about it?"

"Yeah, that might help."

"I'll get her."

Penmark came back with her. When she came into the room, she looked at Hastings with a little bewilderment and some guarded hostility. But she had come without Rook and that was at least a partial victory.

But the first thing she said when she sat down was, "Have I done something wrong?" Her tone clipped and a little surly.

"No," Hastings said. "I just wanted to check something out."

"Okay," she said. Her legs were crossed.

"I wanted to know if you knew what Cordelia's plans were the night she was abducted."

"You want to know if I knew her plans?"

"Yes."

"No, I didn't. I think I told you before we hadn't seen her since the Tuesday before."

"You did. But did she call either one of you, or e-mail, to let you know where she would be that night?"

Gene Penmark said, "She didn't tell me."

Lexie said, "She didn't tell me either."

Hastings said, "Would you happen to know if she told anyone?"

They looked at each other and both shook their heads. Gene said, "She could have told any number of people. We honestly don't know."

"She didn't come here before going to the party?"

Lexie said, "I guess she could have and we didn't know about it. But I was back here by three and she wasn't here then. And Gene got home around six that evening. He changed and we went to the dinner party."

Hastings said, "I know I've gone over this with you before, but I think that the people who kidnapped your daughter knew where she was going to be that night. That they knew her plans. The drop with you"—Hastings gestured to Gene Penmark—"that was very well planned. I'm sorry, but it was. If they planned that so well, they must have planned the initial abduction with the same care."

Lexie said, "You think they knew her?"

"I don't know," Hastings said. "They knew who she was. Who she went to the party with. They knew who she'd leave with."

Lexie said, "What about the man you killed?"

It surprised Hastings, the ex-reporter popping him with a question like that. And she asked it like a reporter too, her tone dispassionate and professional.

Hastings said, "Excuse me?"

"The man you killed at the train station," she said. "Haven't you gotten anything from that?"

Hastings avoided eye contact with the victim's father. "No," he said.

"If you hadn't killed him," Lexie Penmark said, "maybe he could have given us some information."

"Yeah, maybe," he said. He would give the woman that.

But it wasn't enough. Lexie said, "Was saving yourself more important than saving her?"

The woman was giving him something of a nasty smile now. Enough that he felt sorry for her husband. He could ask the husband if he could be alone with his wife so that he ask her what her fucking problem was. But then that would bother the husband, maybe even emasculate him, which was what probably what this woman wanted.

Hastings said, "Mrs. Penmark, if I'd been killed, it wouldn't have made your stepdaughter any more safe. Yesterday you asked me if I wanted to work for your husband's company. I said no and you've been trying to undermine me ever since. Is there something behind this?"

Her face flushed with anger and her expression was tight when she answered him. "No," she said. "Are you accusing me of having something to do with her abduction?"

"No, ma'am."

"Because if you are, I'll—Gene, are you listening to this?"

Gene Penmark's mouth was open. "I, uh,—"

But she was back on Hastings. "I happen to be on very good

terms with the chief, Lieutenant. Very good terms. And I will be taking this up with him."

"That's fine, Mrs. Penmark."

"You screw things up and you try to put it off on me by suggesting I, that I—for Christ's sake, that I would have my own stepdaughter kidnapped."

"No, ma'am, you misunderstood me."

"You're a cheap, second-rate bastard," she said. She stood up and walked out.

After she was gone, Hastings turned to Penmark. He still felt sorry for the man, his wife having put him in this position.

He was relieved when Gene Penmark finally said something and put his fears to rest.

Penmark said, "She offered you a job at my company?"

TWENTY-EIGHT

Hastings saw Lexie Penmark conferring with Rook as he walked out of the house, Lexie murmuring something to the security specialist, and Rook probably assuring her that yes, reporting him to the chief would be a good idea. Chief Grassino, a man Hastings respected, might or might not act on it, depending on how he felt at that moment. If he did act on it, Hastings would be questioned by his captain, Karen Brady, and he would have to sit and nod quietly as Karen would tell him about using appropriate social skills with people like Lexie Penmark. As if he had talked smack to her.

Hastings didn't suspect Lexie of anything except being a controller and a busybody and a heartless gold digger, none of which was a crime. It was she who had decided to create that dramatic scene back in the house—*How dare you*—and Hastings took a little comfort in knowing that when she did report him, she would exaggerate what happened and undermine her own credibility in so doing. *He accused me of having Cordelia abducted.* He didn't enjoy lowering himself to having a dialogue with her, but he thought it was necessary to give her a little shove so she would stay out of his way. At least for a while. And as he walked to his car, he believed that he had acted with admirable restraint, because if he hadn't been watching himself, he could have told her, *Your stepdaughter may be dead.*

She could be dead right now. And if she was still alive, her time was limited. The kidnappers had not released her. Hours had passed since they'd gotten the money, and there still had been no word about the girl. They had a dead man at the medical examiner's and they didn't know who he was. They had a sketch of a man in a raincoat and they didn't know who he was either. The dead man had come at Hastings with a knife with a determination that chilled even after he had been killed. Hastings believed he would have nightmares about that bathroom the next time he slept and maybe for a while after. A man damn near takes your life in combat and unless you're a hard-bitten soldier you don't forget it anytime soon. But that was for later. The concern now was that the Indian's willingness to kill a cop extended to the people he was working with. That is, if he would be willing to kill a cop, his cohorts would be willing to kill a rich girl they had abducted. This was the reality that Lexie Penmark didn't seem able to recognize. This was the dread that was slowly but surely overwhelming Gene Penmark. They had the money now and nothing would be able to stop them from doing it.

But they had planned things, Hastings thought. They had planned out the drop. The drop had been thought out in advance and well executed. They had sent a man to pick up the money and another man to guard him. And Hastings, the expert crime solver, had not even known about the second man until the man tried to gut him with a knife. So more than one man was involved. Hastings wondered now about the man with the knife, wondered how long he had been the man's prey. Was it on the train that the Indian had decided he would kill Hastings? Hastings the hunted, Hastings the prey without knowing it.

Cordelia Penmark hadn't known she was the prey either. Hadn't known that she was being tracked.

Hastings had done most of his hunting in Nebraska. He liked all of it, the rituals, the cold, the smell, the getting up at 4:00 A.M., the draw of the silent places. He had learned at a young age that a gun was a tool to be respected. He remembered some girl at college calling him an "animal assassin," something he'd never heard back home. He read books about hunting too. Books about professional hunters who went after big game in Africa, India, and South America. Guys going after not deer but lions that if you missed your shot would turn around and come after you and tear your scalp off. Hastings had learned that for the hunter in Africa, it is motion that gives you away, not color.

In the city, there was no long grass to hide in. Had the man who tracked Cordelia Penmark remained concealed? Did he keep his movements hidden?

Hastings called Gabler on his cell phone.

"Hello."

"Gabe, it's George. Hey, I understand Cordelia has a roommate in her apartment in the loft district."

"Yeah, that's right. One of our agents interviewed her. Didn't turn up anything."

"What's the girl's name?"

"Uh, can you hold on a minute?"

"Yeah."

Hastings started the Jaguar. Let it warm. The sun was coming down now, the beginning of a cold night. Maybe Cordelia Penmark's last. There were only a couple of days left until Christmas.

Did the Penmarks celebrate it? Would there be a Christmas dinner at their home, with Cordelia, Lexie, Gene, and Edie?

Then Gabler was back on the phone. "Yeah," he said, "her name is Lynn Akre. She's a student too, working on her master's in speech pathology. You want her cell number?"

TWENTY-NINE

When Terrill awoke, Maggie was still next to him sleeping. He watched her for a few moments. Then he quietly slipped out of bed. He stepped out into the dark hallway and slowly closed the door behind him.

"Hey."

Terrill jumped.

"Jesus!"

It was Lee.

Terrill said, "What are you doing here?"

She stood there in the dark, clad in gray corduroys and a dirty yellow T-shirt. Terrill noticed that she had lost weight. She said, "I've been walking around."

Terrill said, "Inside?"

She shrugged.

"You're supposed to stay inside," Terrill said.

"Don't worry about it."

She remained there in the dark, looking a bit like a ghost. Perhaps for the first time, Terrill felt uneasy around her.

Terrill said, "Have you slept at all tonight?"

"No."

"What about last night?"

She shook her head.

Terrill said, "When was the last time—"

"I told you, don't worry about it. What are you doing out here?"

The sharpness in her voice was new to him.

"I'm going to take a piss," he said. "Okay?"

She was staring at him now.

Shit, Terrill thought. She's speeding. Walking around, not sleeping, getting hostile and weird. He had started giving her amphetamines a couple of weeks after they left Oregon. He and Maggie had started her out with acid; ten strips dissolving on her tongue, and when that was done they would suggest things to her. Tell her that she was beautiful and clean and try to put her in a different place. After she came down, she would tell them about her hallucinations. The bluish light at the top of her screen, square at first, but then widening out into an onion shape, fat on the sides, and then slimming back down to the base. She said that the onion was the earth, Greenland and Russia large at the top and Antarctica icy and clean and smooth at the bottom. She said it was beautiful at first, but then it became dark and black, the ocean not quite fluid, but gelatined, the continental masses between jagged and rocky. She said she was up there looking down on it and then she was down there herself; seeing herself, in this fucking country, this place, this desert...seeing herself curled up, coiled. She was naked and strong in this vision. She was feral and unbound. They told her, yes, she was wild and free and lovely and aware.

But when she came down, she said she felt gross and dirty. And she was tired. So tired. Terrill started feeding her speed. She started out with a couple of pills a day. Then it was three. And in the weeks preceding the kidnapping, the daily dosage had been increased to seven. Though Terrill himself had not kept track.

Now he said to her, "Hey." His nice-guy tone. "You're beautiful. You want to come with me?"

"In the bathroom?"

"Yeah. We can share a joint. It's nice in there."

"Why don't we go to my room?" Lee said.

"Okay."

In her room, she grabbed at him in the darkness, her hands at his belt buckle, her mouth furious on his. He wasn't ready for it. She had been a soft, timid lover their first few times. Saying his name a lot and giving out little *oh*s . . . that was before . . . now she was pulling him down on top of her, wrapping her legs around him, her tongue plunging into his mouth, animal-like, loud and passionate, saying dirty things between her kisses. Terrill feared that Maggie would hear them.

It was soon done. Terrill looked down at her.

Lee said, "You like to fuck me?"

Terrill grinned. Goddamn, to think when he met her that she would talk like this. He felt, incorrectly, a pride in this transition. Henry Higgins to little Eliza.

"Sure," he said.

Lee said, "Is something funny?"

"No. No."

"Don't laugh at me."

"I'm not."

"Don't patronize me," she said. "I don't like that."

"Okay," he said.

He rolled off her and lay on his back.

After a few moments, he heard her say, "What do we do now?"

"I can't stay the night here," he said.

"I don't mean that. I mean, what do we do tomorrow?"

It occurred to him then that when she said "we," she didn't mean all of them. That she didn't mean Maggie and Ray and Jan, all the rest. He pretended he hadn't caught her meaning and said, "I don't know. We'll have a discussion."

"You and I?"

"No. I meant all of us. Look, it's late and I'm tired. Do we have to talk about it now?"

"We need to talk," she said. "About a lot of things."

Shit. Terrill said, "Why don't we go to sleep?"

"I don't want to sleep."

"You need to sleep, babe."

"You want to leave, go back to her, then do it. But if you do, I don't want you telling her about this."

"There are no secrets here, Lee. We're a family."

"I *don't* want you telling her about this. I don't want any black stares. I don't want people talking about me. Do you understand that?"

"No one's talking about you, babe."

In the darkness, silence. Terrill looked over to see her staring right at him. She held her stare but did not smile. He could stare back at her, outstare her, stare her down . . . but goddammit, he was tired. She had the advantage of taking all those fucking pills. Christ. He needed to weed her off that shit before she locked herself in the toilet and started banging her head on the wall or something. There was no talking sense to her when she was zonked out.

He said, "No one's talking about you, honey. We love you. You're one of us now. We need you and we love you. Okay?"

She held her stare for a few more moments. Then she turned and looked back up at the ceiling.

"Go back to her," Lee said. "We'll talk about it later."

THIRTY

There were parents with children, some of them unsteady because they were on skates for the first time. The Steinberg Skating Rink in Forest Park. It was dark now, but the rink was lighted up. It was crowded, people feeling the spirit of the season, and it was cold enough to keep the ice frozen, but not so cold you didn't want to be outside. The rink was near the edge of Forest Park, near Kingshighway, and you could see Barnes-Jewish Hospital looming in the distance.

Hastings walked to the fence separating the rink from the spectators. He watched until he picked out a young woman in her early twenties wearing a red-and-white scarf and a black turtleneck sweater. She was holding a little girl's hand. The little girl wore glasses and she was talking to the young woman, the young woman nodding her head and responding. A young boy, older than the girl, was skating by them, calling out "whoa, whoa" while he pretended to stumble, but was actually showing off, showing them how much in control he was. The nephew, Hastings thought. And the little girl was the niece. Hastings held up his hand and waved to the young woman. She paused, hesitating, then waved back. Then she came over.

They stood on opposite sides of the fence.

The girl said, "Are you the detective?"

"Yes. George Hastings."

"I'm Lynn," she said. "But I guess you knew that."

"You said you'd be here with your niece and nephew."

"Yes." Lynn Akre looked down at the little girl with the glasses. "Sadie, this is Mr. Hastings. He's a policeman."

The little girl looked up at Hastings. He was in plainclothes, so she didn't process it right away. Hastings estimated that she was the age Amy was when he married Amy's mother.

"Hi," the little girl said.

"Hi," Hastings said.

Lynn Akre said, "I know this may sound paranoid, especially with all these people around, but I don't want to leave her alone while we talk."

"It's not paranoid."

"But I don't want her to hear what we talk about either."

Hastings said, "We'll talk quietly."

Lynn Akre smiled.

•

They sat at a circular table, the little girl drinking hot chocolate while the grown-ups sipped coffee. The noise of people having fun on the rink, anticipating the beginning of the Christmas weekend, time off work and with family, in the distance, traffic passing back and forth on Kingshighway.

Lynn Akre sat close to Hastings, both of them keeping their voices low as adults do when they want to hide things from children. Though Hastings was aware that Lynn Akre was probably young enough to be his daughter as well.

She said, "I feel bad, being out like this."

"Why?"

"I mean, out having fun. I should be home, waiting to see what's happened to Cordelia. But I promised the kids that I would bring them here before Christmas. We had it planned before, you know—"

"I understand."

"She's still gone, isn't she?"

"Yes."

"Didn't her dad pay the ransom?"

"He did. But it looks like they haven't kept their end of the bargain."

"Does that mean—"

"We don't know. We don't know yet."

The young woman put her hand over her mouth. But then it passed and she was looking at him again. "Tell me what I can do," she said.

It occurred to Hastings that the she may have been the most mature person he had dealt with so far in this investigation. Certainly she was brave.

"I know you've already talked with Agent Kubiak," Hastings said. "But there's some things I'd like to go over with you."

"Okay."

"How long have you known Cordelia?"

"About two years."

"Is she a close friend?"

"Well, not real close. We room together and we get along. But we don't hang out together much socially. She bought the condo in the loft district and she wanted a roommate. She was a friend of a friend, Christie Kriko, and Christie told me she wanted a roommate. So we hooked up."

"You didn't know her before then?"

"No. God knows she doesn't need the money. I think she just wanted to have someone living there with her. It's got three bedrooms and two bathrooms. Sometimes, we'd go two, three days without even seeing each other."

"When did you see her last?"

"I saw her before she went to the party with Tom."

"The night she was abducted?"

"Yes."

"Tell me about that."

Lynn Akre shrugged. "She came home around five or five thirty and she was wearing jeans, casual clothing. And she changed for this party. I saw her in the kitchen when she came out of her room. She was wearing a dress. A nice dress. And I asked her where she was going, and she said she was going to a Christmas party with Tom."

"You'd met Tom before that?"

"Yes."

"Did you like him?"

"No, not really."

"Why not?"

"Well, I didn't think he was scary or anything. But he seemed like one of those guys that's only nice to people he thinks are important. When she first introduced me to him, it was all he could do to make eye contact." She looked at Hastings now. "Do you think he had something to do with it?"

"With her being kidnapped?"

"Yes."

Hastings said, "No." He didn't either. He said, "You'd met him before that night?"

"Yeah. I think a couple of months before."

"Did Cordelia ever tell you what she thought of him?"

"Oh, not really. But it was obvious she wasn't in love with him. Listen, I want you to know that she wasn't like that."

"Like what?"

"Like him. You know, a snob. Yeah, she had all that money. But you wouldn't have known it if you didn't know it. When I first moved in with her, I was sort of defensive. I mean, I come from Belleville, you know?"

Hastings nodded.

Lynn Akre said, "But after a while, I realized that she didn't really care. I don't think the money meant much to her. Or if it did, she didn't show it."

"Yet," Hastings said, "you two didn't become close."

"No. I mean, it shouldn't make a difference, but it does. It's a different class structure. The money, I mean. It makes a difference. Last March? She went to Switzerland for spring break. Switzerland. She asked me if I wanted to come and I said no. And then she said that she would pay my way. I still said no. I mean, I couldn't do that. It'd be like I was the nanny, you know. And I don't want to feel that way. You know what I mean?"

Getting to, Hastings thought. "Sure," he said.

"And that's the funny thing," she said. "I felt like I was snubbing *her* then. But I had to."

"I understand," Hastings said. It made him think of something. "Her mother," he said.

"Her mother or stepmother?"

"Her mother. Adele."

"Yes?"

"Was she close to her?"

"Oh, I don't think so. Adele seemed out of it."

"Out of it, you mean—?"

"Just out of it. Like she had taken too much prescription medication or something. You know, like one of those people you meet at a dog park or something. A nice lady, but, you know, socially inept and unable to deal with things. I'm sorry; that sounds terrible."

"I understand."

"I'm not like that."

"I know."

"I mean, in a way, both of her parents were like that. Socially retarded. But it was like her father could come out of it, sort of, and her mother couldn't. You know?"

"Was she closer to her stepmother?"

"Lexy?"

"Yes."

"Oh, God no. She thinks Lexy's vile. Can't stand her."

"So she wouldn't have confided in Lexy?"

"Never." Lynn Akre said, "I remember one time, Lexy and Mr. Penmark were over before they went to some society event and Cordy put on this strapless dress and Lexy said, 'Ooh, strut it.' You know, trying to sound young and with it. And Cordy gave her this look like . . . well, Cordy just thought she was gross."

Hastings found himself smiling.

The Akre girl noticed this. She said, "She's a good girl, you know. In spite of everything."

"I see that."

"Cordy, I mean."

"I know."

Lynn Akre turned to her niece. "You doing okay, sweetie?"

The little girl nodded, still shy in the presence of the policeman.

It made Hastings uncomfortable, the sweetness and innocence of that exchange. He liked being around this young woman and her cute little niece. He was aware that their presence was refreshing after his time with the Penmarks. But it wasn't his place to judge them and he knew that he would be doing a disservice to everyone, himself included, if he started thinking that the rich got what they deserved. But that wasn't the reason he was uncomfortable now and he knew it.

He leaned closer to Lynn Akre and said, "I'm sorry, but I have to ask you this."

"Ask me what?"

"Cordelia. Did she—have other lovers?"

"You mean, other than Tom Myers?"

"Yes."

"Why must you ask me that?"

Detective Skye Washington, a friend of Hastings in the sex crimes unit, had once investigated a complaint of an alleged rape. A white girl of nineteen reported that a black guy had raped her at a party. Skye took the girl's statement at the hospital and thought there had been some holes in her story, certain parts vividly remembered, other parts suspiciously vague. Then the evidence from the rape kit showed that the girl had had intercourse with three other men as well. In the same hour that she claimed she'd been raped by one. All four of the boys admitted that they had been with her, but all of them said it had been consensual. It was a mess, but the girl herself later acknowledged that she had consented to be with the first three, but "I never said it was okay for Jesse to do it." She never said yes to Jesse, but she never said no either. The district attorney declined to file charges.

It caused something of a stir for the girl's family. Mainly, because the girl's dad owned a construction business and had a lot of money and he was not about to accept that his daughter was much wilder than he'd ever imagined. He hired a high-dollar lawyer who filed a lawsuit, which was dismissed after a judge ruled that the police officers had done nothing improper. Skye Washington would later tell Hastings, "You could have shown *video* to that girl's daddy and he still wouldn't have believed it."

Cordelia Penmark came from a wealthier family than that girl's. And it would have been easy for her to hide a wild, unhealthy lifestyle from them.

Hastings said to Lynn Akre, "I need to know if she did. I need to see if she was kidnapped by someone who knew her."

Lynn Akre said, "You mean by someone she might have slept with?"

"Not necessarily slept with, but was associated with."

"I understand," she said. "No."

"No?"

"No, she wasn't promiscuous. She wasn't wild. She didn't take drugs and I don't think was associated with people who did. If there was a hidden pathology in her, I never saw it. If she associated with lowlifes, I never saw them."

"You never saw them," Hastings said. "But do you think she did?"

"No, I don't. I would be very surprised if she had."

"And you're not protecting her now?"

"You mean, am I lying for her?"

"Yeah."

"Well, I wouldn't very well be protecting her by lying, would I?" She was smiling at him now and again Hastings noted that she was mature beyond her years.

He said, "No, I guess you wouldn't. Did you tell anyone where she went that night?"

"You mean before I told Agent Kubiak?"

"Yes."

"No. I didn't tell anyone."

"Did she ever say anything about someone maybe stalking her?"

"No."

"No one following her or watching her?"

"No. She never said anything to me."

The little girl with the glasses was starting to get restless. She was a good kid, but her chocolate was getting cold.

Hastings said, "I need to ask you a favor."

Lynn Akre said, "What?"

"I want to retrace where Cordelia went that night. Starting at her condo. Can you take me there?"

"Yeah," she said. "Let me get the kids back to their parents, and I can meet you there. You know where it is?"

"I know."

"I'll get her brother. Can you stay with her a minute?"

"Sure."

Shortly, she was out on the rink, skating across the ice smoothly and gracefully, moving toward her nephew to rein him in.

Hastings turned to look at the little girl with the glasses. She was looking at him, comfortable with him in the way Amy had been when she was that age, the child recognizing the natural parent in him. Her hands were in her pockets. She said, "Are you married?"

Hastings smiled. It was little girls who thought in terms of marriage and men and women. They were curious about such things in ways boys were not. Perhaps she was too young to discern the age difference between him and her aunt. Amy had been inquisitive too and early on had hoped that Hastings would marry her mother.

Hastings said, "No. But I have a little girl of my own. She's older than you."

"How much older?"

"She's twelve."

"That's old," she said. Then she was looking back at the people on the rink, her interest in him dwindling.

A half hour later they were in Cordelia Penmark's condominium. It was a two-story job with a lot of glass and modern appeal. There was a gas fireplace and an entertainment center and matching furnishings. The windows were huge and Hastings could see traffic going up and down Washington Avenue. Nice and high-cost, but Hastings knew he would not like to live in a place like this. Not much privacy; though you could look out the window, people outside could look in at you. But maybe that was the point.

Lynn said, "Would you like something to drink?"

They were standing in the kitchen area, a large island counter with a finished wood top. On top was a coffee cup that had been left there that morning.

Hastings said, "No, thank you. You were here when she left for the party?"

"Yes."

"Did Tom Myers come up here to pick her up?"

"Yes."

"You saw him?"

"Yeah. For a minute. I was in here making something to eat. He came in and went and stood over there."

"You didn't talk to him?"

"He didn't talk to me. I told you how he was." She stopped. "I'm sorry; I guess I should be more respectful."

"Don't worry about it. Did they have a drink or anything before they left?"

"No. She came out of her room and they left."

Hastings gestured to what effectively was a glass wall. It was too big to be called a window. He said, "I don't see any sort of curtain or way to cover that. Is there one?"

"No," she said. "It's not very private. But we didn't walk around here naked."

Hastings avoided eye contact with the girl then. He said, "Did they say they were going to go anywhere before the party? Say for a drink or dinner?"

Lynn seemed to think about it for a moment. Then she said, "No, they didn't. But it was fairly early when they left here. Cordelia liked Dressel's."

"In the Central West End?"

"Yeah."

"You think they might have gone there?"

"I don't know. But I wouldn't be surprised if they did."

"Okay," Hastings said. "I'm gonna go."

"Do you want me to go with you?"

"No." Hastings handed her a business card. "If you think of anything else that you think would help, call me."

"I will."

When they were at the door, she wished him luck. He turned and saw that there were tears in her eyes.

"Hey," Hastings said.

Lynn Akre said, "Do you think she's still . . ."

"Yes," Hastings said. "I do." He held her gaze then in such a way that he believed it himself. He had to.

•

The Jaguar was parked across the street so he had to wait for a break in traffic before he could cross over and get to it. When he did, he stood next to the car and looked up and down the street.

Friday night. The beginning of the holiday weekend, Christmas Eve on Monday, Christmas on Tuesday. The beginning of a vacation for most people. Christmas.

"Shit," Hastings said. He pulled out his cell phone and dialed a number.

Eileen answered after a few rings. Recognizing his number, her voice was familiar.

"What's up?"

"Hi. I just wanted to make sure you had Amy with you."

"Of course I do. I picked her up from school hours ago." Eileen sighed. "Christ, George." All through their marriage there had been arguments about her irresponsibility. Hastings saying, Where were you? She saying, It must be nice to be perfect, and when was he going to write his book on parenting? She resented his second-guessing, but he felt that she usually didn't leave him much choice.

"I wasn't doubting you," Hastings said, though he was. "I just wanted to check."

"She's here, George. We even gave her dinner."

"Okay, Eileen." Hastings stopped, told himself to relax. He wasn't in the mood for argument. Not tonight. He said, "When are you leaving for Jamaica?"

"We're leaving Sunday afternoon. Can you pick Amy up by ten?"

"It shouldn't be a problem." Hastings hesitated. Then he said, "Listen, Eileen. I'm working a kidnapping. The Penmark girl."

Eileen said, "Oh." Her tone different then. She was no fool and she didn't need everything explained to her. Hastings was trying to put himself in the frame of mind of a kidnapper. Asking himself, If I planned to kidnap Cordelia Penmark, what would I do? It made him think of Amy.

Eileen said, "I understand. Listen, she's okay. Do you want to talk to her?"

"No, that's all right."

"George?"

"Yes?"

"There was something on the news about a police officer involved in a fight with one of the kidnapping suspects. Was that you?"

"Yeah."

"Oh, Jesus. I'm sorry I was such a bitch. Are you all right?"

"I'm fine. Look, I gotta get going."

"Okay. Listen: be careful, okay?"

"I will, sweetie. Bye."

"Bye."

Eileen, he thought. Can't live with her. Can't hate her either. No matter what bad thing she did—and there would be plenty more, knowing her—he would always forgive her. It would forever be his plight.

•

Presuming the kidnappers were watching Cordelia and the lawyer that night. Watching them through the glass, as if they were actors on a stage. The rich girl and her lawyer boyfriend descend out of their glass box into the street, where Tom Myers escorts Cordelia to his BMW. Presume that . . .

Why wouldn't they just take Cordelia then?

Hastings looked up and down the street again.

Too much traffic. And too much glass up above. Maybe someone would see. And the area itself was within a half mile of the central police department. Wait. Patiently wait until the girl and her escort are in a less populated area. Wait until the prey have had a few drinks and slowed down their defenses.

Hastings started the car. The engine burbled to life. Hastings put the car in gear and started west.

•

He imagined following Tom Myers's BMW. Trailing them as they took the ramp up to the interstate and drove west. The lights of

Union Station coming into view on their right, then even with them, then behind them. Then Midtown and Saint Louis University, so changed from when Hastings had gone there. Hastings took the exit at Kingshighway and turned north. He doubled back on Lindell and then made the left turn on Euclid, taking him into the Central West End.

It was crowded and he had to park almost two blocks from Dressel's.

He showed photographs of Tom Myers and Cordelia to the manager and asked about the night in question. The manager said, yeah, she was a regular, but he couldn't remember if she had been in that night. He looked at the schedule to see who had been on shift then and soon Hastings found himself in a dialogue with the bartender and a waitress.

The waitress said, "She's okay. A little quiet, I guess. But not rude. I didn't much like the guy she was with."

Hastings said, "So they were here that night?"

The waitress said, "Yeah. They got a light dinner and had a couple of drinks. I got the feeling she would have liked to stay longer, but he kept looking at his watch. And he asked me for the check like he was in a hurry."

"Do you remember about what time they left?"

"Not exactly," she said. "But I think it was before eight o'clock."

"This is a longshot," Hastings said, "but do either of you remember someone else being here that night that seemed to be— watching them?"

The waitress said, "Watching them?"

"Yes."

She looked at the bartender, who looked back at her. She said, "Well, sir, I don't know. I don't remember anything like that."

Hastings turned to the bartender. "How about you?"

The bartender said, "I ... don't remember anyone," he paused, searching for the proper television-cop lingo, then said, "suspicious."

The waitress said, "She was kidnapped later that night, wasn't she?"

"Yes."

The waitress said, "You think the kidnappers were here, watching her or following her?"

"I think they might have been." Hasting felt a little awkward then, wondering if the waitress or the bartender would tell their friends how little he had to go on, the sort of things he was reaching for. But the bartender and the waitress were looking at each other again, trying to see if the other one could remember anything.

The bartender said, "I'm sorry, man. I can't remember anything like that."

"That's all right," Hastings said. He handed the bartender a card. "If you think of anything, call me."

•

He walked back to his car, again looking at the intersection and the sidewalks, asking himself if the kidnappers had been sitting in a car that night watching Cordelia and Tom Myers as they walked to his BMW. Sitting in a car, eyeing their prey, waiting to pounce. Predators.

They knew who Cordelia Penmark was. They had her marked. It was possible that they knew she would be at a party in Ladue, possible that they knew of it in advance. Possible, but not likely. They knew who Cordelia was, but they probably did not know her schedule. So they must have followed her.

His cell phone rang.

An unidentified number. Hastings answered it.

"Hastings, it's Fenton Murray."

"Yes, sir."

"Where are you now?"

"I'm in the Central West End. I'm going over Cordelia Penmark's tracks the night she was abducted."

Silence. Hastings waited for Murray to ask him what the hell good that was going to do. It irritated him now, the thought of a higher-up interfering and second-guessing.

Maybe Murray sensed this in the quiet moment, because he said, "Well . . . the girl hasn't turned up, has she?"

"No, sir."

Another pause, Fenton Murray debating whether to make a suggestion, Hastings guarded and resentful. Murray said, "All right. Well, you know what you're doing."

"Thank you," Hastings said. "Did the chief ask you to call me?"

"Yeah. It's FBI's case and he realizes that. But the media doesn't really understand and they keep calling us for answers."

"I understand," Hastings said.

"Yeah," Murray said. "Well, call me if you need anything."

"I will. Thanks."

The call ended and Hastings started the car. He looked at his watch. Well into night now, but he was getting his second wind. The staff at Dressel's hadn't seen anyone suspicious, but they had confirmed that Cordelia Penmark had been there the night she was kidnapped, so Hastings took it as a sign that he was onto something. It was all he had for now.

He started the drive to Ladue.

THIRTY-ONE

She wore artificial flowers, artificial flowers...

They were piping music into the basement. In the last couple of days, she had discerned where the speakers were, but she had not determined the source. There were no commercials, but it was on some sort of oldies loop. Bobby Darin, the Four Seasons, the Platters, Bill Haley and the Comets, Ricky Nelson covering "Fools Rush In." Music that was unfamiliar to her and would forever be unpleasant. They meant to disorient her as to time and space. Or maybe they meant to comfort her. No, that was not likely.

Cordelia heard them celebrating earlier. Whooping, cheering, people saying, "Fuck, yeah." Celebrating something. They must have gotten the money, she thought. She didn't know what else could have made them that happy. That had to be it, she thought. That had to be it, and it would mean that they were letting her go. The guy had said they would. He had said, "It's up to your father." Something like that. *He has to pay us before we'll give you back. It's up to him.* Now they were cheering upstairs; it had to mean that they had the money and now were about to let her go. They had told her that they would. Surely, they would not have misled her. Surely they would not have been so cruel as to give her false hope. No. No, she would not nurse that thought. They would not do that. They would have killed her already if they were going to kill her.

They had taken away her watch. Her sense of time was limited.

All she had was the music. She decided that each song was approximately three minutes, so she would count songs. Ten songs were thirty minutes, another ten and an hour had passed. It was something to focus on and maybe it was making her go insane or maybe it was holding her together. It was getting harder to tell the difference.

But she remained aware of the passage of time. And she was aware that one hour had passed after she heard the cheers, after she heard the celebration. They would set her free now. Maybe take her out to some field, someplace desolate and remote. Or maybe someplace crowded where she would just be another face. A shopping mall parking lot or the Savvis Center. They would have to let her go. They had gotten what they wanted now, they had gotten all they needed out of her. The sensible thing to do was let her go. They didn't have to be nice. They didn't have to be humane. But they could be reasonable. There was no *need* anymore. No need to kill her.

But the hour passed and no one came to see her. No one came to tell her that they had gotten the money and would be letting her go. No one came to tell her that they *hadn't* gotten the money. No one came to tell her anything. No one shared anything with her.

I'm still here, she thought. I'm still here and I'm the reason you got that money. I'm relevant. Can't you at least tell me what you're going to do to me?

"Please," she said. She was talking aloud now. Talking just to herself. The way you would do if you were driving and someone did something stupid in traffic and you said, "Thank you," aloud, being sarcastic, but the only one who would hear your voice would be you.

"Please," she said again.

Please what?

Please let me go, she thought. Please tell me if you got what you wanted. Please tell me what you're going to do. Please tell me you're going to let me go. Please tell me you're not going to kill me. Please deliver me from this place, from this despair.

Another hour went by, and then another. Three hours since she had heard them whoop and cheer because they had gotten their ransom. It had to be that because what else would they be so happy about? It could be that her dad had agreed to give them the money and that in itself was cause for celebration. *He's agreed to pay us.* Hooray. Maybe it had been that that caused them to cheer. If all it was was that, then it would explain leaving her down here. It would explain their not letting her go. They couldn't let her go yet, see, because they hadn't actually gotten the money yet. They had only secured an *agreement* from Daddy to give them the money. And that wasn't the same thing as actually having the money. It was a reason to be happy, but not a victory.

But . . . but—why would they cheer over an agreement? Were they stupid enough to say, *We've won. He's* agreed *to give us the money?*

God.

Tears were rolling down her cheeks now. Because even trying, she could not persuade herself to believe something so silly. If they were celebrating, it was because they had the money. Not just an agreement. They had the money, they had secured their ransom, over three hours ago and she was still down here.

Cordelia thought, I have no control. It angered her more than it frightened her. She had absolutely no fucking control over her fate. None. She was powerless. Whether she lived or died was totally at the discretion of the monsters beyond the door. She was nothing to them. A piggie, the girl had said. An object, a thing they kept down in their basement.

She thought briefly of her stepmother, a woman she pretty much loathed. Lexie's buzzword for the twenty-first century was *proactive*. *How do we get proactive on this, Gene? We need to be proactive.* Using a stupid, meaningless word to sound smart. Classic Lexie. How do we get proactive here, Lexie? Let's see, I can bang my head against the cement wall until I'm unconscious. Or I can scream bloody murder so that they turn this fucking music up even louder and I go completely insane. I can beg for my life, beg for it from savages who shot bullets into poor Tom like he was a large bag of cooking rice. What do you say, Lexie? Shall we have a meeting? Shall we have a tea party? Maybe put out some wine and cheese? What? You say there's no peanut butter and Wonder Bread? Well, holy fucking shit, what kind of host are you? Don't you realize I've formed a taste for peanut butter sandwiches? Who's in charge of this meeting, anyway? Take down notes, Lexie. Take down this, you stupid dipshit whore: These People are Going to Kill Me.

Cordelia allowed herself a grim smile. God. Maybe she was going insane. Thinking these nasty thoughts about her stepmother had actually eased some of her despair. The things you think of when you're terrified.

Music still being piped in. What were they playing now? "Where the Boys Are?" Connie Francis singing it. Hadn't that been a movie? Yes, she had seen it on cable with her mother and Edie. They had laughed at it together, Edie and Adele laughing more than she had. Adele had told them that the main actress went on to become a Catholic nun after leaving Hollywood, and Edie said she wasn't surprised.

But it was a good song, Cordelia thought. Its strains and movements and build still holding up well today. And as it came to its end, she found herself singing along with Connie Francis as tears rolled down her cheeks.

•

Hastings took the McKnight Road exit off the interstate, drove south to where it intersected with Litzsinger, and turned right. Twenty-minute drive out of downtown into paradise. Twisty black roads, mansions, trees, lawns. He envisioned the kidnappers following Tom Myers's BMW down this road, the kidnappers looking at the grand houses and country club golf courses, thinking, Look at this shit. Smelling the money.

Klosterman had once told Hastings a story about Murph that Murph had never denied or confirmed. Apparently, Murph had been something of a stud when he was a younger man. Girls liked him and he liked them. When he was about twenty-two, he had met a girl at Mississippi Nights. They had been drinking and not asking too much background from each other and before the night was through she gave him her number. When he went to pick her up a couple of nights later for a date, he was driving his primary vehicle, a 1977 Chevy truck with the two-tone paint. Murph was a smart kid, even at twenty-two, and when he pulled up to the house and saw that it was a high-dollar home in Kirkwood, he sensed the onset of a culture clash. Still, he had to hold his temper when the girl, and her mother, told him she would be ready to leave in a few minutes, but would he mind parking his truck around the corner so people wouldn't see it? Murph being Murph said, "Not at all, ma'am." Walked outside, got in his truck, and drove away, likely back to Mississippi Nights. There was snobbishness and there was pride.

Maybe it was true, Hastings thought. Or maybe it was working-class-hero horseshit. If Murph had made it up, he'd have to be given credit for having a good imagination. Hastings's ex-wife had apparently been raised with money or had gotten used to it. When Hastings fell in love with her and married her, he told himself that it wouldn't matter. But years later, he figured out that Murph was probably smarter than he was about such things. Eileen was openly supportive of class distinctions and, perhaps to her credit, did not hesitate to share this sentiment with Hastings when they were married. Not ironically, Murph, born and raised in the Dogtown section of St. Louis, probably felt the same way. It was perhaps unusual, but Eileen had always said that no one was more in favor of the British class system than the British working class.

Hastings himself was by no means immune. He was a homicide detective, one of the elite, and though the term *glory boy* nettled him at times, he did take a certain pride in it. He had no desire to have his rank reduced, no desire to return to street patrol. He remembered returning to Lincoln to visit his mother and seeing a group of meatpacking workers in a sports bar and thinking, Oh, Jesus. But for an athletic scholarship to Saint Louis University, he could have been one of them. They were laughing and drinking and enjoying themselves, talking about Cornhusker football and that week's lottery number. They *seemed* happy, and who was he to think they shouldn't be? Yet he had dreaded the thought of being one of them.

He was coming up on the Fisher house now, the house where Tom Myers had brought Cordelia Penmark. The street was empty now, no Christmas parties tonight. Hastings slowed the car and pulled it over to the side of the road. In the darkness, he estimated the place where Myers had parked his BMW. On the north side of the road.

Maybe the kidnappers had slowly driven by, marking the place, then turning around to find a place to park themselves. Watching the young couple get out of the car and move toward the house where they would drink and schmooze. They would stay at the party for at least two hours, maybe even three. The kidnappers would wait that long.

There had been footprints of two people, probably men. One on the passenger side of the BMW, grabbing Cordelia Penmark, the other on the driver's side, holding a gun at Tom Myers's side, then pulling the trigger twice, and once more when Myers was on the ground.

And then they were gone.

Probably driving west, Hastings thought.

And then where? Christ, a party with over two hundred guests and no one had seen the abduction. It was dark and late and people had been drinking. It could have happened in front of them and they would have had several different descriptions, but no license tag.

And why her? Why Cordelia Penmark? She had not been a high-profile girl. There was no twisted Paris Hilton vanity in her, no grasp for the spotlight. No flattering pictures in the society pages. She seemed like she was trying to live a normal life, in spite of everything. Not ashamed of her money or her background, but not flaunting it either.

Hastings wondered if he had been following a spoor to no end. He was at the place where the abduction had occurred, trying to think like a predator to catch one, but nothing was coming to the fore. He could go back to the blind and hope for the deer to pass in front of it for an easy shot, but that wasn't going to happen. Or he could give himself busywork to make himself believe that he was doing something to save the girl, but that wouldn't help her if he wasn't making headway.

He flicked on the overhead light and started to go through his notebook. He was searching for a telephone number when the dome light was overpowered and the back of the car was filled with the illumination of headlight beams.

Hastings looked in the rearview mirror. His heart skipped a beat, and then he relaxed.

Christ. It was a police car.

A Ladue patrol car.

A patrolman walked up, holding a flashlight. Hastings was patient, waiting to get it over with. The patrolman was young.

He said, "Is there a problem, sir?"

Hastings said, "Hi. I'm a cop. Let me reach into my jacket here and I'll show you my ID."

The patrolman flashed the light in the car and saw the police radio and the flashing light that could be set on the dash. But he was cautious and he said, "Okay. Well, uh, let me see your ID anyway."

Hastings gave it to him. The patrolman looked at it and handed it back.

"Sorry," he said.

"It's all right," Hastings said. "It doesn't look like a police car."

"What are you doing out here?"

"I'm investigating a murder. The one that—"

"Oh, yeah. I know about it. Well, I'll let you get back to work."

"Thanks. Hey," Hastings said, "Were you on patrol that night?"

"Yeah. I didn't see anything though." The young cop said, "We don't get much out here. We look for signs of robbery, traffic violations . . . I remember there were a lot of cars parked along this road that night. A party."

"Yeah, there was a party."

The patrol officer said, "It was a good night to do it."

Hastings stopped and looked up at the man. "How do you mean?" he said.

"I mean, all these cars were parked on the street that night because of Mr. Fisher's party. Any other night, a car on this street would have stood out and me or someone else on patrol would have stopped and questioned them. Like I just did to you. You're not really supposed to park here. But we let it slide once a year for Fisher."

"Fisher has a Christmas party every year?"

"Oh yeah. At least as long as I've been here, and that's coming up on six years."

"I see."

"Well . . . anything else?"

"No. Thanks."

"Good luck."

The cop was walking back to his car. He reported back to dispatch and then pulled past the Jag and was driving away; the sound of his engine dissipating was replaced by the ringing of Hastings's cell phone.

"Yeah?" Hastings said.

"George, it's Murph. We got something on Edie Penmark."

"Yeah? What is it?"

"Well, it's not drugs. But you were right: she is mixed up in something. I downloaded some things and you should probably see it."

THIRTY-TWO

Murph was already at the Penmark house when Hastings got there. He got out of an unmarked Chevy Impala with a brown file holder in his hand. He and Hastings went over them together. A few minutes later, Hastings said, "She's in one of the bungalows in the back. We'll go around."

The blue water in the swimming pool rippled as a large snake-like tube curled around in it. A heated pool, warm enough for a swim on a December night.

They got to the bungalows and Hastings rapped on the door. Edie Penmark answered it after the third series of knocks.

She looked first at Hastings and then at Murph, whom she'd never seen before. Murph's presence indicating that Hastings had not returned for any improper purpose. She said, "What do you want now?"

Hastings said, "You've been keeping something from us."

"I don't know what you're talking about."

"Ernie Shavers, to begin with. Do you want to have this conversation here, or in your father's office?"

The alarm appeared on her face when Hastings said the name Ernie Shavers. She backed away from the door and let them in. Then she went straight to the couch and took a seat, waiting for what she was pretty sure she knew was coming.

The detectives followed her, remaining on their feet for the time being.

Hastings gestured to the packet Murph held. He said, "You know what we've got here?"

"What?" Edie said.

"Downloads of porn. From a Web site you own." Hastings picked a couple of the stills out, young, rough-looking girls with men. "Do you need to see it?"

She shrugged. "Local whores and strippers. Nothing I bet you haven't seen before."

"You're a co-owner with Ernie Shavers. He's already confirmed that for us."

"So what?"

"So what?" Hastings said. "For Christ's sake, how can you do this?"

"I'm not in any of those things," she said. "We hire those girls. It's just a business opportunity."

"Whether or not you're in it is not the point," Hastings said. "You're selling it."

Edie Penmark shrugged again. She was looking straight ahead, avoiding eye contact.

Hastings said, "Do your parents know about this?"

Edie Penmark smirked. "What do you think?"

"I think they'd be sick if they knew."

"I told you," she said, "it's just a business investment. People pay for it."

"A business investment," Hastings said. "Like you need the money?"

"I put up some of the money. And we had an okay return."

"But why invest in something like this? What's wrong with you?"

"Oh for Christ's sake," she said. "You're a cop. You telling me you haven't seen this before? And what does it have to do with anything, anyway? Aren't you supposed to be finding my sister?"

"Unfortunately," Hastings said, "this may relate to your sister. Are you aware that Ernie Shavers is involved in prostitution?"

Edie Penmark wanted to retain her tough exterior. "It doesn't surprise me," she said.

Hastings wanted to hit her. Her nonchalance might have been a pose, but it was getting to him. He wanted to reach out and slap the smug expression off her face. He said, "He's a fucking criminal. Did it ever occur to you that it was a bad idea to mix with people like that?"

"He's harmless."

"He's not harmless. He's done a couple of stretches in prison." Hastings sighed. "A couple of my men are questioning him now to see if he had any involvement in this matter."

Edie Penmark said, "Ernie doesn't know Cordelia. Do you think I'd ever introduce him to her?"

"I don't know what to think about you," Hastings said. "I'll tell you this, though: he probably wouldn't have known who she was if not for you."

"Check him out then," she said. "You won't find anything on him."

"We will," Hastings said. "And we have to check out all these other people you did business with too. That's the task you've presented us with, young lady."

"It's none of your business," she said. "It's nobody's business."

"It is now," Hastings said. "And you better—goddammit, why didn't you tell us that you were involved in this?"

"I didn't think it mattered," she said. Her face no longer smug now, tears coming to her eyes.

"It very well may. You're in a seedy business with seedy people. Criminals. Don't you understand you may have exposed your sister to them?"

Tears were rolling down her cheeks now. "I don't think there's a connection," she said.

"Did you tell Ernie Shavers where Cordelia was going to be that night?"

"No."

"Are you sure?"

"Yes."

"Did you tell anyone?"

"No. Jesus, I didn't know myself." She sobbed. "Are you going to tell my father?"

Hastings sighed. "I don't know," he said. "Right now, that's the least of my concerns."

"Are you going to arrest me?"

"I would if I could," he said, still angry.

"Christ," she said, "you act like *you're* my father." Her sobs were mixing with her voice now. She said, "You're the one that hasn't found her. You think I don't care about my own sister? I do. More than you'll ever understand. I think you're just trying to find someone to blame for this."

———

Later, he and Murph stood by their cars talking it out. Hastings glancing from time to time at the Penmark house, apprehensive that Gene would come out and ask him what it was all about.

Murph said, "George, she doesn't know what she's talking about." He was referring to her last comment, Hastings looking for someone to blame.

Hastings himself wasn't so sure. That she was involved in such things had offended him in ways he could not quite explain. He kept thinking, But you have money. Why would you do this if you had money? It all seemed so pointless and destructive.

Murph said, "She's upset. We all know you've done everything you can."

"Not really," Hastings said. "Klosterman's still interviewing Shavers?"

"Yeah. They've got him down at the station. Rhodes is helping him."

Hastings said, "I'm going to call Agent Gabler. He'll probably want to be there. Or Kubiak will."

"Okay."

It was getting colder. Away from the city and the city lights, starshine lit up the cars. It was quiet.

Hastings said, "Murph?"

"Yeah?"

"Did you hear her say that she didn't know her sister was going to the party?"

"Yeah. You asked her if she told Shavers about it. And she said, no, she didn't even know herself." Murph put his hand over his jacket pocket. "I wrote it down. Why?"

"I'm not sure yet," Hastings said. "Go back downtown, tell Joe about what we found out here. If the feds want to question you, give them your full cooperation. I'm going back to Ladue."

THIRTY-THREE

Hastings rang the doorbell until the lights came on and he could see a man looking at him through a window. It was Sam Fisher and Hastings could see that he had gotten the guy out of bed. Sam Fisher opened the door, looking cross in his bathrobe and pajamas.

Sam Fisher said, "What do you want?"

"I'm sorry to get you out of bed," Hastings said, though he wasn't much. "But it's very important that I talk to you."

Fisher said, "Tonight? Can't it wait till morning?"

"I'm afraid it can't. The Penmark girl, the kidnappers still have her. They've got their ransom money, but she hasn't been released." Hastings waited.

"I don't understand," Fisher said.

"They may kill her soon."

"You think."

"Yeah, I think. Can I come in?"

Fisher sighed and backed into the house. Hastings followed him in and Fisher closed the door. He said, "What is it I can do?"

Hastings said, "I've been thinking that the kidnappers knew about your party in advance. That they planned on taking Cordelia when she left here."

"That they knew about this party in advance?"

"Yes."

"But that could have been anybody. It could have been somebody she told."

"I've thought about that," Hastings said. "But there doesn't seem to be any evidence that she tipped anyone off."

Fisher crooked his head, lawyer skepticism on his face. "You think it was someone Tom Myers told?"

"No, not directly. Maybe it was someone from your firm."

"My firm?" Sam Fisher laughed. "The kidnapping was masterminded by someone at my law firm?"

Hastings sighed. Athletes retire from competition, but lawyers never do. He could stipulate to Sam Fisher that Fisher was smarter than he was, and maybe that would move things along. Hastings said, "No, not exactly. What I mean is . . . well, how many people are employed by the firm?"

"About two hundred lawyers with at least as many staff." Fisher was still looking at him like he was slow or something. Like, *You really want to continue this line of questioning?* He was a bully, this one. But that wasn't the point.

Hastings said, "Are you the managing partner?"

"Yes. I'm senior managing partner." His tone was almost defensive then, Hastings having hit some sort of nerve.

Hastings said, "Do you have any employees, perhaps recently terminated, that have been in trouble with the law?"

"Well . . ."

"You do?"

"Well, we don't make a practice of hiring criminals, if that's what you mean."

"That's not what I mean. You know what I meant."

Hastings was looking at him directly now. A high-powered lawyer to be sure, but no match for an experienced con when it came to lying. Sam Fisher was worrying about something now. Something was bothering him and he was too smart a man to be able to put it aside.

"Well," Fisher said, "yes, there was someone that we had to let go a couple of months ago. But I really don't . . ."

"You seem to be concerned about it."

"I . . . I really doubt that she, that she would . . ."

"Tell me about her anyway." Hastings was sensing the lawyer morphing into a witness, seeming almost frightened now because he was afraid of his instinct being correct.

Fisher said, "Her name was Jan Rusnok. Or Janet Rusnok. She went by Jan. We hired her about a year and a half ago. Legal assistant. She worked in the employment litigation department, which I used to run. She was a good worker, most of the time. About a year ago, she got arrested for possession. She told us about it. And I went to bat for her. It was just marijuana. I'm from the Baby Boomer generation and most of us had—well, you know. It was just a misdemeanor and I said we should give her a second chance. No big deal. She stays with the firm and for the next couple of months, everything's fine. Then she starts getting . . . weird. Political. Like left-wing political. Well, that's nothing new at our firm. We've got plenty of liberals, myself included. I say shit about Bush all the time. But this wasn't just some tree-hugger bullshit. This was something more. She was getting radical. Which is fine, but the bottom line is, we're a corporate firm. We defend the big corporations when they get sued by the little guys. Me, I don't apologize for it.

Corporation's entitled to a fair trial and a defense as much as anyone else, right?"

He was looking for reassurance and Hastings saw no reason not
to give it to him. At least, not now. "Right," Hastings said.

"Well, Jan gets to where she doesn't see it that way. I mean, she
was starting fights with her bosses over what sort of things we
should turn over in discovery. Not just mild disagreements. I mean
fights. Screaming matches." Sam Fisher sighed. "So, I called her in
to talk to her about it. I didn't want to fire her. I really didn't. I'd
gone to bat for her before and I thought...well, I thought she
might be having some sort of breakdown."

"Was she?"

"I don't know. It was like she was ... under some sort of spell or
something. Like a cult."

"You called her in."

"Yes. I told her what the firm was about, that she had always
known what it was about. That we valued her as an employee, but
that she had to get back in line. I'll tell you, I was expecting an apology. Contrition. I've met with plenty of employees over the years
and that's what usually happens."

"Was she contrite?"

"Not in the slightest. She attacked *me*."

"Physically?"

"No, not physically. I mean, she attacked me personally. She said
I was just a bullshit liberal. She said I didn't give a fuck about people. I didn't give a fuck about the poor or the working class. She even
told me I didn't give a shit about my own children. By the way, that's
the language she was using when she talked to me, the managing

partner. She said I was the worst sort of hypocrite there was." Fisher paused. "I tell you, I was kind of shaken up by it."

"Why?"

"I just never imagined she would talk to me that way. It was like she was possessed. No, I take that back. What I mean is, I didn't know that she had that sort of hatred in her."

"She threaten you?"

"No. But that was pretty much it for her. I told her she was terminated. I had to have her escorted out of the building. It was an awful scene."

"You never reported this?"

"What was there to report? She didn't break any laws. She told off her boss. All I could do was fire her. And I tell you, I did not enjoy doing that."

"I believe you," Hastings said. "She didn't threaten you or anyone else at the firm?"

"No."

"Yet," Hastings said, "you find yourself thinking about her now."

"Yeah, I do," Fisher said. "I'm not sure why, but sometimes you feel things, you know?"

Hastings nodded.

"The thing is, no one ever heard from her again. She had friends there. She did when she worked there. And usually, a legal secretary ends up at another firm. Even when they tell a boss to go fuck himself."

"Really?"

"Oh, there are some lawyers out there who would have hired her *because* she told me off. But she sort of ... disappeared."

"Anyone at the firm know where she ended up?"

"I don't think so. I mean, people joked about her living on some sort of lesbian commune. But I don't know where she ended up."

"Would she have known that Tom Myers was dating Cordelia Penmark?"

"Of course. Tom wanted everybody to know that."

"And she would have known that he would bring her to your party?"

"Well, yes. She would have known that he would come. Some-one like Tom, he's not going to skip the firm party. She would have known that." Fisher straightened and said, "Listen, Lieutenant. This is all very speculative. I mean, we're talking about a legal assis-tant who may have been a little unbalanced. She's wacky, but . . . to plan a kidnapping, murder . . . really."

Hastings knew that what Fisher was saying was sensible. It *was* speculative, maybe even silly. But Fisher himself said he had felt something, even though he was now trying to talk himself out of it.

Hastings said, "You don't have a forwarding address?"

"I don't. I'm sorry."

Hastings said, "Did she file an unemployment claim?"

Fisher stopped. He said, "Yes, as a matter of fact. I had to write out a statement to the unemployment office. Her claim was denied."

•

Fisher told him he could pull his car into the driveway so that it wouldn't get hit by another car or investigated by another cop. Hast-ings moved the Jag and was sitting in it when he reached Murph on the phone. He told Murph about Janet Rusnok and her unemploy-ment claim, which meant that she had to have left an address on some government record. Murph said he would do a quick NCIS search too to see if there was anything on the girl. Hastings, hedging himself, said the girl was probably just a person of interest at this stage, but he had to nail it down before he could move on.

Murph got off the phone and Hastings sat in the car in the dark driveway. He put his head back on the headrest and closed his eyes. Time drifted off and when he opened his eyes he looked at his watch and saw that almost twenty minutes had passed. He cursed at the lost minutes, then he started the car and drove to a 7-Eleven and bought a large coffee.

His phone was ringing as he was walking outside.

He set the coffee on the roof of the car and answered the phone.

"Yeah?"

"George. We may have something."

"Okay."

"Janet Rusnok was listed as a witness on a County PD report. She was the roommate of a girl named Gabrielle Bersch. About three months ago, Gabrielle Bersch disappeared."

Hastings said, "Permanently?"

"Looks that way. They haven't found her yet, anyway. She called her mom one night, crying, said she 'had had enough' and wanted to come home. Apparently, she'd started hanging out with a new group of friends. Some bad apples, her mother told the police. And she got scared and called and asked if she could come home. Mama says yes, come on home. Gabrielle Bersch hangs up and they never see her again."

"What about Janet Rusnok?"

"They got a statement from her. She said she didn't know where she had gone. But the report noted that Gabrielle had lost her hair-dressing job about three weeks before she disappeared. Lost her job, quit her family."

"You got a copy of the County report there?"

"Yeah. They faxed it to me. George, it seems the most helpful statement they got here is from her manager at the salon."

"Why do you say that?"

"It's the most detailed, the most thoughtful. The mom was too beside herself to be much help."

"Give me the guy's number."

"Okay. His name is Mitchell Raines. . . ."

THIRTY-FOUR

Mitchell Raines told the waiter to bring him and his friend Del Glickman another bottle of wine. The waiter, whose name was Robert, asked Mitchell Raines if they were celebrating anything. Mitchell Raines said that Del's son had just gotten accepted into medical school. Which wasn't true. Mitchell Raines liked to make things up on the spot, get people to stop and look at him to see if he was serious. Saying he couldn't read or that he had had a fight with someone while they were in the restroom or that he had been Jeanne Tripplehorn's first husband. The waiter was used to this sort of joking around from Mitchell Raines. But he was glad that Mitchell and his friend had taken a table in his station because Mitch Raines always tipped well.

They had just opened the second bottle of wine when Del Glickman called the maître d' over. The maître d's name was Mark, and Del and Mitchell knew him from La Baguette off Brentwood Boulevard. Mark was British and he usually had something for them.

Del Glickman said, "Mark, tell us what you think of this new French restaurant they opened on Euclid."

"It's . . . acceptable, I suppose."

"What't the clientele like?"

"Oh, the usual. Poofs and trollops. They get all a-bother if a fork is dropped on the floor, even though two hours later they'll go home with a complete stranger and put his cock in their mouth."

Mitch and Del loved this. Mark could usually deliver. Droll and British. Fag jokes were okay coming from him.

A cell phone rang. Rang again and the maître' d said, "You're not going to answer that, are you?"

"Yes," Mitchell said. Then he said, "This is Mitch."

"Mitchell Raines?"

"Yes. Who am I speaking to?"

"George Hastings. I'm a lieutenant with the St. Louis Police Department."

"Oh. What can I do for you?"

"A few months ago, you gave a statement to the County Police Department regarding the disappearance of one of your employees."

"Yes. Gaby."

"Gabrielle Bersch."

"Yes. We called her Gaby. Have you found her?"

"No. I'm sorry, we haven't. You gave a very helpful statement to the police."

"Did I."

"Yes. It was very comprehensive. But I'm wondering if there was something else."

"Like what?"

"Well, the report said that she called her mother and said that she'd had enough and she wanted to come home."

"Yes."

"I was wondering if you knew what she wanted to come home from?"

Mitch Raines sighed. "I'm sorry, but I don't."

"Did she quit or did you fire her?"

"I fired her."

"How come?"

"Oh, she was fucking up. She was preaching to the customers, starting arguments. Liberal shit. I mean, that's nothing new at our shop. But she was getting militant. And it was putting off the clients. It was too bad because she was a real sweet girl."

"Did you know her roommate, Janet Rusnok?"

"No. Never met her."

Hastings said, "You said 'militant'."

"Yes."

"What do you mean by that?"

"I don't know. Radical. Tree hugging. No, wait. Not tree hugging. It wasn't about the environment. I mean, like communist."

"Had she joined some sort of group?"

"She was into something called— Del?"

"Yes?"

"What was that group Gaby used to talk about? The one she said she met up with at Cicero's?"

"Liberation . . . Earth?"

"Liberation Earth?"

"No. Not Earth. Fuck. . . . Front. That's it. Liberation Front."

Mitch said into the phone, "Liberation Front."

Hastings wrote it down on his pad. "Liberation Front. Is that right?"

"Yes."

"Did you discuss this with the County police?"

"I don't think so. It never came up. I mean, I didn't think it would mean anything. Half of my staff is into weird shit I can't keep track of. You know how that is."

"Yeah," Hastings said. "Thanks for your help."

•

Hastings called Gabler on his cell phone.

Hastings said, "Where are you?"

Gabler said, "Craig and I are at St. Louis PD. Craig's in the interrogation room with your man interviewing Ernie Shavers. I'm on the other side of the glass. Hey, why did you have Klosterman bring the guy here?" Gabler sounded irritated, suggesting Hastings was trying to scoop him.

Hastings said, "I'm sorry about that. It was just something I was having them check out. I wasn't trying to hide it. I had Murph call you."

Gabler sighed. "Yeah, I guess you did."

Hastings said, "How's it going?"

"Lame. No offense, but I think it's a dead end. The guy's got an alibi and even if he didn't, I don't think he had anything to do with this."

"What does Klosterman think?"

"He think's the same thing," Gabler said. "You want to ask him yourself?"

"No, I believe you. Listen, write this name down: Jan Rusnok."

"Jan Rusnok. With a *k* or a *ck*?"

"*K.* R-u-s-n-o-k. Rusnok. She used to be a legal assistant at Tom Myers's law firm. She got fired a couple of months ago. She knew that Tom would be taking Cordelia to Fisher's Christmas party."

"So what?"

"Well, it may not mean anything. But Fisher seems awful nervous about her. She was apparently part of some left-wing radical group called the Liberation Front. And she had a roommate named Gabrielle Bersch who disappeared."

"The Liberation Front?" Gabler seemed interested now. "Was that all? It wasn't the Earth Liberation Front or the Green Front?"

"No, just the Liberation Front. Why? Have you heard of it?"

"Yeah, I have actually."

Hastings was standing next to his car again. He put his hand on the roof. "You think we got something here?"

"We might," Gabler said. "Jesus, we might. Where are you now?"

"West of the city."

"There's a file on this group at our field office. Can you meet me there?"

•

Minutes later, Hastings was racing the Jag down the interstate, the speedometer hovering between eighty and eighty-five, the burble of the engine sounding contented as the red police light on the dash flicked on and off. Driving fast because he could feel that they had something now. Not knowing in fact, but feeling that the prey was in sight, was near. The fear in Sam Fisher's voice as he spoke of Jan Rusnok, not having any proof that she was connected to it, but being scared that she was, the fear that comes from a gut feeling of dealing with a person. Maybe she was just a misfit. A loser who couldn't hold on to a job at a law firm even when the managing partner was going out of his way to give her a break. A person could be misguided and self-destructive, but that didn't necessarily make them capable of kidnapping and murder. We're all misguided and self-destructive at times, but few of us can murder with ease. At least that's how Hastings saw it.

But Hastings hadn't sat across a desk and stared into the hateful eyes of Jan Rusnok. Sam Fisher had, and whatever it was he'd seen, it seemed to have scared him. And Sam Fisher had not seemed, to Hastings, a man who was scared easily. Jan Rusnok had rattled him, though. Enough that he had felt it was important to tell Hastings about it tonight. And then a roommate of hers had disappeared.

Janet Rusnok. What was she? A loser? Or part of something bigger, scarier? What would the FBI have on this group that she was associated with?

"Oh, shit," Hastings said aloud.

The guy who telephoned Judy Chen had called himself Carl. A pseudonym, right? But there was Karl Marx and there was a disgruntled girl who had joined a radical, left-wing group that the FBI had a file on. Maybe it was just a coincidence. A piece of a puzzle that wasn't really a piece, but something that Hastings wanted to fit. Deduction, my dear Watson. Deduction, bullshit. What if they were all off the mark? Desperate, well-meaning men grasping at straws because, as Edie Penmark had said, they hadn't yet found Cordelia.

They had been concentrating on her. Who was in Cordelia's life? Who was near to her, near enough to know who she was and track her, prey upon her? Using that premise hadn't gotten them anywhere. Now, they were presented with a theory that just had a couple of pieces, just a handful that could mean something. And the presumption this time was not that they knew about Cordelia from Cordelia's world, but from Tom Myers's world. Tom Myers, a young ambitious lawyer, a social climber who might have been using Cordelia. Not for sex, but for the status she could bring him and for her money. Who at his law firm would not be aware that he was courting Cordelia Penmark? What an accomplishment that was. She wasn't a raving beauty, but she was one of the richest of the rich, a penthouse away from a young lawyer from a modest background. Being with her gave Tom Myers a pass; a bypass of sorts over the Sam Fishers of this world, over the middlemen. Would Tom Myers have let people know that? If not directly, then indirectly? Cordelia's roommate had indicated that Tom Myers was a run-of-the-mill toady. Perhaps smarter and better-looking than most, but a toady all the same. He would kiss up to those above him and ignore or bully those below. Kiss up to Sam Fisher, at least for the time being, but treat the legal assistants like field hands.

To Tom Myers, maybe Jan Rusnok was a field hand. But maybe she was the sort who remembered and wrote down grudges in her own little book.

The book. Murph had once explained that concept to Hastings. He said it was an Irish thing. If someone wronged you, you didn't necessarily have to get vengeance right away. But you would remember. It would not be forgotten. "It's in the book," Murph said.

An SUV up ahead caught the flashing police light in its rearview mirror and moved out of the passing line. Hastings pressed the accelerator a little harder. Forest Park passed by on his left now, the Arch coming into view.

———

Kubiak and Gabler were in a workroom, files and photographs spread out on a conference table. There was something in the air, an anticipation of sorts. A lead that might finally mean something. It was Kubiak who spoke to him first.

He said, "Lieutenant, you may have hit on something. You ever hear of something called the Liberation Front?"

"Not till today."

Kubiak slid a photo over to him. It was a picture of Mickey Seften.

"Recognize him?" Kubiak said.

"Yeah. He was the man on the train."

Kubiak looked over to Gabler.

Gabler said, "God damn."

"What?" Hastings said.

"These are the jackal bins," Kubiak said.

Hastings said, "The what?"

Gabler said, "It's an inside joke of sorts. A small left-wing group was formed over the last couple of years. They call themselves the Liberation Front." He pushed another photograph over to Hastings. "That's Terrill Colely. The leader. He was arrested for destruction of property and negligent assault last year by the Portland police. Before his trial, he was busted out. They used a journalist to sneak in a couple of gunmen. Two deputies were murdered, and Colely escaped. After it happened, the local sheriff held a press conference and called them Jacobins, but another journalist wrote it down wrong. Jackal bins."

Hastings grunted. Hard to laugh now.

Kubiak handed another photograph to Gabler. Gabler looked at it for a moment, then slid that one over to Hastings.

"This is Maggie Corbitt. Also believed to have been involved in Colely's escape. Probably his girlfriend. Colely grew up in Peoria, but has been traveling the country since then. A drifter, living underground. Maggie Corbitt lived here for a time. A runaway from Arkansas, she's been arrested a couple of times for prostitution and drug possession. Nothing much stronger than that."

Hastings thought briefly of Edie Penmark. Then slid her offstage. He said, "What about the other man in the bathroom?"

Gabler said, "We don't know. Craig's suggested that he may have been a Canadian, maybe from Alberta. The Portland police said that there was a lot of drug-running activity over the border in the Pacific Northwest. Maybe that's why they were up there in the first place."

Hastings said, "Who else?"

"A young lady named Lee Ensler. The journalist. A graduate of Brown University. Comes from a wealthy family. Before the breakout in Oregon, she had no past record of criminal activity. The Oregon State Police think she just fell under Colely's spell. Terrill Colely's a handsome dude, apparently, and a practiced con. She visited him once, just once, before helping break him out. And she's been underground ever since."

Kubiak said, "We've reexamined the ransom message they put on their videotape and compared it with some of Lee Ensler's writings. I've only had time to look at a couple of samples, but I think it was her creation."

Hastings said, "You think they're still around?"

Gabler said, "We have to hope they are. They were here for the drop."

And that was this morning, Hastings thought. Hard to believe it had only been this morning.

Gabler said, "I think you've hit on it, George." He was giving Hastings a look of admiration now, the professional sort. "But we've still got to find them."

Kubiak said, "We can fax photos of the suspects to all the local law-enforcement agencies. Give them to the media tonight. Media will run them starting tomorrow morning. But..." He refrained from saying that the girl might be dead by then.

But Terrill Colely was already a wanted man. He had had two deputies killed in Oregon months ago and no one had caught him for that. He or someone associated with him had killed Tom Myers and then abducted a girl. They had their money, and the history gave no evidence that they were going to show the girl any mercy. It was on Hastings's mind and he knew it was on the agents' too.

Kubiak said, "Maggie Corbitt and Jan Rusnok have ties to St. Louis. We have that."

Hastings said, "Are Rusnok's parents living in St. Louis?" He had asked about her, not Corbitt, because they had already said that Corbitt was from Arkansas.

Kubiak looked through the file. "Yeah," he said. "Ten twelve South Gray. That's near the Bosnian neighborhood."

Not far from my own, Hastings thought. He turned to Gabler and said, "Why don't we go there, see what they know?"

Kubiak said, "She's got a brother too. Lives near the airport. I'll go talk to him."

Gabler said, "Craig, it's your command. Don't you think it'd be better to send a couple of agents instead? I think you need to be here to coordinate." Gabler made a conciliatory gesture. "It's your command."

"Okay," Kubiak said. "I'll send Crider and Dolworth to the brother's. You guys go to the parents'." He turned to Hastings. "Can you spare a couple of men to look into Maggie Corbitt?"

"Yeah. I'll call 'em."

•

Gabler and Hastings drove south by southwest on Gravois Road, the street narrow, sloping down under a railroad bridge, the engine increasing volume as Hastings throttled it back up the other side. Soon, the faux German architecture came into view. South Gravois neighborhood, not really German anymore but Bosnian. Fifty thousand refugees having settled there since the Serbians had officially and unofficially declared war on them. They were a tough people, used to harshness, and Hastings wondered if they knocked on the wrong door at this hour of the night, would they be answered with a shotgun blast? A good many of them didn't speak English.

He drove past the Croatian-owned video shop next to the Quik-Trip, slowed, then turned down a narrow street with tightly packed little row houses. He made a couple of turns and then he saw the address they needed.

Hastings double parked the Jaguar, blocking the road. He left the police light on. He looked at his watch. It was almost midnight.

They rang the doorbell and rapped on the front door until the porch light came on and they saw an old woman's face peering at them through the window. Looking at two white men in jackets and ties and a flashing red light in a car in the street behind them. It's a frightening thing to be awakened in the dark of night by sharp knocking on your door, even if you're not old, but Hastings hoped that she would see the view through her window and figure out they were police.

She didn't open the door and now they could hear her raised voice from behind the door.

"What do you want?"

"Police, ma'am. We need to speak to you immediately. It's an emergency."

"Let me see your identification."

They held their badges up to the glass so that she could peer at them. She gave them an old woman's scrutiny, then took in the sight of the unmarked police car beyond. But said again, "What do you want?"

"Ma'am, it's about your daughter," Gabler said. "Please let us in."

She unlocked the door and chain and opened the door. They walked in. It had the smell of a retired person, the heat turned up. The woman was holding her robe closed at the neck. She looked like she was in her sixties. She said, "Is Jannie dead? Is that what you've come to tell me?"

"No," Gabler said.

The old woman blinked at him. "Is she in trouble, then?"

"She may be," Hastings said. "We'd like to try to help her. Do you know where she is?"

"I haven't seen her in a couple of months. What's she done?"

"We don't know if she's done anything wrong," Gabler said. "But we do need to speak to her immediately."

The woman looked at the FBI agent and then at the police officer. She said, "Why?"

Hastings said, "A girl has been kidnapped. She may be killed if we don't find her in time."

"What's that have to do with Jan?"

"Maybe nothing," Hastings said. "But we need to speak to her."

"You think she's involved?"

"Maybe."

The lady's jaw was quivering now. "No," she said. "No."

Gabler said, "You said you don't know where she is."

"No, I don't."

Gabler said, "When's the last time you saw her?"

"It was before Thanksgiving. She was supposed to come to her brother's on Thanksgiving. She knew about it."

"But she didn't come?" Hastings said.

"No. She didn't. She came the year before, though. But didn't stay long. She said there was no place there for her."

Jan Rusnok's mother looked as if this had not surprised her.

Gabler said, "Where is Mr. Rusnok?"

"He died last year." There was little emotion in her voice then. Perhaps she was relieved.

Hastings said, "Did Jan live here before?"

"She moved in and out. She'd come back here after some boy would dump her. But she never stayed long. She said we were common."

"But she stayed here?" Hastings said.

The old lady shrugged. "What are we supposed to do?" It was their daughter.

Agent Gabler said, "Ma'am, it's very important that we speak to her. A young girl's life may be at stake. And if your daughter is mixed up with the people that kidnapped her, she's in danger too."

"Sir," Mrs. Rusnok said, "I don't know where she is. She didn't even come to her dad's funeral."

"We're sorry about that," Hastings said. "But we have to find her. Please help us."

The old woman was shaking her head. "She doesn't . . ."

"Pardon?" Gabler said.

"She doesn't talk to us." The woman looked up at the FBI agent. "She doesn't tell us anything."

Gabler said, "You said that she would move out when another man would come along. Is that right?"

"Yes."

Gabler said, "Who was the last man?"

She was looking down at the ground again, perhaps because of a bad memory. But then they saw that she was trying to remember, trying.

She said, "There was a boy that brought her to Kenny's that Thanksgiving. He was a loser, you could see that. No manners. A bad egg. His name was Ray. Ray something."

Gabler said, "Can you remember the last name?"

The woman was shaking her head again. "I'm sorry," she said. "I'm sorry, I can't."

Gabler looked at Hastings and then looked back at the woman. "Excuse me," he said. He moved down the hallway and made a call on his cell phone.

"Craig, this's Gabe. Who did you send out to the brother's

house? ... Charlie? ... Give me his number. ... Yeah, we've got Jan associating with a Ray something, but we don't have a last name. ... All right."

Gabler placed another call, to Agent Charles Crider. Hastings turned back to the old lady. She caught his expression and said, "You're not going to hurt her, are you?"

Her face in itself told a story. Not a clueless old lady, but probably pretty sharp. She knew that her daughter was capable of being involved in such a thing. Hastings wondered how long the woman had been able to see her daughter clearly, how long she had resisted closing her eyes to it. She was maybe sixty, but the despair made her look older. Her words told more. *You're not going to hurt her, are you?* Resignation in that question, a hard acceptance of what her daughter had become. She had likely seen the same hatred and nihilism as Sam Fisher had seen. She had lived with it and was decent enough to wonder if she'd had some part in forming the girl's character.

Hastings said, "We don't want to."

The woman was looking directly at him now, in a way that almost shamed him. Though he didn't know why.

Mrs. Rusnok said, "She wasn't always that way."

Hastings didn't say anything. He heard Gabler say, "Oh, that's great, Charlie, that is great. Okay. Call me if you need anything."

Gabler walked back to Hastings. He said, "Ray Muller. That's the guy's name. Charlie's calling Craig now."

Hastings looked at Mrs. Rusnok. He said, "Does that sound right?"

She said, "I still don't remember. He never told *me* his name. I guess Kenny remembered, though."

Hastings said, "Would you mind if we took a quick look through her room?"

"Go ahead." She seemed very tired now. "But it's not really her room anymore. I doubt you'll find anything."

She was right about that. Her daughter hadn't left any clothes or personal effects or notes to Ray Muller with a home address. It was a free hotel room for Jan Rusnok and little more. Soon they were finished and walking through the kitchen, where Mrs. Rusnok was sitting at a small red covered kitchen table. She looked up at them, wondering if they could share anything with her, and they couldn't.

Hastings said, "Thank you for your cooperation. We'll let you know if we need anything else."

She didn't respond.

Five minutes later, they were back in the car, heading back downtown.

•

Craig Kubiak was standing behind another agent, who was sitting in front of a computer screen. Agent Crider and his partner, Shelly Dolworth, got back to the field station just a few minutes before Hastings and Gabler; they still had their overcoats on. Kubiak turned to make eye contact with Gabler.

Kubiak said, "We've got him."

"Ray Muller?" Gabler said.

"Yes," Kubiak said. "He's drawing a government disability."

"For what?"

Kubiak said, "He was in the army and he got stabbed. Not in combat, mind you. A fight with another soldier. Listen, he was trained in electronics and telecommunications. He was discharged in ninety-eight and he's been drawing the disability since. He's thirty years old. County records show that he's divorced and actually had custody of his son for a couple of years. His ex-wife was paying child support to him until she proved to the court that he was spending it on himself and leaving the kid with his mother. A turd."

Craig Kubiak in his white shirt and spectacles was sounding more like a beat cop now than a federal agent. He said, "The disability checks are sent to a farmhouse in Illinois. Near White Hall. Off State Highway 9." Kubiak looked at Hastings. "You know where that is?"

Hastings nodded.

Gabler said, "Have you called Shellow?"

"No," Kubiak said. "Not yet."

Hastings said, "What's the problem?"

Gabler said, "We want all the toys, we have to get authorization. Probably from our SAC. At a minimum, our ASAC."

"For what?" Hastings said.

"Explosive entry, Hostage Rescue Team, stun grenades, and vehicles disguised so that we look like we're delivering flowers or some shit."

Hastings sighed.

Gabler said, "Listen, about fifteen years ago, a bunch of FBI agents tried to take two guys armed to the teeth after a vehicle pursuit. Two, that's all. All but one of the agents were killed in the firefight. This was before Waco, before Ruby Ridge. Ever since then, they've more or less taken . . . conservative approaches. They don't like agents getting killed."

The agent at the computer screen was turned around in his seat.

Agents Crider and Dolworth were still with them, Hastings the only Metro cop.

Hastings said, "Well, how long will it take to get authorization?"

"It's not so much the time," Kubiak said. "It's what we have to get authorization. Or don't have." He looked at Hastings now. "I wonder if it's too—speculative. A girl who used to work with Tom Myers..."

Hastings said, "We've got more than that and you know it. Craig, it's right there in front of you. I know you see it."

Kubiak looked around the room at the other agents and read their expressions and body language. He returned his eyes to Hastings.

Kubiak said, "Are you going to go around me?" Meaning to St. Louis PD and the Illinois State Police. Craig Kubiak wasn't trying to talk tough now and his tone was not disrespectful. He was asking a straight question.

"I'd rather not," Hastings said. "But you need to make a decision. Now."

A few moments passed, no one in the room saying anything.

Then Kubiak said, "Okay. I'll get the authorization."

THIRTY-FIVE

Between three and four in the morning, Lee got out of bed and went and stood by the window. There was a full moon out. Lee looked up at the moon and felt it looking down on her. Seeing her naked and bright. A Kiowa moon, Lee thought. That was when the Kiowa would attack the settlers—under a full moon. Light to guide them in the slaughter, yes, but it was good medicine too. An inspiration. A sign.

She thought there had been such a moon when Gabrielle ran away. The dumb girl probably thought the moon would help her, give her light to escape back to her piggy hairdresser world. She only got about a mile. Stayed near the road and stopped at a convenience store. That's where they found her. Jan and Terrill had found her there and Jan had gotten out of the car and walked over to her and told her they loved her and they were family and talked her into coming back. And then Terrill and Mickey took her out to a field and killed her. She was still there now, buried in her own sod.

It's all sod, Lee thought. Sod, dirt, and ashes. She pictured herself in another place. Another time. Inside the settlers' sodhouse as the Indians tried to get in ... opening shutters and pointing rifles out, but they keep coming ... and then she pictured herself on the outside, astride a horse, pointing a rifle at the sodhouse, waiting for a head to appear in the window ... She wondered vaguely if she had been there when it happened. If she had been a man, a warrior in another time.

She had not slept since her husband left her room. Her man. Her man needed her, she knew. He had come to depend on her. She had not slept in days. The effects of the speed would start to wear off and she would feel sick, feel that awful, horrible coming-down feeling, a feeling of hunger, of knowing you should eat something, but knowing too that food would make you sick. A sandwich . . . two pieces of flour and shit white paste that was Wonder Bread with that disgusting sweet brown frost of peanut butter in between . . . get dry heaves just at the thought of it. And she would take another tablet and the nausea would pass. Speeding onto the entrance ramp, and then slipping back onto the highway and falling back into a comfortable rhthym.

She could talk about this . . . this *thing* with her husband. But it would make her a drag if she brought it up now. He didn't need a drag while this was going on. He needed to work, to lead. He needed—he *thought* he needed—to help his sister. Sister Maggie. For that's what Maggie was to Terrill. She was a big sister. An annoying, bossy one. She thought she was helping Terrill, but she wasn't helping him. She was retarding him. Hindering him. Defiling him. It was gross. Deviant. A sister screwing her little brother. Screwing another woman's husband. It was unclean, unhealthy. It was not beautiful or edifying to do that to him.

Sometimes, lying in bed at night, she would visit dark places. And in those dark places she would see them together as children. See them growing up together. See Maggie approaching Terrill when he was still a child, a beautiful boy. She was doing things to him. Teaching him to be strong, but doing awful, nasty things to him too. Bad things. Once or twice, Lee had cried out for her to stop. But she wouldn't listen. She didn't listen to people. Not even to her own brother.

Lee put a T-shirt and underpants on. She walked out into the dark hallway, oblivious of the cold. Downstairs, she cleaned the kitchen. Then she cleaned the living room. And when that was finished, she thought about cleaning the little piggy's room downstairs. But the piggy would try to talk to her, bother her if she did that. So she went back to the kitchen and this time cleaned the cupboards and drawers. Around five, she went back upstairs. She saw her jeans hanging over the chair and she didn't like the way they lay there. She took the jeans off the chair and pulled them on. Then she got back in bed.

THIRTY-SIX

At dawn, she awakened him, shaking him in bed. His back was to her and he turned and said, "What?" Too loud, the dumb ass.

Maggie said, "Ssshh."

Terrill said, "What is it?"

"You need to get going," Maggie said. Her voice was a whisper, conspiring.

Terrill turned over to look at her. "Now?"

"Yes."

After a moment, he said, "You mean Mickey?"

"I mean Mickey and the girl. You can't do it here. You'll have to take both of them away."

"The girl too?"

"Yeah. She saw you shoot that lawyer, didn't she?"

"Yeah, she did."

Maggie shrugged, as if to say, *Okay then.*

"Okay," Terrill said. And like that, it was decided.

Maggie had thought it out while Terrill was sleeping and before that as well. She was usually thinking. They couldn't kill Mickey in the house. There couldn't be witnesses. Maggie, with Terrill's help, had spent months conditioning them to think in terms of the group. Always it was the group and whatever was best for the group. The individual was to be forgotten. Individuality was to be suppressed. They had taught their followers that and their followers had been prime subjects for conditioning. Losers, misfits, misanthropes wanting to belong, little girls with daddy issues. They had been good subjects, easily suggestible. Even Toby Eagle had come around. It had been easy. Yes, they had been good subjects. But they weren't robots. They could still bicker and resent and nurse grudges about whom Terrill liked better and who had last done the dishes. They hadn't shut down all their emotions. So the sight of Terrill putting a couple of bullets into Mickey's head was bound to cause problems. *What did you kill Mickey for, man? Mickey was all right. Mickey was a good dude. Mickey loved you. What did he do to you?*

What did he do? He fucked up, you stupid cows. He let a policeman live when he should have helped Toby kill him and now the policeman had given all the other pigs and the media a pretty good description of Mickey and all the other fuck whores. Mickey had become a liability. As much as the girl had.

Maggie could tell them that. She could explain to them that their collective welfare was more important than Mickey's. That the needs of the many outweighed the needs of the one and all that other bullshit. Maybe they'd buy it...maybe...but Mickey would surely have something to say in his own defense, maybe with a gun, and even if they locked him up during the show trial, there wouldn't be time for the dialogue. They had the money now and they needed to move.

Her voice still a whisper, Maggie said, "Tell Mickey you need his help with the girl. You know him. You know he'll want to be alone with you."

Terrill said, "Now?"

"Now. I'll be waiting here for you."

———

Cordelia lifted her head up when she heard the door open. She didn't know if she'd been sleeping or if she had just passed out. She had stopped counting songs. The songs would fade and she could hear them in her sleep, going in and out, but she would lose count, and when she came to, she didn't know how much time had passed. She didn't know if it was day or night. She was weak. She was hungry. She was struggling not to lose her sanity, but it was getting harder, not easier. She felt ashamed. She had told herself to kick away at panic and then maybe the panic would start respecting her, acknowledge that she was not so easily dominated. But it was not panic that was threatening to overwhelm her now; it was despair. She had not been raped, she had not been tortured. Yet she felt a mess.

When she heard the door open, she wondered, What next? What else can they do to me? Would they just leave her here to die, like the dog tied to a tree and left to starve. Would they send someone down just to shoot her? Thanks for the cash, be-yotch. Would they turn off this incessant, godawful music? Brian Wilson morphing into Frankie Valli into Bobby Darin and then Bobby Goldsboro until blood poured out of her ears. Big girls *do* cry, motherfucker, and they pee and shit and wonder if they'd be better off dead.

There was someone coming down the stairs.

A form taking shape. Tall man wearing a black stocking cap, dark hair coming out of the sides. Dark in the basement, but Cordelia knew who he was now. He'd been wearing that cap when he shot Tom Myers.

She could call him on that. Try to eke out some dignity amid the smell and the dank and the worthlessness. Tell him: *I saw you. I saw you murder Tom, you fucking creep. You fucking monster. Are you going to shoot me too? Do it then. Do it, you worthless piece of shit.*

But she didn't. She didn't say what she was thinking. Coward, she thought. You can't even die with dignity. You can't even give yourself that.

"Please," she said.

Terrill stopped at the bottom of the stairs.

"Please," she said, her voice remote and small. "Please don't kill me."

Terrill said, "Did I say I was?" His voice hard, even now.

Cordelia sobbed and lowered her head. She didn't think she had anything left.

Terrill moved behind her and unlocked the chain that bound her to the pipe. He lifted her up. She was unsteady on her feet. Then she slipped and he caught her.

"Come on," he said. "We're leaving."

He had to help her up the stairs. And then they were out of the basement. The morning light assaulted her eyes and she put her arm up to shield herself. She could see a carpeted floor. Dirty. The smell was better than the basement, but it was still rank. Where was she? Was she in St. Louis? Was she in the United States? She could have been anywhere.

She lowered her hand and exposed her eyes to the light. It stung. She covered her eyes again.

She was being guided. She was aware of another person. A man in front of them, opening the door, and she felt the cold air rushing onto her. They were going outside.

Once they were outside, she opened her eyes again. Rural. They were in a rural area. Propane tanks and trashed-out vehicles. She wanted to ask them where they were taking her, but she was too weak and frightened to speak. She didn't want to ruin things. Maybe, if she misbehaved, they'd turn around and march her back into the house and throw her back into the basement, and she'd rather face the unknown than do that. *Complaining, are we? Fine, we'll just go right home, young lady.*

She was squinting now. Opening and closing her eyes by degree, adjusting to the light, keeping them open longer each time. She saw the other man now walking in front of them. Going toward an old blue Volvo, the boxy sort. Now he was opening the trunk.

"Oh, no," she said. "No." Her voice seemed small and unfamiliar to her.

"Relax," Terrill said. "We're going to let you go."

He wanted her to believe it. It was early and he wasn't in the mood to struggle with her. If he shot her here, it would wake up everyone in the house, and Mickey would still be here. They needed to get away from the house.

She was a little thing, weakened from hunger and thirst. It didn't take much to get her into the trunk. They didn't even bother tying her up.

Terrill said, "I'll drive."

"Okay," Mickey said. He seemed like he was in good spirits. Like he had been worried that Terrill was mad at him or something, but now knew that everything was okay between them.

Terrill leaned close to him now, his voice low. He said, "We're going to take her a couple of miles from here. The woods next to the pasture."

Mickey nodded. "You think that may be a little close?"

Terrill shook his head. "We're not staying there long." He said it in a way that made Mickey think he was being let in on something. An intimacy.

Mickey nodded, glad to be in the inner ring.

Mickey had a .380 Ruger semiautomatic in his coat pocket. Racked and ready to go. Terrill had the big .357 revolver he had used on the lawyer. There was a Browning bolt-action rifle on the floorboard behind them.

They drove on a long flat road, going a smooth fifty, until they passed a sign that said PASTURE FOR RENT and took the next right after that. Then they were on a narrower road, between wheat fields. They would wave pretty and green in the late spring, but now they were pale and cold.

Terrill slowed at a cut in the field that formed a sort of driveway through the wheat. He turned in and drove about thirty yards until the wheat formed walls around them. He shut off the car's engine.

"Okay," Terrill said.

They got out and moved to the back of the car. Mickey unlocked the trunk and popped it open. The girl was there, pale and a little shrunken, but still alive.

"Take her out," Terrill said.

Mickey obliged, half lifting her, half helping her get on her feet. Then he took her by the arm and led her away from the car. He was standing next to the girl and about fifteen feet away from the car when he looked up and saw Terrill.

Had Terrill just been taking his revolver out to kill the girl, Mickey would not have said anything. Had Terrill merely touched the revolver, Mickey would not have thought twice. But Mickey Seften had the survival instincts of a ferret and sometimes he noticed things. Terrill was touching his gun while he looked, not at the girl, but at Mickey. Like he was drawing a bead.

Mickey was looking back at Terrill now. Mickey let go of the girl's arm.

Terrill was busted and he knew it. He decided the best thing was just to bluff it out. He frowned at Mickey and said, "What?"

Mickey Seften's hands were at his side. "You tell me what," he said.

Terrill said, "What are you, fucking paranoid? You been smoking too much dope, man." He tried a smile.

But it wasn't working. Maybe the guy had been smoking too much dope, getting paranoid. Or maybe Mickey had seen the glint in Terrill's eye before and he knew and saw in the way that killers know and see, and Terrill said, "Mickey" in a conciliatory way, like you would use to try to talk someone off a ledge, but it was a bluff and Mickey knew it because he was reaching inside his coat pocket and Terrill didn't see that he had any choice and then he was drawing his revolver, and then Mickey was drawing too, hippy cowboys, and shots cracked out in the cold morning as they exchanged gunfire.

They were neither one of them marksmen and it's not an easy thing to draw and fire even at a stationary target. Their hands were shaking and adrenaline was surging and then they both started moving, involuntarily, as they kept firing at each other, Terrill retreating behind the Volvo to take cover, Mickey with nowhere to go except turn and run into the wheat field, but that didn't occur to him at the moment, and then Terrill's body was behind the Volvo and Mickey felt something tear at his shoulder and he got another shot out of the .380 before he went down and was looking up at the sky.

Terrill was ducked behind the rear of the Volvo now and he could hear Mickey groaning, his breathing rasped and irregular. Terrill kept to the ground as he moved on hands and knees to the front of the Volvo. He crept around and saw that Mickey was on his back. Terrill came out then and fired his last two shots into Mickey's body. He saw Mickey twitch and buck and he knew he was dead.

Terrill sighed. His heart was racing. It was done. He moved up to Mickey and took the .380 away from him. Mickey had a bullet in his shoulder and two in his body. Terrill stood over him with the .380 and put another bullet in his head, more out of anger than a need to be sure.

Terrill turned around and looked into the wall of the wheat field. It didn't tell him anything, except that the girl was gone.

Terrill gave the corpse a good kick and said, "Shit, Mickey. Now look what you've done."

•

After she heard the Volvo pull away, Maggie Corbitt sat cross-legged on the bed and smoked a joint. She was enjoying the moment. Wake and bake, as Terrill used to say. A peaceful morning.

Soon the girl would be taken care of and Mickey would be too. That would leave three of them in the house, outside of her and Terrill. Three, and three was not so difficult to handle.

Two million dollars. Two million dollars and it had been easy. You want to steal, steal from the rich. They've got it, and if you've got something they want, they'll give it to you. It really was that simple.

It seemed silly now, all that fuss. The Gene Penmarks of this world even debating whether they should pay the ransom. The man probably spent two million dollars last year refurbishing his house. Ten times that on a yacht. Half that for his "sumptuous" wedding. Fuck him. He could spare two million.

Maggie didn't need a mansion up on a hill. She and Terrill would take the money and maybe settle for a beach house in California. Blue sky and water and waves breaking on the surf. Get away from this midwest shithole. You say you worked hard for your money? Yeah, well, try sharing a house with a bunch of hippy-dippy ass-holes for a few weeks. Like babysitting grown children. Lee with her Ivy League worldview, spacing out now. Acting like Europe made her smart. Ray, talking about hitting "the man" while taking a government disability check. Jan talking tough feminist bullshit but sulking if Terrill or Ray didn't give her enough attention. Christ, it could wear on you.

Maggie put the joint out in the ashtray on the night table. She got off the bed and pulled her pants on. She pulled on a white T-shirt and her green jacket. Then she went downstairs.

It seemed more relaxed to her at first. The Penmark girl was gone and it made her feel better. She could have died down there and they would have had to haul her out and dispose of her some-where. But it was taken care of now.

Ray was leaning up against the counter. Jan was standing nearby. They stopped their conversation when Maggie came in.

"Hey," Maggie said. "Where's Lee?"

Ray said, "How should I know?"

"What?" Maggie said, her tone tough. She was sensing an inso-lence here.

"I said, how should I know."

A definite insolence. Maggie wondered if she should ask them what they had been talking about. They probably wouldn't answer her truthfully. Though all three of them knew it was about the money.

"What's up?" Maggie said, immediately regretting that she'd said it.

Ray said, "Where did Terrill go?" His voice was a little harder than Maggie was used to. Not asking, but questioning, and there was a difference between the two.

Maggie said, "He and Mickey are taking care of the girl."

"Taking care of her?" Ray said, "Or returning her?"

Maggie gave him a direct look. "What do you care?"

"I don't care if they kill her or not," Ray said. "But you might have checked with us before deciding."

Maggie said, "You knew it would come to that." She was getting impatient now. Ray drawing distinctions when he had already mur-dered a deputy in Oregon. Maggie shrugged. "Is there a problem?"

Jan started to speak, then stopped. She tried again, saying, "We were just wondering what—what happens next."

Ray said, "We were wondering where the money is."

Maggie thought, I knew it. It was just a matter of time. So predictable, all of it. The chickenshits couldn't go right to it, but had to act like they were miffed about the Penmark girl. Like they cared whether she lived. It was the money they were worried about.

"Don't worry about it," Maggie said. She went to the counter to get a coffee cup, showing them that she wasn't that concerned. But she could feel their eyes on her back.

Ray said, "Are you going to meet up with them?"

Maggie turned around. "Meet up with who?"

"With Terrill and Mickey? Is that what you've got in mind?"

"Man," Maggie said, "what is this?"

"It just seems funny," Ray said. "We wake up this morning and the girl's gone and Terrill's gone and Mickey's gone. And we don't know where the money is. That's all I'm saying."

Jan sensed the hostility between Ray and Maggie. She was on Ray's side, but she felt something coming, so she tried to sound like a mediating voice of reason when she spoke. She said, "We just want to know what's going on, that's all."

"Shut up," Maggie said, keeping her eyes on Ray. To Ray she said, "If you think we're trying to double-deal you, why don't you just say it?"

"Did I say that? When did I say that?"

Maggie said, "I think you are saying it."

Ray said, "Where is the money now?"

"What?"

"Where is the money, Maggie. Did Terrill and Mickey drive off with it? Where is it? Where is the fucking money?"

"What is this? Huh? No. They did not drive off with it. Terrill—
they'll be back in a minute. And then we can all talk about what happens next. Like we always do."

Ray Muller was giving her a long look now, appraising her in a
way that she had never quite seen before. Maggie thought about the
man she had sent to kill deputies in Oregon. It was the same guy,
she thought. The same Doberman she had sicced on a dumb-shit
cop, but now the Doberman was looking at her and the usual com-
mands didn't seem to be working.

Ray said, "Like we always do." Mimicking her, but calling her
out too. He said, "Is that really how it works?"

Maggie said, "Man, what is with you?"

Ray went on as if he hadn't heard her. "Or isn't it you and Terrill just telling us what we're going to do? Isn't that how it usually
works?"

Shit, Maggie thought. Ray growling now, tensing for a spring.
She saw it now, saw it coming, and the man was leaving her little
choice. Part of her hoped that Terrill would come back and help
her reason with this asshole. But another part of her hoped that
Terrill wouldn't come back soon because if he did, he would not
have Mickey with him and there would be more questions then.
An insurrection was what it was. A fucking insurrection.

Maggie gave out a sigh. "Do you want to see the money?" she
said. "It's still here. I can show it to you, okay?"

"Yeah," Ray said, "why don't you do that."

Christ, Maggie thought. He was *ordering* her now. The dumb
shit.

"It's upstairs," Maggie said.

She began walking out of the kitchen. Then she was in the living room walking toward the staircase. She could feel Ray walking behind her. Not right behind her, but following her into the living room, making sure she wasn't going to try to run out the front door. He stopped before she went up the stairs, though. There was no fire escape, so if Maggie wanted to leave, she would have to come back down the stairs. And Maggie could feel it then. The two of them holding her accountable. My, my, she thought. My, my.

She took the money out from under her bed. It was still in the black bag Mickey had given to Terrill. Maggie set it on the bed. Then she opened the top drawer of the chest and took out a Beretta 9-millimeter semiautomatic. She racked the slide and put one in the chamber. She looked at the bedroom door. It was still closed. She stuck the gun in the front of her pants and then lifted the black bag up in front of her. It was big and heavy and it hid the butt of the gun above her belt.

She was a cool cat, she thought. A very cool cat. Cool and calm as she thought it out. She would be holding the bag with two hands when she went down the stairs. They would be waiting there and when they saw the bag, that's where they would focus their attention. Ray would say something like "ah" or "now that's better" or something else stupid and Maggie would toss it down the stairs, let it land at their feet. Ray would keep his eyes on it and that would be when she shot him. Pull the Berretta out of her pants and plug him in the chest. Maybe see his eyes go wide in that moment when he realizes what's going to happen and that it's too late to stop it . . . the moment between life and death when he realizes he's been played.

Shoot him and then shoot Jan for siding with him. She would

probably cry out some sort of plea before getting hers. *Maggie, no!* Sorry, Jan. You play, you pay, bitch.

Maggie stepped out into the hallway.

"Where are you going?"

Maggie turned and looked down the hall. It was Lee. Christ.

"I'm going downstairs," Maggie said. Using the tone she generally used with Lee. "Something wrong?"

Lee stood there in the hallway, her expression blank. She took in the bag.

Lee said, "You're going to run away with him, aren't you?"

"Who?" And after Maggie asked that, she saw the revolver Lee was holding down at her side. Using one hand, Maggie began to reach for her Beretta.

"Lee...?"

Lee raised her arm and fired three shots. Two of them took Maggie in the chest and knocked her down. Lee walked to her and fired two more shots into her torso, twitching it, though Maggie's face registered the same initial shock. Lee pulled the trigger three more times on empty chambers. *Click, click, click.*

Lee stood over the body. Early dawn now, the Kiowa moon gone.

She looked over to see Ray standing nearby. He had come up the stairs.

Ray Muller looked at the dead body and then over at Lee, still holding the pistol.

"Jesus Christ," Ray said.

Lee vaguely pointed the spent pistol at Ray. Ray put his hands up. "Lee," he said.

"She was going to take him away from me." Lee looked at the gun and tossed it on the floor.

Ray picked it up. Then he took the Beretta that was near Maggie's hand. He pointed it at Lee. Debated it for a moment, then said, "It's okay, Lee. No one's mad at you. Go back to your room. Okay?"

Lee looked at him, her eyes something feral. "Don't tell me what to do," she said.

She stayed there for a couple of moments, then walked back down the hall to the bathroom. Ray heard the door slam shut.

"Jesus Christ," he said again.

THIRTY-SEVEN

Protocol was such that they had to alert the U.S. Marshals, the Illinois State Police, and Alton PD. The Springfield PD would have liked to have a piece too, but they were far enough away that they could be left out of it. It was necessary to alert these people so that they wouldn't show up because of reports of shots being fired and local deputies wouldn't mistakenly shoot at federal agents. Still, it was the FBI's show and every law enforcement officer there understood that. The secondary law enforcement was positioned in the rear. Agent Kubiak had left express instructions that he didn't want police cars in the immediate vicinity. If they saw police cars, they might shoot the girl right away.

The Hostage Rescue Team was stuffed into a white Ford van that said HUDSON ELECTRICAL AND MECHANICAL on the sides. The slogan on the back read, QUALITY DOESN'T COST, IT PAYS! Eight federal agents inside wearing Kevlar jackets and carrying automatic rifles. They had VHF handsets and when they got to the house they would surround it and then commence an explosive entry and move in with stun grenades and tear gas. The hope was that it would go so quickly that there wouldn't be time for the suspects to reach Cordelia Penmark. They didn't want the suspects inside while the HRT were outside and the negotiator tried to talk them out of killing someone they had probably already killed.

About a mile down the road was a line of three cars, two Ford

Crown Victorias and a 1987 Jaguar XJ6. Klosterman and Hastings sat in the Jaguar.

They watched as Curtis Gabler walked down to them and opened the back door to the Jag. The door shut and Gabler said, "Cold out this morning."

"Yeah," Klosterman said.

There were two shotguns up front. One of them in the stand against the dashboard, vertically positioned. The other one lay across Klosterman's lap, the muzzle pointing to the door.

Gabler said, "Okay. We just got word from the team commander. They've got the house surrounded. But we're not sure Muller is at home."

Hastings said, "Why's that?"

Gabler said, "Department of Motor Vehicles says that Ray Muller's got a 1991 Volvo 240. But we don't see it there. So we don't know."

Hastings looked in the rearview mirror. He caught Gabler's eye. "You thinking we should wait till he comes back?"

"I don't know. What do you think?"

"If we think the girl's in there . . ."

"Yeah," Gabler said, "that's what I thought." He drew a cold breath. "Okay." He got out of the car and walked back to the first Crown Vic.

•

Jan said, "Maybe we should wait until Terrill and Mickey come back."

Ray said, "I don't know who's crazier, you or Lee. Terrill finds out Maggie's dead, he's likely to kill us for it."

"But we didn't—"

"I don't know if he'll believe that. I don't know if he'll believe what actually happened." Ray sighed. "I'm not sure I do."

"She's been fucking tweaking for days. If anyone should've seen it, he should have."

"Well, he didn't. Look, I'm leaving and I'm taking this money with me. You can come with me or you can stay here."

"But the movement—"

"*There is no movement.* There is no cause." Ray held the bag. "*This* is what it's about. Terrill and Maggie knew it all along. Don't you see?"

Jan looked around the house. She looked to the stairs, Maggie's corpse at the top. Lee still up there somewhere . . .

Jan said, "Let me get my coat."

•

They walked out the front door, Ray holding the keys to the Toyota. They got about twenty yards from it when they heard a voice calling out to them.

"Hold it!"

And Ray knew it was a cop.

He turned to his left and saw an FBI agent in a blue military uniform. He was holding an M-16.

Ray still had the Beretta in his jacket pocket. He made his face passive and normal and said, "What's going on?"

The agent had his rifle raised, the barrel pointing at him.

Ray kept it up, saying, "What is this?"

The agent's voice was a shout. *"Drop that bag and put your hands on your head. Do it now. You too, lady."*

Ray saw just the one agent. He had the money and the car was near and he figured his odds were good. He took the Beretta out of his pocket and had it halfway raised when the first shot took him in the back. And Jan was screaming when the agent in front of them pulled the trigger and shot Ray in the forehead. A third agent, positioned in front of the house, also took a shot, which caught Ray in the right shoulder. Ray dropped to the ground, dead before he hit.

•

Within five minutes, the unmarked Crown Vics were racing down the dirt road, trailed by Hastings's Jag. They scrunched to a halt in front of the farmhouse and were out with guns drawn, fearful and anxious even though all the shooting was done. The team commander of the Hostage Rescue Team, a tall man who had been a Marine, kept saying, "Chill, chill," before some overexcited cop shot another. Two suspects were handcuffed, both female. One of them was crying hysterically, saying they had taken the kidnapped girl someplace she didn't know. The second suspect seemed to be in an almost catatonic state.

Gabler was standing in front of the team commander, saying, "The girl, where is the girl?" Still saying it when Hasting came up nearby.

The team commander said, "She's not here."

"She's dead?"

"I don't know. She's not here."

Hastings said, "What about Mickey Seften? Is he here?"

"No," the team commander said. "Neither is the leader, Terrill Colely. There's a dead body in the house, but we can't find Colely or Seften or the girl."

Gabler turned to Hastings. "They've taken her out to kill her. Or bury her."

Hastings said, "A ninety-one Volvo, is that what you said?"

"Yeah."

Hastings took a breath. He said, "The roads around here, if you stay off the highways, the roads are more or less on a grid. Like a checkerboard. We run back and forth and . . . see what we can find."

"Yeah," Gabler said, "if they didn't go far."

Hastings pointed to the black bag. "They'd want to come back for that."

"Okay," Gabler said. "I'll tell Craig to give the order."

Hastings said, "I'll get started." He ran to his car, leaving the corpses and the feds behind.

•

Terrill gave up about forty yards into the wheat. He couldn't see the girl anywhere. He couldn't even hear her rustling about because the sound of his own crashing was too loud. He stopped a couple of times to see if she would cry out because she'd stepped on a short stalk and hopefully punctured a hole in her foot, but it didn't happen. He had Mickey's little semiautomatic, but it wasn't the sort of gun you could use for long-distance shooting and he couldn't see anything. If they had a combine, they could cut it all down, wait for her to try to scurry out of its path, and then shoot her when she presented herself. But they didn't have a combine and Terrill wouldn't have known how to operate it anyway.

After spending precious minutes doing this horseshit, Terrill thought, *She's running and she's going to come out the other end. Use your head, man, and wait for her on the other side.*

Terrill went back to the Volvo. He got in and backed out onto the road. He took a look at the wheat field, now on his right. It spread up a couple of hundred yards where it would stop at the next road on the grid. Terrill told himself that she was not going to stay in that wheat. It would be too cold for her to do that and she would be too scared, thinking that he was coming through the wheat after her. She would be scared and she would try to make a run for the road and flag down a driver. *Help me, please. Help me.* Yes... yes. Better to be there when she came out. A welcoming party.

He got the Volvo up to about fifty, but slowed when he came to the next intersection. He told himself that it was not easy to run through a wheat field. The terrain was not flat and was difficult to cross. She would have to push her way through it, and it would not be easy for a girl who was exhausted and weak with hunger. He would get to the other side before her.

Terrill made a left at the intersection. There was about a twenty-yard stretch between the wheat field and the road, long prairie grass and scrub filling the gap. Terrill stopped the car. He got out and took the Browning bolt-action rifle out of the backseat. He put a 7.62-millimeter slug in the breech and bolted it into place. It clicked home and was ready.

And then he saw it. *There.* A black shadow among the yellow and gray. She was coming out of the wheat, about fifty yards ahead and up to his right. She came out of the wheat and into the tall grass and scrub. Looking toward the road like it was a beacon of hope. Then she turned and saw him in the distance.

Terrill raised the rifle. He put the front sight on her, saw her begin to move, and he pulled the trigger. He saw her go down.

•

Hastings drove fast enough to eat up the roads that lay flat and long. He made loops, going four intersections down before turning down one, then coming back down the other. Looking for a 1991 Volvo, looking for two white males, looking for a girl who he hoped was still alive. Looking and hoping.

They had two more cars out there: Klosterman with a federal agent in one, other federal agents in the other. The U.S. Marshals would send men out too, in time. They had split up the area into boxes.

But it was a big goddamn area. They needed a helicopter to sweep over these things. Looking for the same thing he was looking for and doing it much better and quicker than he could. He had not spoken to Gabler about a helicopter, but Gabler would figure that out on his own. For now, all they could do was drive up and down the lines separating this checkerboard of fields until they found something. They had to do something because the alternative was to give up.

One dead girl at the house, one male killed by FBI agents. Radicals, revolutionaries, fighters of the establishment, whatever you want to call it, but finding out soon enough what Bogart had had to deal with in *The Treasure of the Sierra Madre*: that money does things to people, makes them paranoid and watchful and sometimes murderous.

But the money was still at the house. They would have to come back to the house to get the money. At least try. But they had the girl and they weren't going to come back until they took care of her.

Hastings would slow enough at the intersections to take a quick look left and right. See if the lines between the checkerboard would give him something to go after, something to pursue, something to stop him from going nuts from driving and seeing nothing worth seeing.

And then he saw it.

He had lost track of how many intersections he had counted. But it didn't matter. He saw a flash of darkness. A car. A boxy car. A Volvo.

Then he was past the intersection.

Hastings stomped on the brakes, the wheels trying to grip the gravel before coming to a stop. Hastings put the gear in reverse and backed up to the intersection.

And there it was. A 1991 Volvo pulled off to the side of the road. A man with dark hair holding a fucking rifle. And in the distance he could see the girl on her knees.

•

Did I get her? Terrill wondered.

He had seen her fall. Had seen her fall after he fired.

Terrill squinted into the distance. There was no scope on the rifle, only the front sight. The front sight was sufficient for aiming, but it wouldn't work as a telescope. At first, he thought he had hit her with the bullet. But now he wasn't so sure. Maybe she had just tripped or fainted.

Terrill pulled the bolt back and then shoved it forward again, putting another slug in the breech. He could still see her. She had not gone back into the field. She was on her knees now, maybe preparing for another dash back into the wheat for cover. Terrill raised the rifle to fire.

He heard tires on gravel then and then the sound of a car's engine. Not steady, but accelerating and getting closer. Terrill turned. A brown Jaguar—

"Christ," Terrill said.

—Bearing down on him.

Terrill raised the rifle again, as Hastings pressed the accelerator to the floor. The engine roaring as the Jaguar veered off the road and slammed into the back of the Volvo. The impact punched the Volvo off its wheels and into Terrill Colely. The force of it swatted Terrill about twenty-five feet through the air, unconscious before he hit the ground.

Hastings ran to him after he got his seat belt off. He was holding the shotgun on Colely. He checked for a pulse and found one. Colely would later die of internal injuries, but he was alive then. Hastings knew that the man was in bad shape and wasn't going anywhere. Still, Hastings checked him for other weapons, and when he left Colely he took the rifle with him.

Hastings walked toward the field. His heart was racing.

"Cordelia," he called out. "Cordelia!"

Hastings turned and looked back at his Jag, the front all smashed in. In front of the damage, a man on his back, crushed and bloody. She wouldn't know it was a policeman's car, Hastings thought.

Hastings dropped the shotgun and the rifle on the ground. He took out his police badge and held it up.

"Cordelia," he said. "I'm a police officer. My name's Lieutenant George Hastings. I'm a police officer. It's okay."

That's when he saw the girl stand up. She was coming toward him.

Hastings said, "Are you shot?"

She was about thirty yards from him, stumbling a little but coming to him, saying something.

"What?" he said.

"No," she said. "I'm not shot. Is he dead?"

Hastings said, "I don't think so. But he's unconscious. It's okay now."

There was an awkward moment, the two of them complete strangers, but she knew what he was and her face was crumpled with fright, on the verge of collapse. She rushed to him quickly, a stranger, but needing human contact then. She wrapped her arms around him, crying and shaking. And Hastings was aware that if he let her go she would drop to the ground.

"It's okay now," Hastings said.

THIRTY-EIGHT

Within a half hour, they were back at Muller's house and all the emergency vehicles had converged onto the grounds. Ambulances, police cars, federal vehicles, and then a police helicopter. Hastings looked up and shook his head at it, wondering where it had been earlier. The helicopter landed and Hastings saw Jim Shellow step out with a couple of other federal agents.

Cordelia Penmark said she would get in the ambulance even though she felt she was not hurt. But before she did she asked Hastings who he was again, and when he told her she said, "I saw it. I saw that man in the field shoot Tom. It was him."

They were standing in front of the house. The ambulance was nearby. Cordelia had told them that she didn't need a stretcher.

Hastings said, "That's what we thought."

"I want to help," Cordelia said.

"You have," Hastings said. He gestured to a woman in uniform. "This is Gerry Willis. She's a U.S. marshal. She's going to ride with you to the hospital. You'll be all right."

Cordelia said, "Okay."

Hastings had decided that Cordelia Penmark was not in shock. He had thought she would be. He said, "Your parents will be waiting for you at the hospital. We've telephoned them."

"My mother too?"

"Your mother too. And your sister."

"Oh," Cordelia said. "How are they?"

Hastings stopped. The girl worrying about her mother and sister at a time like this. Amazing. "They're overjoyed," he said. "They look forward to seeing you."

Hmmm," Cordelia said, a slight smile on her face. She reached out and placed her hand on his arm. "Thank you," she said.

"Forget it."

He wanted to say something else. Something like, *It's over now.* Which it was. But he knew she would have nightmares over it for years to come, would flinch at shadows in the night in the following months at least. It would take a while before she would be able to heal. Some never did, and there was a line between healing and nursing grief unnecessarily that was hard to discern. Grief was to be respected, not bowed to. Closure was an illusory concept; you just had to carry on.

It was on Hastings's mind when he looked at the young lady and told her what he thought she needed to hear. He said, "It's good to be alive. Remember that."

"I will," Cordelia said.

The U.S. marshal led her away to the ambulance.

•

Hastings joined Gabler and Klosterman. They were leaned up against a car. Gabler had a cigarette in his mouth.

Hastings said, "You smoke?"

"Once in a while," Gabler said. "When I'm stressed."

"But it's over."

Gabler shrugged.

Klosterman said, "Probably Virginia Slims."

"Well," Hastings said, "there are no children watching. Give me one too."

Gabler did and handed him a lighter to go along with it. Then Gabler said, "Well, hotshot, now that you wrecked your car, how're you going to get home?"

"We'll figure something out. Maybe I can buy another one with the reward money."

Klosterman said, "There is no reward money."

A uniformed agent came within shouting distance of them.

"Gabe," he said. "There's a Jeffrey Rook on the phone. He says he wants to talk to you right now."

"Tell him to go fuck himself," Gabler said, his voice raised. "I'm working here."

"Yes, sir."

To Hastings, Klosterman said, "Quick-tempered, these feds. Very volatile."

Agent Gabler was smiling, an expression of intoxication brought on by exhaustion rather than alcohol. Gabler said, "You guys had lunch yet?"

The cops said they hadn't.

"Let's go into town," Gabler said. "It's on me."

THIRTY-NINE

On Christmas Eve, he awoke on his couch from a long nap. He had intended to sleep for about twenty minutes or so, but it had stretched into two and half hours. His arm over his eyes to ward off light. Sounds coming in and out and then he opened his eyes completely and looked over at his daughter. She was sitting in the recliner, her legs draped over the arm. She was eating some sort of yogurt granola mix from a bowl. The sort of thing Hastings didn't even like to look at.

Amy said, "Did the television wake you?"

"No," Hastings said. He looked at his watch. "Hmmm," he said, acknowledging the passage of time.

Amy said, "I can turn it off if you like. I mean, if you want to go back to sleep."

"No, that's all right." He sat up and rubbed his face with his hands. Came out of the hands and looked at the television screen. Cary Grant and Loretta Young skating around on an outdoor ice rink. A seasonal film, Cary Grant playing an angel who falls in love with David Niven's wife, yet somehow also teaches Niven the true meaning of Christmas.

Hastings said, "Haven't you seen this before?"

"Yeah." Amy shrugged. "I like it. Do you want to watch football instead?"

"Not really." He stood up and went to the kitchen. Thought, Beer or coffee? Then decided on coffee. A couple of minutes later, it was brewing and he went back to the living room and stood behind Amy's chair.

"Amy."

"Yes." Her attention still on the movie.

"I know it's short notice, but Joe asked if we'd like to come to his house for Christmas."

Amy turned to look at him.

"We'd have dinner with him and his family," Hastings said. "You like them, don't you?"

"They're okay."

"So what do you think?"

A pause. Then she said, "Would we have to do it every year?"

Hastings smiled. She was trying to be funny. And in being funny, being brave. He said, "Well, we'll see how it goes."

Amy was a twelve-year-old kid, but aware in her way. She had watched the news for the past couple of days and had seen footage of the poor girl who had been kidnapped and she had some knowledge of her father's role in it, but only some. Too much for a kid to process, but she knew he was tired and would probably need more rest. More important, she knew he was trying.

"I think that sounds fine," Amy said and gave him a smile.

"Good."

Hastings came back to the living room with his coffee and sat on the couch. He picked up the newspaper and began reading the sports page. Amy sat in her chair and returned her attention to the *The Bishop's Wife*. The cab driver had joined Cary and Loretta on the rink.